The Black Cat Detectives

The Black Cat Detectives

A MYSTERY

Kit Gray

CROOKED LANE

NEW YORK

Books should be disposed of and recycled according to local requirements. All paper materials used are FSC compliant.

This is a work of fiction. All of the names, characters, organizations, places, and events portrayed in this novel are either products of the author's imagination or are used fictitiously. Any resemblance to real or actual events, locales, or persons, living or dead, is entirely coincidental.

Published in the United States by Crooked Lane Books, an imprint of The Quick Brown Fox & Company LLC.

Crooked Lane Books and its logo are trademarks of The Quick Brown Fox & Company LLC.

Library of Congress Catalog-in-Publication data available upon request.

ISBN (hardcover): 979-8-89242-552-0
ISBN (paperback): 979-8-89242-553-7
ISBN (ebook): 979-8-89242-554-4

Cover design by Natalie Shaw

Printed in the United States.

www.crookedlanebooks.com

Crooked Lane Books
34 West 27th St., 10th Floor
New York, NY 10001

First Edition: May 2026

The authorized representative in the EU for product safety and compliance is eucomply OÜPärnu mnt 139b-14, 11317 Tallinn, Estonia, hello@eucompliancepartner.com, +33757690241

10 9 8 7 6 5 4 3 2 1

For every cat who ever chose to spend their life loving a human.

For Kit, Turtle, Nora, Trace, and Lyra: I wrote this story so you would live forever.

For Mom, who taught me to love mysteries, and for Dad, who taught me to love books.

For my writing soulmate, April, who inspires me, challenges me, and always believes in me.

And for Kaya, kitten in human form & light of my life.

For readers who would find it helpful, Content Warnings and a list of Names and Places are available at the end of the book.

Chapter One
The Opportunity

Mila.

Mila tried not to think about Brandon, but it was no use. *Is he going to do it?* The question echoed in her mind over and over. *Is it going to happen?* Her determined footsteps faltered and she wheeled her bulky case to a halt in the middle of the Corvin's Crossing town green.

Spring was in riotous bloom all around her. Rolling her shoulders and closing her eyes, she breathed in the blossom-scented air of the crisp April morning. She'd been lucky to get a parking place right on the little square at the center of town. The allure of a rest in the trellised gazebo nestled between redbuds in riotous magenta bloom and fragrant poplar trees with flowers like porcelain teacups seemed irresistible. Besides, maybe nestling herself on its comfortable bench would calm her anxious thoughts.

She sighed, flexing the strain from her sore hands as a breeze lifted her long, coppery brown hair from her neck and shoulders. The ever-present tang of the sea air wove fingers through the sweet spring zephyr. It called to mind sails snapping in a sharp headwind, children racing along the beach as shells spilled from their overstuffed pockets, and the crash and roar of the surf breaking itself on the bluffs that rose up along the southern coast. Mila loved to imagine what it would have been like to grow up here. She couldn't imagine a happier, safer, more carefree place to live.

Drawing in another deep lungful of the refreshing morning air and blowing it out slowly, she felt the knots in her shoulders begin to loosen. Her eyes traveled across the quaint shops that lined the four cobbled streets bordering the green.

On the Northwest corner was Q Tea Pie, with the comfiest sofas and the flakiest pastry in all of New England. Q's bakery was the heart of the little island community. Mila could almost hear the merry jingle that met her every time she pulled open the door, always accompanied by friendly smiles and warm laughter drifting to her on sweet, cinnamon-scented air. Her mouth watered at the thought of Q's new raspberry saffron poundcake. That would really hit the spot on a bright morning like this, especially with a steaming mug of ginger peach rooibos latte and Q's wide, friendly smile.

The Corvin's Crossing United Church of Christ sat on the Northeast corner, its white clapboard austerity softened by a beautiful stained-glass window depicting a dove in flight. If she gazed at it long enough, she felt like something inside of her was soaring, too. Tucked between the bakery and the church lay a neatly cultivated herb and flower garden dotted with quaint benches. An elaborate wrought-iron fence with an arched gate gave it an old-timey apothecary feel.

Mila's childhood town couldn't have been more different from Corvin's Crossing. Her heart filled with warmth as she wrapped fond memories of her adopted home around herself like a quilt.

With a happy sigh, she looked eastward, to the aged brick face and golden marquee lights of Mugsy's Club where she was headlining her magic show tonight.

Beyond was a narrow alley that ended in a parking lot. On the other side of the alley was the pillared front edifice of the town hall. She stiffened.

Brandon's flashy green convertible turned up the alley, vanity plates that read *COMDORE* gleaming in the sun.

What's he doing here? She went cold. *Maybe he's heard back . . . Maybe it's bad news.*

No, she told herself. *Calm down. He's probably just going to see the mayor.* She nodded. *That makes sense. He's the only lawyer in town. There are plenty of reasons he'd have business in one of the town offices or public works departments.*

Still, she couldn't shake the nervous feeling rising in her belly. Maybe he'd already heard whether Mr. Cavendish would be coming to scout her tonight. Or was he planning to meet her at Mugsy's?

Oh no!

Instead of feeling rejuvenated by her morning reflection, she was more nervous than ever. Especially since she'd kept Mugsy waiting. He was opening up just for her, and he'd be grouchy as a woken bear if she made him wait too long. She leaped to her feet, hauling her case along in her wake as she hurried across the green.

Mugsy was already standing by the red lacquered door, eyes stormy beneath beetled brows as thick as wooly caterpillars. His black porkpie hat was askew on his grizzled head, and he grunted as Mila trotted up.

"You're late."

From his unintentionally crushed velvet vest and rumpled trousers to his scruffy goatee slowly disappearing into cheek stubble that was more gray than brown, Mugsy looked like a fancy older gentleman someone had left in the dryer for way too long.

"Sorry, Mugsy. I took a minute to admire the flowers and enjoy the peace of the morning, and I guess I lost track of time."

He held the door for her to enter the club, muttering about woolgathering and common courtesy and going out of his way to be dressed and downstairs by ten just for her when he could have used that extra twenty-odd minutes of sleep.

Mila peered into the darkness, hoping to spot Brandon waiting inside. Her shoulders slumped when she saw the empty club. She shook her head. She was going to put on a great show, regardless of whether Brandon came through or not.

A wet nose bumped her palm. "Hi, Brutus." She smiled down at the broad-chested brindle pit bull. "How are you, buddy?" He shoved his massive head into her hand, flinging his whip tail around gleefully as Mila scratched behind his ear.

Faint smile lines appeared at the corners of Mugsy's eyes as he lifted Mila's case. His mouth quirked. "Come on, kid. Let's get your props backstage before you lose track of them too."

As Mila followed him through the club, the tightness in her shoulders began to ease. The familiar musk of beer and wood polish somehow fit perfectly with the club's motley blend of old country Irish pub vibes and glitzy off-Broadway theater camp. A broad bar carved from honey-colored oak lined the left side of the dim space, and the hardwood floor was liberally scattered with sawdust, but the cushions of the armchairs set behind gilt iron tables were crimson velvet, just like the stage curtains tied back with gold-tasseled rope.

Signed headshots from dozens of performers who had trodden these storied boards filled the walls: musicians, actors, comedians, poets, dancers, and of course, Mila's personal hero, the world-famous illusionist Samuel Pickwick.

Mila raised her chin. Time to focus. She had a lot of work to do setting up her props for tonight's show. A magician always had to practice to stay sharp. She was honing the blade of her trick knife when a ping sounded inside her patchwork crossbody bag. Her thoughts raced. It had to be Brandon. And it had to be good news. She rooted around with suddenly cold fingers. It *had* to be. She whipped out the phone.

It was him. His text read, *Got an update. I'm behind Mugsy's. Come out and meet me.*

Her hands were shaking so hard, it took three tries to type a legible response. *Is it good news? Just tell me!*

Come out back. Only have a minute.

Her heart thundered in her ears. She'd been performing magic for as long as she could remember, but for the past five years, she'd been working herself ragged trying to make a name for herself as more than just a party entertainer. She drew in a shaky breath and blew it out slowly, forcing herself not to run as she veered behind the stage-right curtain and across the back of the club, walk-jogging for the rear exit.

"You good, Mugsy? I've got to go. Brandon has news. But I'll be back later to finish setting up."

"Sure, kid." His gravelly voice drifted to her from the shadowy depths of backstage. "Good luck."

When Mila pulled the door open, Brandon's BMW was already idling in the alley with its top down. His tailored beige suit and green pinstriped tie matched his car perfectly. Everything about Brandon's slicked back blond hair, designer wraparound shades, and flawless tan shouted money.

She wasn't normally into flash, but Brandon had worked hard to build his lucrative firm, Jameson Law, from the ground up. She respected that. Besides, she couldn't quell a little flutter in her belly at the sight of his full lips curving into a smile as she appeared.

The rumble of his engine echoed off the cobblestone alleyway, which was barely wide enough for a single vehicle to pass between the right side of Mugsy's club and the two-story cinderblock side of the municipal complex.

"Hey." He gave her a nod. "You ready for the show tonight?"

She rushed over to his door, staring down at his face desperately. "Just tell me!"

"I did it." He grinned. "I got him."

Mila shrieked. Elation bubbled through her, making it impossible not to jump up and down. "Oh my gosh, Brandon! Really? Mr. Cavendish is going to come to my show tonight?"

Brandon lifted his sunglasses. "Yep. You, Ms. Mila MacAllister, may just be the new headliner for the Luxe Hotel and Resort's grand opening show." He winked. "Pays to have friends in high places, doesn't it?"

"I can't believe it!" She was elated, her preshow nerves forgotten. "I'm finally getting my shot!" Mila reached down to hug him. "Oh, Brandon, all my dreams are about to come true!"

"There's just one thing."

A weight dropped in Mila's stomach. She released him and stood. "What is it?"

His eyes flitted away from her. He straightened his already perfect tie. "I might not make it tonight."

"What?" She hadn't intended to sound so shrill, but the little nervous hum in her mind was suddenly louder than a chainsaw. Her voice was ragged as it left her throat. "Brandon, I need you there! I need—"

"Hey, hey, no need to shout!" Brandon's sharp voice echoed above the growl of the BMW.

"I'm not shouting!" she shrieked. "I need my manager to look out for me, and I need my boyfriend to keep me calm. I can't do it without you, Brandon." Okay, maybe she *was* shouting, but if so, she couldn't help it. His was the face she found in the theater whenever she started to falter. A sob caught in her chest. "I need you."

His lips curled. "Nothing is ever good enough for you!" he sneered. "I was hoping for *thanks*, not a melodramatic scene."

Mila gasped, tears filling her eyes. She knew he'd been under a lot of pressure ever since he got the contract to handle permitting, subcontracts, and supervision of the Luxe construction project. Still, it hurt when he belittled her feelings.

"Everything okay out there, Mila?"

She looked up to see Sheriff Pete Goff's suntanned face sticking out the window of his office in the municipal building down the alley. His sea-blue eyes were filled with gentle concern. Forcing herself to grin, Mila waved.

"It's fine, Pete. Brandon was just telling me some good news. Mr. Cavendish is coming to scout me at my show tonight."

Joy lifted the corners of Pete's mouth. "That's great! I'll be there cheering you on like always!"

"Thanks." She barely managed the syllable and a nod to go with it.

"Ugh," Brandon groused. "Why are you friends with that small-time rent-a-cop? I don't see the big appeal."

"He's nice," Mila shot back. "What's your problem with him?"

"He's always looking at me like I pissed in his beer or something."

Mila pressed her lips together. "Not everyone in town is excited about this huge construction project on our little island, you know."

"Well then," he snapped, "they're ignorant. We need the business for our tax base. We—you know what, never mind. I've got things to take care of."

Her face crumpled. "Look, Brandon, I—"

He lifted his palm to stop her. "I've got to go. I'm going to give you some time to process. See you later."

Before she could react, his BMW was roaring down the alley.

Mila flung herself to the far side of Mugsy's dumpster, where Pete wouldn't see her crying.

The smell of stale alcohol and rotting food rose up around her as she slumped against the cool brick wall, collapsing under the weight of her misery.

Everything was falling apart, and it wasn't even noon yet.

Chapter Two
The Rescue

Kitten 1.

We wouldn't survive for much longer. My siblings and I were too small to leap over the walls of our cardboard prison, and our claws weren't thick enough to penetrate the coarse material. Without Mother's tender ministrations, our fur was all filthy and clumped, but there was nothing I could do about it. My mouth was so dry that my tongue-combs felt hopelessly stuck together, and my muscles were getting weak. At this point, Mother probably wasn't coming back, which meant that we were all alone in this world. Trapped. All three of us knew it, but nobody wanted to say it.

"She's not coming back! We're all alone!" The plaintive wail had me turning my head. "She's probably dead, sis! Dead!"

Okay, fine. My brother was more than happy to say it. Over and over, in fact. At first, I'd told him to shush. Mother always went to find food after evening milk-time. She always licked our ears and told us she loved us, and as soon as she left, my brother always started wailing that she'd abandoned us forever. And he was always wrong.

Except . . . maybe not this time. I couldn't stop remembering her glossy black tail vanishing over the top of the box we called home. But try as I might, I couldn't picture her bright blue eyes peeking over the rim as she returned.

She'd left four and a half days ago, and with each passing hour, it seemed more and more likely that she was gone forever. That meant I was responsible for keeping my family alive. I was the one who taught my two siblings to lap dew from the cardboard walls of our box in the coldest part of each night. I was the one who stopped them from eating shreds of our newspaper bedding when the ache in their bellies got to be too much. Each time she left, Mother had reminded me to look out for them. After all, I was the smartest.

I looked at my siblings, trying to convince myself that I was up to the task. My brother was lean and muscular, with a long tail and huge paws. He paced back and forth in the cramped space, his tail poofed out like a haggard and slightly crooked bottlebrush. I couldn't imagine where he got the strength to move around so much.

My other sibling had always been far more languid. They loved to lean on anyone they could get into contact with, their eyes half-shut in anticipatory bliss, purring as loudly as they could. The sound reminded me of tires crunching on the gravel that lined the alley where our box sat. If they couldn't get into direct contact with my brother or me—or our mother before she vanished—they'd lie down nearby, gazing at their chosen target and purring as if they could draw us inexorably toward them with their love.

Which, frankly, worked more often than not.

Then our alley filled with a loud, terrifying roar. Cars and trucks growled through our alley periodically. Mother had taught us to fear the sound. To hide. But now, there were voices rising over the noise. Humans.

"—ever good enough for you!" The voice was sharp with fury. It wasn't the voice of the human Mother had used to teach us their word-language. He always grumbled, and he smelled of dog. But this one sounded meaner. "I was hoping for *thanks*, not a melodramatic scene."

"Guys!" I shouted, forcing myself to sit up tall. I even used my voice to be sure I got their attention, rather than communicating with body language like we cats usually did. My brother froze midpace, one broad paw lifted in the air. His tail wobbled as he struggled with gravity and was nearly defeated. His gaze raced to and fro, searching for an enemy to attack. Our snuggly sibling's ears twitched. They opened their eyes most of the way, then squeezed them shut affectionately.

"Guys!" I repeated. "Get it together. There are people nearby. Humans! This may be our last chance to be rescued." I raised my voice as loud as I could. "Help!" I meowed, trying to sound like a big cat. "Help! Save us! Please!"

"Shhhhhh!" hissed my brother. "Humans are dangerous. Mother said so. Didn't you pay attention to her stories? They'll steal our skin for their fancy handbags."

I glared at him. "Let them try. It's better than dying of thirst and hunger in this box. Mother isn't coming back, and we won't make it much longer."

"Mother isn't coming back," he moaned. He raised his voice in a desperate, heartbroken cry. "Motherrrrr!" Not exactly what I'd been hoping for, but it was loud enough to hopefully get the attention of the humans.

My sibling opened their eyes, stretched, and yawned. They waved their tail in the air and looked between us as I began to shout for help again, my voice mingling with my brother's.

"We are meowing!" called our sibling joyously. "We are meoooowing!"

The humans continued to shout at one another. A new voice joined in. "Everything okay, Mila?" I wasn't familiar with this voice either, and it was farther away. But it didn't matter who heard us, just as long as someone did.

"It's fine, Pete . . ."

"Helllllllllllp!" I cried.

"Motherrrrrrrrrrrrr!"

"Meowing is fuuuuuuunnn!"

The sharp voice came again. "I'm going to give you some time to process. See you later."

Oh, no. Were the humans preparing to leave? We couldn't let them get away.

"Louder, siblings!" I exhorted.

The low rumble of the car's engine grew into a throaty roar, then vanished. The humans had driven away. They were gone. Our last chance was gone.

We really were going to die here.

I felt my legs tremble and collapse under the combined weight of my hunger, thirst, and despair. My empty belly hit the cardboard with a hollow-sounding *plop*.

Immediately, my sibling was atop me, purring and rubbing their whiskers and jawline across the top of my head. But under the sound of my sibling's purrs . . . behind it . . . there was something else.

A human sob.

One of them was still here. Which meant we still had a chance. I forced myself up onto my paws. My sibling slid down my side in an awkward sprawl. They sat up, blinking curiously.

"One more time, kittens," I exhorted. "Loud as you can!"

"HELLLLLLLLLLLLLP!"

"MOTHERRRRRRRRRR!"

"WE ARRRRE MEEEOOOOOOOOWIIIIIIING TOGETHERRRRRRRRR!"

There was a sniffle, then a crunching sound. I held my breath. The crunching . . . Was it . . . coming closer?

Something tickled my whiskers, and I twitched them in irritation. With a thud, my sibling landed atop me again. They chewed idly on my ear, purring.

I was about to hiss out my frustration when a face appeared over the edge of the box. It was wide and pale and flat, like the moon, with a short, upturned nose and full lips that parted with a gasp. "Well, hello, there. I'm Mila," said the human in a voice as soft and perfect as Mother's belly on a cold night.

I stood, and my sibling fell into the nest of crumpled newspaper pages mother would bring back whenever she found some. She had used them to teach us how to read their odd human words, and most of our knowledge about their ways came from these pages.

I understood why my brother feared humans, but this one was our last hope. Her hand reached toward me. Long, straight hair that nearly matched the cardboard, except that it was shot through with gleaming copper, slipped past her shoulder and whisked into the box. A smell flowed over me, like sun after a rainstorm.

I took a wobbly step toward her outstretched fingers. Then another.

"Intruderrrrrr!" growled my brother, leaping. He extended his front legs as he flew at her, wrapping his paws around her long tresses and clinging on for dear life, shouting a battle chant only he understood.

No! He would ruin our chance at salvation!

But the human giggled, curling her fingers around his body. He nearly disappeared into her palm, his face barely visible above her thumb. His tail poked out below her smallest finger, stiff with rage. He pinned his ears and hissed, an impressively fierce sound.

Oh no.

She was in for it now.

Until her other hand lifted up to the soft place just beneath his left ear, and she ran her fingernail around in delicate little circles. His eyes went all dewy and glazed and his tail went limp.

"What are you doing to him?" I shouted.

She set my brother on her generous chest and reached down to me and my sibling, who was already purring in anticipation, lifting us up beside him. One arm curled around us, holding us gently but firmly in place, and the fingers of the other hand returned to my brother. He was blinking in confusion, but sank back into his inexplicable stupor as soon as she touched him again.

I wriggled out from beneath her arm and stalked up her shoulder to confront her.

"Thank you for the rescue, truly, but I demand that you explain immediately what you are doing to my bro—"

Before I had time to realize what was happening, her fingers arrived at the base of my neck and began doing . . . something indescribable. My muscles went limp as bliss washed through me.

Abruptly, my gut lurched. My eyes flew open and my limbs flailed. Terror gripped me in its icy claws. I had slid off of Mila's shoulder and was plummeting toward the pavement, twisting to get my paws organized. But the ground was too far away. This was going to hurt.

If I even survived. My stomach clenched at the thought.

The fall seemed to last forever.

Until her hand caught me, sinking slightly as it absorbed the impact of my weight. The air was barely even knocked from my lungs. She set me back on her chest and my rump slid down until it rested in the crook of her elbow. My siblings pressed into me, and to my surprise, I began to purr.

I looked up into Mila's face, my blue eyes meeting her green ones.

"I don't understand the meaning of this, human, but I am grateful." Remembering how Mother had taught us about the simple minds of humans, unable to understand any language but their own, I decided to clarify my message as much as I could. I squeezed my eyes shut, a gesture of trust and affection, and when I opened them, her entire face had shifted, softening.

"Three little kittens, all perfectly black. The Goddess must be smiling on me." She grinned, touching each of our noses in turn. "I'm in need of a little magic, and suddenly here you all are."

"It's an auspicious beginning indeed, human," I agreed. "Your timing couldn't have been better."

"I don't trust her," my brother muttered.

"She's soft," purred my sibling.

Mila smiled down at us. "What do you say? Shall we adopt each other?"

"Why not?" I flicked an ear forward to signal agreement.

"Hmph," grunted my brother.

My sibling was too busy licking her to answer.

She began to walk, wrapping her arms around us a bit more snugly as we bounced and slid across her chest. Our journey was long. We squinted at the brightness of the morning sun as the human carried us out of the alley and into what I knew must be the vast wilderness of the wide world.

"Trees," I breathed in awe. They were larger than anything I could have imagined, and far more beautiful. The air was cool and crisp. I felt a pang for the comforting miasma of our box, but as Mila took us across a sea of soft green that had to be grass, my whiskers tingled with hope and joy.

My brother leaped at her hair again, but she caught him and set him back between my sibling and me, tutting gently.

When the human finally stopped walking, there was a strange chirp, then a metallic clunking sound, and we found ourselves inside of a space far, far larger and more luxurious than our box had been.

I recognized some of the objects around me from the newspapers, but many more were utterly strange to me. Obviously, our education had significant gaps in it.

There appeared to be multiple tiers of living space, all covered in soft, plush fabrics. The structure was metal like the dumpster beside our box, but incredibly shiny. Its upper level was enclosed in gleaming glass. Two large sofas sat one in front of the other, and took up most of the space inside.

Overhead, we saw not the sky, but a sturdy roof with a light in the center of it. The rain and wind couldn't touch us here. I remembered Mother's stories about human homes, full of food and comfort and secure from danger, but this was beyond anything I had ever imagined.

Mila's home—our new home—felt . . . safe.

It was odd, to suddenly be filled with a sensation whose absence had been so normal, I hadn't known anything was wrong. But now that I knew what safety felt like, I found myself hoping I'd never have to be without it again.

My eyes couldn't stop moving from wonder to wonder. There was so much to explore. For instance, what was the purpose of the large wheel Mila was setting her hands on? And what were those little silvery things dangling down behind it?

And why was the whole home suddenly making a noise like a thousand giant cats growling simultaneously?

Then it moved, and my stomach felt like it was being yanked out from inside of me again. I yowled. This was no home, it was a trap.

We were doomed.

Chapter Three
The Battle

Kitten 2.

My sister was screaming her head off.

Usually, *she* was the one acting all calm and in charge. Telling *me* to stop shouting. I tossed her a disdainful glance. She was always ignoring me when there was a threat to our safety. Now she was caterwauling about doom. But for once, everything was fine. Better than fine.

This new home was *awesome.*

I was flying through the world like a bullet. I wasn't totally clear on what a bullet was. Something fast. And deadly. Something from Mother's stories about human battles. The thought of Mother brought a sharp stab in my chest, but if this situation had anything to do with battle, I needed to be in warrior mode. Warriors didn't feel, they fought.

So what was this thing we were in? It was fast. Deadly. Oh no. We were in a car. I went cold inside. Cars were the most dangerous things *ever*. When they smashed, everyone died. If ours smashed, that would be the end of us.

Which would make my sister right.

That wouldn't do. Not at all.

I needed to keep us safe. That meant helping the human.

She was talking into a shiny rectangle. I thought back to an advertisement I'd seen in a corner of my favorite bedding, *Popular Physics* magazine. A smartphone. I wondered how it could be smart.

"Brandon's seat has the card underneath," the nice human was saying. "No, he said he might not make it. I'm going to need you to make sure someone is seated there. No, it doesn't matter who. Great. Thank you, Mugsy. I appreciate you."

A good warrior stayed informed, which meant paying attention to what the humans were saying. That's why we learned their noise-language. In truth, though, it would be better for this human to pay attention to what *I* had to say.

I leaped onto her shoulder, clinging to the slippery film of fabric the poor thing had instead of fur. It slid around, unbalancing me, so I stuck out my claws to get a better hold.

She yelped in distress and her body lurched. Thinking fast, I hopped to a superior vantage point: the nest of long, shiny fur atop her head. I didn't quite make it, but I persevered, pulling myself to the top and shouting directions to her.

"Dodge! An attacker is coming! *Dodge!* Yes! Excellent evasive maneuvers, human! This is *exhilarating!* Here comes another—"

I found myself scooped up from my captain's perch and deposited in the bowels of the car.

From such low ground, there was no view of the outside world. I set off to regain my former position, but the terrain was wooly and warm. My sibling sidled up to me, blinking hopefully. They batted languidly at my tail.

"You're ridiculous," I scoffed. Still, when they lowered their belly to the floor and nuzzled into the fuzz, purring, I couldn't resist trying it.

I sighed blissfully. It smelled earthy. The warm, soft, vibrating surface reminded me of Mother. The grief that hit me was more than a stab. It shook me all the way to my bones like thunder. My paws flexed and released as I squeezed my eyes shut, lost to everything about the world except the memory of how she had smelled.

I must have fallen asleep, because the next thing I knew, my sibling was being lifted off my face, and I was being hoisted into the air. The human strode through the warm spring breeze. I sniffed, my whiskers twitching. There were a lot of animal smells nearby. Dozens. Dogs and cats, mostly. The scents concentrated even more as the human pulled open a door.

Perhaps there would be a battle inside. My tail poofed fiercely.

A jangling sound brought a gush of air that was strangely tame. Instead of trees or grass or rain, there was a sharp, chemical smell. The human was talking in a bright, cheerful tone.

"Hi Jenny. Thank you for fitting us in right away!"

"Of course!" a new human responded. She was sitting behind a half-wall. Dark brown hair hung around her pale face, which was covered in hundreds of fetching little brown dots. She looked up at Mila. "Hey, everything okay?"

"Yeah," our human answered. "Why?"

"Your mascara is a little . . ." Jenny drew a line under one of her own eyes with a fingertip. The gesture made me itchy to pounce. I wondered if I could leap far enough to land on her face.

"Oh. Yeah. No. Brandon's not going to make it to my show tonight. I just found out."

The spotted human's eyes widened. "Really? He never misses your shows. Did you ask why?"

"Didn't get a chance to." Mila pressed her lips together.

The human's spots faded as her cheeks grew pink. "Listen. I need to tell you something. It's about Becca and the club . . . And Brandon." She made a sound halfway between a growl and a hairball-cough. "Do you want to sit down?"

Mila froze, eyes darting back and forth like she was tracking prey. She got a pinched look on her face. "No. It's okay, Jenny. Just tell me."

"Becca and Brandon are . . . that is . . . they . . ." Jenny broke off, looking worried.

Mila squeezed her eyes shut and gave a tight nod. "How do you know?"

"I saw them together at Mugsy's. I'm really sorry."

"Ouch." Mila blew out a breath. "Okay, yeah. That feels bad. I can't say I'm completely surprised that Brandon is fooling around. But Becca?"

"I know," Jenny nodded. "She's your best friend. I don't think she meant to hurt you. Anyway, I'm sorry. I just figured if it was me, I'd want to know."

"Yeah. Thank you for telling me." She shook her head as if to shoo something away. Was a fly bothering her? If so, I would eat it for her. I couldn't see one, though. She rolled her shoulders, jostling us. "I can't be thinking about this right now. I have the most important show of my life tonight."

"Luckily," Jenny offered, "you have the best distraction imaginable! I can't believe these kittens. Adorable! What are their names?"

Mila gave her a bright smile. "I don't know, Jenny, I haven't had a chance to think about names yet. What do you think I should call them?"

She must be talking about us. Finally, something interesting.

Mother hadn't given us names. My throat tightened at the realization she never would. Kittens received their names on the night of the third full moon after birth. We'd only seen the moon wax and wane twice, and now Mother was gone. But I needed to be on my guard. No time to feel sad.

I accidentally yowled.

"Well, he's a vocal one, isn't he?" offered the spotted human.

Mila took a step forward, bringing the counter between her and the spotted human into range.

I leaped. It was slippery, so my paws went off in their own directions. I gathered them neatly. Battle-readiness was always important.

Our new terrain was cluttered with a variety of bizarre-looking accessories. Any of them might have been a trap. I heard my siblings land behind me. Neither of them managed their paws particularly well.

The humans emitted a bubbly sound that seemed like a cross between a purr and a song.

If they were trying to be fierce, they were *extremely* bad at it.

Suddenly, I smelled something utterly beguiling. What could it be?

"We need a name for the file, even if it's something temporary," the spotted human said. "You could name them something magic-y. You know, considering what you do." She raised her hands in the air, wiggling her fingers in a way that made me want to pounce. "Like hocus and pocus, except there's three of them. Think about it while I fill in some of these forms for you."

Now she was poking at little clicking squares in front of her. No doubt about it, this new human was trying to distract me from whatever treasure she had. What was it? What was that hypnotic smell?

Suddenly, I knew.

Water.

My tongue darted hopefully. "Psst! Guys!" I signaled with a wiggle of my tail, then shot my eyes in the direction of the water. They twitched their ears attentively.

"Okay, here's the battle plan," I told them. "You two distract the new human. I'll liberate the water. Meet me there once it flows free."

My sister's eyes narrowed in irritation that I was taking command, but her tail stood crisply at attention. "Got it."

She pounced on the spotted human's fingers, which were dancing faster and faster over the small, raised squares. Each square held one of the letters humans used to make their words.

Trrrrrrn? she queried.

Then she began to leap about, her back arched. It was, I had to admit, an excellent assay.

When the spotted human reached for her, my sibling charged to the rescue, hurtling themself through the air and wrapping their paws around her wrist. "We are playing!" they shouted, then opened their mouth wide and nuzzled their face into their target.

Their tactics were decent, but all the purring undermined their fierceness. And they needed to work on their biting.

I'd speak to them about it later.

The spotted human lifted her wrist, my sibling clinging to it with great tenacity. When they got close enough to her face, my brave warrior reached out a paw and smacked at her nose.

"Boop!" Mila chimed as my sibling landed another blow. She emitted that strange musical purr again. The spotted human joined in the ruckus.

Both enemy combatants were completely distracted. This was my chance.

I darted over to the tall, half-full drinking glass I'd identified as our strategic target. It was so smooth. I touched it gently and felt its coolness against my paw-pads.

It did not respond.

I poked it again, harder. This time, when my claws made contact, it made a light *tink* sound. Excellent.

Gravity would be my best option. I reached out my arm, curving my paw into a hook shape. I slid it along the ground toward my target and poked harder, but it remained entirely stalwart.

My tail twitched. It was sturdier than I had hoped.

I tapped it a few more times, my tail whisking about, but to no effect.

My siblings were still distracting the humans, but I knew their attention could turn to me at any moment. I gave myself a count, for strength and courage.

One. I crouched low.

Two. I pinned my ears to my neck in preparation.

Three. I wriggled my hindquarters, gauging the distance.

"Now!" I shouted, leaping at the glass and swiping my hooked paw at its rim with all my might.

My combat-mind was flawless, my awareness crystal clear.

I could feel the forces of physics at play in the target. Momentum. Gravity. Friction. Its system swelled with the energy I'd pushed into it. My whiskers twitched in fascination.

The trajectory of the target's fall vibrated in my mind so that I knew the exact lines of fracture and the directionality of each shard of glass and each droplet of water before the massive collision even happened.

I smirked.

Both humans jumped at the sound, and my siblings and I rushed to the edge of the counter, leaping in harmony.

"Danger! Sharp!" my sister shouted.

For a moment, time stretched like a spine, and I could see through three pairs of eyes.

The floor rushed up toward us in slow motion. Our threefold mind easily unlocked the scatter pattern of debris and water. Each razor-sharp crumble of glass seemed to glow. Our awareness highlighted all the dangers, mapping the terrain in perfect detail. As one, our three backs twisted and our twelve paws reached, finding clean, dry patches of floor to land on.

As soon as we touched down, I shouted, "Charge!"

We rushed forward, tongues tossing droplets of water into the air as we began to gulp down the clear, fresh liquid.

"That's dangerous!" The spotted human lifted us from the loot that was rightfully ours, handing us to our human.

Fury lanced through me. I puffed out my coat and growled fiercely.

"Poor things must be thirsty," Mila responded.

The spotted human had turned her back and was busy with something, but our human continued talking.

It was an advantage of such a noisy language, I supposed. Easier to force someone to hear you even when they're shunning you. Though what our human had done to anger the spotted one, I couldn't guess. "But did you see them all jump in unison like that?" Mila asked. "They were quite a little team. They remind me of the mice in that princess movie . . . you know, the one where—" her eyes went wide.

"Jenny! I've got it!"

The spotted human turned back toward us, opening a door in the half-wall between herself and our human. She was carrying a large silver bowl filled with more water. I pawed at it, but it was maddeningly out of reach.

"Got what?" the other human asked, jutting her chin toward a corridor and striding away with the silver bowl full of treasure.

"Their names," Mila said. "I'll call them Bippity, Boppity, and Boop."

"That's perfect," the spotted human agreed. "It sounds a little bit like the fairy godmother's song, if you mashed up each of the words with a different comic book battle sound effect." She opened a door and set the silver bowl on a huge steel plateau in the middle of a large, extra-sharp-smelling room.

Mila set my siblings and me down on the table one at a time. First was my sister.

"You'll be Bippity," she said as my sister raced over to the bowl, putting her paws on the edge and dipping her face into the water with a sneeze. "I get the feeling you're the leader."

I bristled at that. Ridiculous human. *I* was obviously the leader.

She set me down next. "I'll call you Boppity." She touched my nose. "I saw your fierce paw when you pushed over that glass of water. I can tell you're a warrior." I smacked away her finger and raced to the water.

As much as I hated to admit it, though, my chest swelled with pride at her words.

Finally, she put down my languid sibling. I wasn't watching them anymore. The water was too delicious. But I heard them start to purr as the human said, "You're Boop. Snuggly and mischievous, with a sense of humor."

We all lapped blissfully, our gulps drowning out the delighted murmurs of the humans standing nearby.

Chapter Four
The Vet

Boop.

So I was called Boop. I liked it. It had a nice sound to it, and these humans did love their sounds. I felt better now that my belly was full of water. In addition to our own human, Mila, and the water-giver, Jenny, a third human had appeared.

Mila had a warm, friendly energy with a layer of vulnerability hidden beneath the surface, and Jenny crackled with eagerness. In soothing contrast, the new human was calm and reassuring. I liked her immediately.

She looked at me with dark brown eyes, and I began to purr. I waved my tail invitingly and lifted my back, walking sideways to show her how much soft, lovely fur I had. She probably wanted to snuggle me. Who wouldn't?

"Hello there," the calm new human murmured. "Don't you seem friendly?"

"I do! I do!" I purred as loudly as I could, using the special rumbly one I had always favored when trying to get Mother to lick my ears after milk-time. Something wet and warm dripped onto my paw. Another drop fell on the metal platform where I stood, and more of the liquid was running down my throat. I nearly choked.

Maybe I'd forgotten to swallow the last bit of water I'd lapped from the bowl.

My sister, Bippity, and my brother, Boppity, were watching me with twin looks of disdain. They glanced at one another, then back at me. They were always worrying about unimportant things like dignity and fierceness and who was in charge.

The human brought her kind face closer and reached her hand out toward me. "I'm Dr. Ladonna," she said, "but most people around here call me Doc."

Her hand was so marvelous. I tried to figure out what else I could do to inspire her to pet me with it. Her skin was a cool, silky shade of dark brown. When she uncurled her fingers toward me, I saw that the undersides had a lovely pinkish hue. "Humans are so neat. I love fingers," I told her, adding a friendly trill to my body language as I showed her again how delightful my tail and backside were. "I'd really like to meet yours!"

I whirled around gracefully and leaned toward her, my ribs nestling into her palm as I swept myself off my own feet with all the charm I could muster. Unlike the other humans, she didn't make that tittering sound, though.

Instead, she hummed low in her throat as her fingers moved through my fur. A cloud of gentle concern whirled around her. She turned to Mila.

"This little one is badly malnourished," she murmured. "Blue eyes are rare, especially in black cats, but they're old enough that they'll probably stay this way. How beautiful!"

"You're beautiful, too!" I told her.

She lifted me in her warm, soft hand, stroking my cheek with the back of her index finger. "What do you say, little kitten, will you let me look at your teeth?"

I supposed I didn't see any harm in it. I continued to purr as she gently pulled my jaws apart. My purrs grew louder as my mouth opened wide. What a glorious effect! Mila and Jenny giggled again. My siblings shot me twin scowls.

"Nice healthy teeth," Doc said. "Significant overbite. Explains the . . ." She swiped her finger under my chin and held it up, then wiped it on a nearby towel. I didn't know what she meant, but Mila said, *awwww,* and radiated warm fondness, so it was obviously something loveable.

Doc lifted and probed at other parts of my body, paying me a variety of compliments.

"I heard that bigwig developer is coming to your show tonight," Doc said.

Tension tightened her jaw as she nodded. "How did you know?"

"Oh, you know how it is," Doc shrugged. "Small town. Sheriff Pete posted to the Corvin's Crossing FaceCloud page, asking everyone to come out and support you. I saw the alert just as you were pulling up."

"That's so nice!" Mila's face softened. I figured she was reacting to my cute paws, as Doc flexed my claws one by one. "He didn't have to do that."

"Looks like most folks are coming. Mayor Adams can't make it, but he asked that we send you his best wishes." Doc lifted my tail and peered into my ears. I squeezed my eyes shut and rumbled out my satisfaction with the experience.

"Watch out! You're under attack!" Boppity shouted. I opened my eyes a crack. His ears were flattened against his head again.

He was in full battle mode, his spine arched and his tail poofed out fiercely as he danced sideways, hissing.

"What in the world is that?" Bippity yelped. Concern emanated from her, spiky and alarming.

I tried to turn and look, but Doc had given me to Jenny, who was holding me steady on the shiny metal platform. I hadn't even noticed myself changing hands or my paws touching down.

Though now that I thought about it, I could feel the cool of the metal against my toes. How nice. I redoubled my purring.

There was a strange smell and a sharp prick at the back of my neck, followed by a second and a third. Then fingers soothed the momentary sting. I purred louder.

"What a brave kitten. Good job, Boop." Doc's calm voice washed over me as she lifted me again, dribbling something damp between my shoulder-blades. "Jenny, would you please get one of the cardboard carriers, and while you're in the supply area, bring three kitten starter kits with a bunch of the high calorie canned and crunchy kitten food?"

A moment later, her clever hands lowered me into a . . .

"Wait," I called out, using my voice to be sure all of the humans heard me. "There must be a mistake! Don't put me in here!" But the hands set me down in the cardboard box alone. I didn't want to be trapped again. Especially not without my siblings. I began to cry.

Mila's face appeared above me. Reassurance and love drifted from her in cozy currents, making the box homey, like our old one when Mother was in it with us. "It's okay, little Boop," she said.

A lock of her long hair fell over her shoulder and tickled my nose. It was so enticing, I couldn't resist batting at it. It swayed out of the way, and I fixed it with an intense stare. Ha! It had dared to evade. I'd show it who it was dealing with. I crouched, planning my next move carefully, and pounced.

I was rewarded with fresh waves of affectionate mirth.

In the background, my siblings were hollering about some nonsense or other again, but Mila's joy was far more palpable.

Besides, as the slick, coppery brown hair slipped between my paws, deliciously cool and smooth, I tumbled ears-over-tail across the inside of the box. Woo! That was fun! Mila bubbled with delight.

I was preparing for another leap when Doc's hand appeared and deposited a fizzing, spitting Boppity beside me. Jagged, hot fury sharded out of him, but before he could start to rant, I interrupted him.

"Look, Boppity! Enemy!" I batted at the hair hopefully.

His eyes widened, then narrowed as his rage morphed into ferocity. "Attaaaaaaaack!" he shouted, flinging himself into the air. When he landed, I pounced on his tail. He swung around, slapping at my face a little harder than was probably necessary. But I was used to it. I ducked, then popped up and grabbed his ear. He yelped, so I let go.

"What are you doing?" I looked up to find that Bippity and her prim, spiky irritation had been added to the box. She was glowering at us both. "Honestly, of all the undignified, ridiculous—Oooooo!" She caught sight of Mila's hair and leaped for it, crashing into Boppity.

I began to purr. "I love you guys," I said. They ignored me, tackling one another.

Above us, drifts of worry were gathering around Mila. She tucked her hair behind her ear, but my siblings were too busy wrestling to notice. "I can't afford any of this, Doc. I told Jenny, but . . . I . . . I don't . . ."

Sadness was filling her, and beneath it, fear. I jump-started a fresh batch of purrs with a loud rumble, trying to let her know that everything was okay.

Doc's beautiful, clever hand touched Mila's shoulder.

Somehow, Mila managed not to start purring.

"The important thing is," Doc said in a voice that sounded smooth and cool, like Mila's hair between my paws, "your new kittens are going to be fine. Give them an hour or so, and then you can give them more water and some food. And try not to worry about the money. You'll pay what you can when you can. I won't charge you for the visit. The food, treats, toys, litter, and cat box are all samples we get from sales reps, so those don't cost a thing. You just focus on your show tonight. Especially this new trick we keep hearing about. We're all looking forward to it." I saw her fingers squeeze gently.

Mila must be purring now. How could she resist?

I couldn't hear anything, though. Maybe her purrer was—I gulped—broken.

Poor human.

"Don't worry," I told her with my love-eyes. "I've got you. I'll purr for us both."

"Thanks." Mila nodded at Doc, but I was sure she was talking to me. The chaotic emotions that had been filling the air around her began to calm. She was comforted by my purrs. I increased my volume, opening my mouth a little. I loved this new technique!

"Just listen to that little dear," Doc said, reassurance emanating from her. "That's the right idea. There's a lot to be happy about here, and nothing to worry about. It's all good."

Our new box had a roof, which Mila folded shut, enclosing my siblings and me in darkness. We slid around the slick floor, hollering in protest. Fun was all well and good, but this was just rude.

Still, as I slid into Bippity and then Boppity slid into me, I found myself tucked into a corner, in the middle of a cuddle-pile. That was pretty nice. Maybe boxes weren't all bad.

Chapter Five
The Zone

Mila.

Mila cringed as another ear-splitting wail filled the car. "I'm trying, kittens. I promise. I just need to find a parking—" She gasped in disbelief. The spot directly across the green from Mugsy's was empty! Parking in the town center was always at a premium. Maybe finding this spot open was an auspicious sign. As soon as she turned off her battered old hatchback, the cardboard box went quiet.

"Thank the blessed stars." One of the kittens was obviously terrified of car rides. The entire drive from Doc's back to the green had been punctuated with long, sonorous yowls. Hearing that the whole town was talking about the new trick she hadn't had a chance to practice on stage yet had driven her nervousness through the roof. The chorale of torment and misery had not helped.

To top it all off, Brandon had said he wouldn't be there, and he and Becca—no. Now wasn't the time to think about that.

"I'm so excited to be your new family, kittens." She picked up the box and peeked in through one of the tall, narrow slits that allowed fresh air to circulate. Three sets of blue eyes looked back. "But I need a little calm. I have to get this trick right. A lot is riding on it."

A little trill came from inside the box. The round-faced one with the stubby tail, whose gender she couldn't seem to remember—Boop—padded up to the air hole. One fuzzy paw reached through the slim opening. After waving it in the air for a moment, Boop set it on Mila's cheek. Rumbling purrs vibrated their tiny toe-beans, warm against her cool skin.

A sudden feeling blossomed in her chest, like gratitude, but much fiercer. Somehow, the other emotions battling for her attention, the anxiety and hurt and anger of the day, felt less important. Even if the rest of her life went up in flames, there would be a pile of kittens on her chest when she went to bed tonight.

She drew in a deep breath and squared her shoulders. "Okay, kittens. Here we go."

As she approached, Mila saw that Mugsy had extended the deadbolt before letting the door swing shut to prevent it from auto-locking, giving her easy access. He was thoughtful like that. "Hello?" she called into the darkness. "You there?" There was no response. She blinked as she released the deadbolt and allowed the door to slam shut behind her. "Mugsy?" she called.

He should be here. He could have gone up to his apartment, a little studio above the pub portion of the club, in the front half of the building's second story. The back half was taken up by the fly tower and grid directly above the stage,

But it wasn't like Mugsy to be somewhere else when he'd promised to be here for her setup and prep. Her eyes were adjusting to the darkness now, and she didn't see him anywhere. What if something had happened to him? A chill raced up her spine.

"Hey, kid." Mugsy's voice drifted out from his office, a walled-off room tucked behind the backstage area. "Late again, I see." His voice was barely audible, but growing nearer as he spoke. "I hope you still have enough time to set up and practice." He appeared onstage, still heading toward her. "What's in the box?"

Brutus raced past Mugsy and down the proscenium steps, his tail a patchwork blur. Just before he reached her, Mila's box hissed and a whining growl rose up from inside it. Brutus's feet skidded to a halt. His ears popped up atop his head, which he cocked to the side, shifting his gaze from Mila to the strange sound and back again. Mila burst into laughter at his goofy face and wide, confused eyes.

"K-k-kittens," she chortled. "Found them in the . . . alley out b-b-back." Brutus was approaching cautiously now, nose atwitch. He had almost reached the nearest air-slit when a broad paw reached out and slapped him across the muzzle, accompanied by a sound like miniature fireworks exploding.

He jumped back with a yelp and Mila broke out in a fresh wave of giggles as Mugsy arrived.

"Kittens, eh? Why'd you bring 'em here?" He set a reassuring hand atop Brutus's head. "It's okay, bud," he murmured. "Ignore their nonsense."

"I'm adopting them. Just got them seen down at Doc's." She ran her hand through her hair, trying not to think about the thousands of dollars in vaccinations, vitamin shots, supplements, flea and tick prevention, supplies, and prescription food Doc had given her. Hopefully, someday, she'd be able to repay at least a little of that kindness. "It took longer than I thought, so I didn't have time to take them home."

Mugsy grunted. "Should've gotten a dog. Cats are haughty. Or maybe a rabbit to pull out of your hat." He chuckled to himself. Then he shrugged at the box. "Oh, well. Your life to ruin, I guess."

"Yup." She tried to control her amusement, and mostly succeeded. "It sure is." Her messenger bag rattled with cans of cat food as she hefted it onto her hip. Her shoulder was getting sore. She nudged Brutus with her knee and headed backstage. "I'm going to get to work. There's a lot to do before seven. Did you get the lights set up like I asked you?"

Mugsy nodded. "The main ladder to the fly loft is a bit wobbly and there's a loose railing on the catwalk. If the lights need adjusting, just let me know, and I'll handle it from the control panel. Can't have you climbing up there and getting hurt."

"Okay. Just get ready to be annoyed with me. My new illusion is extremely precise, so the lighting is going to have to be just right to pull off the vanish." She set the box of kittens and her bag in the right wing. Brutus's budding curiosity was quelled with another sharp swat. Mila covered a smile. That broad paw belonged to Boppity, her little warrior. She'd never seen such big feet on such a dinky guy.

She hauled the heavy case off the backstage shelf where Mugsy had stored it. Nerves surged through her. "Oh, and Doc told me that the whole town is talking about the show. Plus, Mr. Cavendish is coming." Her chest tightened. What if she flopped?

She let Brandon's favorite piece of advice play in her head like a tape. "Only a handful have the talent for fame and fortune. Aim for a good, solid B-list career."

B-list, she told herself. *Not perfection, just B-list. I can do that.*

"Don't worry, kid," Mugsy's bushy eyebrows twitched upward, as though he were preparing to dispense a pearl of great wisdom. "Once you get into the zone or whatever you kids call it, you're completely oblivious. The sky could fall, and you'd only notice if it ruined your trick."

* * *

Mugsy turned out to be right. Mila didn't even notice her stomach growling until he pushed one of Q's sandwiches into her hands. The hour Doc had said the kittens needed before they could eat was probably past, too.

She glanced at her phone and her eyes flew wide. Cramming the sandwich into her mouth, she took a huge bite and set the rest aside. She fished in her bag and pulled out three cans of cat food, peeling the tops. Brutus came running, but no sounds arose from the box. Poor little kittens didn't even know the sound of a can of food being opened.

When she unhooked the top of the box and peered inside, delight stole her breath. A tiny pile of black fur with three heads and innumerable paws lay tangled in the corner, sound asleep. Only about half of Boop's round face was visible. Fierce little Boppity lay sprawled atop their head and chest in an X shape, all four of his broad paws splayed out on the cardboard as though he were tethering Boop to the ground protectively.

Bippity lay in a neat curl atop Boop's back half. Her tail was tucked tidily beneath her front paws, and her chin rested on Boppity's back.

She opened her enormous eyes and blinked curiously at the three cans of food Mila set into the box. Then she sniffed the air and let out a tiny, heartwarming trill. It sounded for all the world like a question. Mila giggled.

"Yes, Bippity, I've brought you food. Enjoy!"

The kitten pile lurched, and suddenly kitten faces were shoving and cramming into the cans of food, licking eagerly.

"Don't worry, there's plenty for everyone," Mila told them, pushing the third can over to Boop, who had tumbled onto their side in the rumpus.

She took another huge bite of her own sandwich, then set a teacup from a prop shelf into the corner of the box, and filled it from her water bottle.

One more bite, and she gave the rest to Brutus, who swallowed it whole.

"Now that's a vanish fit for a star," she chuckled, patting him.

She closed the gabled roof of the box over the kittens hungrily scarfing their meal. It was time to set up and make sure everything was organized for the show. She gave her stage marks, black tape on the black floor, a last check. She was organizing her props when Becca walked in.

"You're late," Mugsy scolded.

Becca pressed her burgundy lips together, narrowing dark eyes framed with long, thick lashes. "No, I'm not. I got here early and started in back, finishing up the inventory. Just like you asked."

Her long, glossy black hair was pulled back into a professional bun. She wore the bartender's trousers, apron, and bow-tie with a kind of jaunty, androgynous grace Mila only wished she could achieve. The golden hue of the house lights brought out the warm undertones in her ochre complexion. No wonder Brandon had gone for her. Mila ground her teeth. Feelings were trying to rise up from her gut again, and she didn't have time for them. She turned away, checking over her set one last time.

Wait. Something was wrong.

"Mugsy?" she called.

"Problem with the lighting?"

"No. Mugsy, have you seen my trick knife?"

"I saw it when you were sharpening it earlier today." Mugsy poked his head out from behind the lighting panel in the stage wing. "Not since."

Panic surged in Mila's chest, rising up to choke her. Knife-through-arm was her opening trick. She couldn't perform it without that custom blade. She had a backup one, but it was at home, and there wasn't enough time now to fetch it.

She bit back a curse. What was she going to do? This was the most important show of her life, and she'd somehow misplaced her trick knife. She remembered polishing it, but she'd set it down somewhere when she dashed off to talk with Brandon.

Drawing in a deep, shaky breath, she squared her shoulders. When she blew it out again, it was slow and steady. Nothing to do about the missing knife now. She would just have to open with her backup tricks, the coin and the flowers. Not her finest work, but they'd do.

"I'm going to get into costume." Mila shook out her cape and gown, handsewn from a special fabric called IR flocksheet that absorbed 99.75 percent of the light, rendering it invisible against a black backdrop. She'd painstakingly made them herself, stitching the purple satin lining into the cape to hide the effect of the flocksheet until she closed the cape around herself. They were her favorite possessions in all the world.

Usually, slipping into them would set off her preshow routine where her nerves melted away and she embraced the mystique of the bond she was about to forge with her audience. But this time, anxiety roiled her stomach. Next, Brandon was supposed to give her a hug and tell her to break a leg or at least an arm. Then they were supposed to laugh.

She peeked out from behind the curtain. The guests were arriving. Her eyes fell on Brandon's seat as she watched Ms. Scarborough hand Mugsy a ticket and settle into it. Fondness warmed her heart. The vibrant old lady who ran the local B&B and horse farm was short, plump, and adorable. like everyone's favorite grandma. Her pale face and cloud-like white hair were a perfect frame for her cherubic grin. It was nice that she'd get to have a little role in the show.

Still, her nerves threatened to rise up and distract her. After all, this show was an audition for a headliner gig at a posh new resort. That was the kind of thing that could launch a career. Shots like this didn't come around more than once.

B-list, she reminded herself ruthlessly. *It doesn't have to be perfect. B-list.*

The thought quelled the voice deep within her that demanded greatness. She adjusted her sleeves and checked each of her pockets and props one last time. She imagined Brandon's hands on her shoulders. *No need to grandstand or try to be more than you are. Just put on a good solid show. That's all.*

I can do that.

She smoothed her gown over her middle as Mugsy's voice echoed through the club, introducing her.

When the curtains parted, she gasped. There was not a single empty seat in the house. She'd never had a turnout like this before, and probably never would again. Her eyes scanned the crowd, instinctively looking for Brandon's familiar face to lock onto, and she felt a painful stab in her chest when she saw Ms. Scarborough's gentle smile instead.

It's okay, she told herself. *Mugsy's right. Once you start, you're oblivious. It's just you and your magic. All you need to do is start.*

Aim for the B-list.

Just start the show.

Swallowing hard, she stepped out into the light.

Chapter Six
The Show

Bippity.

I awoke to see Mila's pale, round face gazing down at us. After the poking and inspecting she'd subjected us to, I wasn't entirely sure she was trustworthy, so I watched her closely.

She leaned down and set three containers of strange, mushy glop in the box. It wasn't much to look at, but the bouquet of rich smells caused an earthquake in my belly. I trilled, waking my siblings with the food-song of our mother, and we organized our paws and went to investigate.

There were three distinct fragrances, and one, in particular, was delicate, enticing, and unlike anything I had ever smelled before.

Boppity buried his face in the nearest can, knocking over Boop and making a terrible mess of his whiskers and cheeks. He even managed to get his ears dirty. He growled softly as he attacked with the ferocity of a true warrior, the entirety of his focus devoted to his repast's utter obliteration.

Boop began to purr as Mila slid one of the containers into their reach. The sound of them trying to maintain the ridiculous noise while gulping down facefuls of compelling putty nearly made me snort.

I had basic common sense, unlike my siblings. I sniffed carefully despite my hunger. The scent of my food-lump was reminiscent of a chunk of old tuna sandwich Mother had once brought home.

I sampled the sharp tang of fish oil and the slightly bitter finish from my can. It was good, but Boppity's smelled richer than mine. I nudged him out of the way and helped myself to a morsel. It was dark brown and had a heartier flavor with a round, umami base and oaky, rich top notes. Boppity growled, forcing his face in next to mine and swallowing huge gobs of his feast as if we were in some sort of competition.

I ignored him, savoring the silky taste on my tongue. It called to mind the pot roast with gravy Mother had found in the dumpster one fine evening. While lovely, I couldn't help noticing that it, too, lacked the unique scent that so captivated me.

So off to Boop's container I went. Pushing their face aside, I took a dainty lick of their meal. They leaned against me, purring, and watched me curiously.

As if the heavens had opened up and Mother's love had rained down upon me in warm waves, a superb new flavor washed over my tongue. It was more delicate than the beef and less pungent and floral than the tuna. It had a pale, creamy color and a light, almost musical meatiness, herby and perfectly balanced.

I settled onto my haunches and began to eat neatly. Boop watched me for a moment, then strolled over to my abandoned fish-lump, still purring, and began to eat with undiminished satisfaction.

Partway through my meal, I spotted the man with the furry face and the odious dog at a booth near our box. "Ladies and gentlemen," he intoned. His voice echoed through the sky as if by magic. "We have a real treat for you today. Mugsy's Club is proud to present Mila the Magnificent. Please give her a warm welcome."

Hundreds of raucous smacking sounds rose up out of the darkness. I peered through a slit in the box, and a red fuzzy wall in front of Mila ripped itself open along its middle and whisked itself away. Bright lights streamed down from overhead, blinding me.

I glared at them, willing the disrespectful hordes of photons to leave me alone so I could enjoy my meal.

The little assailants bent slightly in their paths of travel, bouncing off of my cheeks, nose, and forehead instead of troubling my eyes. I shouldn't have been surprised they were obeying me. They ought to, the little scamps. I felt a swell of pride.

Now that only the dimmer ambient light from the room was reaching my pupils, they dilated, and I could see that there was a whole enormous room in front of Mila, crowded with humans sitting at tables. Our part was raised above theirs, clearly indicating that we were more important.

Mila wore a sweeping satin cape, black on the outside and purple on the inside, over a long-sleeved black gown made of some flowing material. Atop her head was a shiny top hat.

She bowed, tipping her hat to the audience and setting it on a table before her.

I continued to nibble at my gourmet meat-feast as I took in the scene before me.

"As you know, friends," Mila announced, her voice filling the room, "Magic is all about energy."

She lifted a flat silver disk, showing it to the room. "With a little effort, I can add friction energy to matter such as this simple coin, and turn it into . . ."

She rubbed her hands together vigorously, then pulled them apart. A puffy mass of weirdly colorful, wobbling paper flowers appeared where the coin had been. "A lovely bouquet."

She whisked them through the air. My tail twitched eagerly. They made a perfect target for pouncing. Why wasn't she inviting us to play with her?

There were more scattered smacks from the room. Mila smiled. "And I can change this beautiful matter into . . ."

She twisted her wrist and flicked her fingers, and a bright light flared. Again, I shooed the offending photons away from my eyes, and again they obeyed. The bouquet vanished into a poof of smoke. "Pure energy."

More smacks came from the humans below.

Mila bowed, then reached into her hat. "And with the right energy, I can bend time and space." She pulled out a small, flat box. "For this next trick, I need a volunteer."

My siblings finished their meat-feasts and joined me in watching Mila. Boppity sniffed hopefully at my food, but I was in no mood to share.

"Good evening, Mr. Cavendish. Thank you for volunteering." A man with fur under his nose in the shape of two slightly curled cat tails nodded at Mila. His shiny black hair was slicked down onto his head, and his skin was the pale color of my meat-feast. I doubted he tasted good, though. Even from this distance, a powerful fragrance wafted from his broad figure and filled the stage.

Mila lifted her little rectangle. "Mr. Cavendish, can you confirm that this is an ordinary deck of cards?"

He unwrapped a compellingly crinkly layer of cellophane from the little object and dropped it to the floor, opening the box inside and inspecting its contents. Handing it back to her, he nodded.

Mila dropped the box and fanned out the cards it held. "Pick a card, please, sir, and memorize it, but don't show it to me. When you're ready, put it in your pocket."

He gave her a questioning look, but she nodded encouragingly. This was far less interesting than the flowers had been. Mila was talking about space and time, swooping her cape, and waving her arms around wildly. The lights even flickered for a moment. Yet nothing fun was happening.

I was beginning to lose interest.

I took another lick of my meat-feast, allowing its flavors to flow across my palate as I savored it. Then Mila lifted two glass bowls filled with scraps of paper. They wobbled as she brought them toward Mr. Cavendish, who reached into one of the bowls.

"Table C," he boomed. His voice was like thunder. A group of humans in the room below waved their arms and made ridiculous, meaningless noises. Mr. Cavendish dropped the scrap of paper, and it fluttered to the floor like a butterfly. My pupils narrowed. I wanted to pounce on it so badly my paws twitched.

"Seat Six," Mr. Cavendish intoned, dropping yet another tantalizing scrap of white to the floor. A white-haired woman with a sturdy frame leaped up, arms in the air, screeching as if she was being attacked. But no danger presented itself.

"Who is it?" Mila asked. "I can't see past the lights."

"It's me! Mary Scarborough!"

Mila smiled warmly. "Ms. Scarborough! Lovely. Please look underneath your chair."

The lady lifted up her seat and pulled out something trapped between the frame and the cushion. "It's a card!" she called out. "The two of hearts!"

"The two of hearts," Mila repeated, smiling broadly. "Mr. Cavendish, was that your—"

But Mr. Cavendish was fumbling around at the inside of his shiny black jacket, tugging at a pocket and scooping his fingers inside. "What the devil . . . Where is it? I put it right here!" His voice was loud, but he smiled broadly, looking pleased. If something had been stolen from him, shouldn't he be upset?

Nobody was upset. In fact, they were all making those smacking sounds with their hands again, which I was beginning to realize meant they were happy with Mila.

Humans were strange. Finishing the last of my meat-feast, I considered our surroundings. We were still imprisoned in this box, and Mila was far away, playing games that occasionally looked fun, but not including us at all. Obviously, she had forgotten us. I wasn't about to allow us to be stranded again. This time, we might not survive. I needed to break us out of here.

The fur-faced human was nowhere to be seen, but his dog, Brutus, was approaching our box, sniffing eagerly. Boppity was about to strike at his muzzle again.

"No," I told him. "Don't." He turned to glower at me, but I would have none of his insubordination. I was the one responsible for our safety, and I had a plan.

"Heyyyy," I yowled. Brutus's big eye appeared at one of the slots. Except for humans, most animals could understand one another across species, provided they could see each other. Body language and even some basic voice sounds were largely universal.

"We have yummy food-cans in here," I told him. His ears perked up with interest. No doubt, the smells from our box had been his main reason for braving the terror of Boppity's paw for a third time. "You want some?"

"I sure do," he said. His body was full of coarse, goofy enthusiasm. I lifted my chin, embarrassed at his indignity, but he didn't seem to notice.

"What? No way!" Boppity protested. "There might be tidbits left. We're not sharing!"

"Sharing is nice," Boop murmured.

"It's a reasonable trade for our freedom," I told my brother sharply. His tail twitched, but he fell silent.

I turned back to Brutus. "If you make a hole in our box big enough for us to get out, I'll lead my siblings away so you can help yourself," I told him.

"Okay!" He wagged happily as he draped a massive paw over the top of the box and began to gnaw. I felt a shiver of apprehension as I watched his huge, pearly teeth pierce the edifice of our prison. His powerful jaws crushed the corner, and his eyes met mine. I nodded.

Terrible shudders wracked our enclosure as he firmed up the hold of his paw and gave a sharp pull. I didn't mean to close my eyes, but I must have. When I opened them, an entire quadrant of the box was gone. Brutus shook it violently a few times to make sure it was dead, then dropped it and turned to me.

"Thanks," I said. He wagged happily as I led my siblings out of the box. "Come on, guys, let's find a way out of here."

Mila was talking again. I felt a pang of regret. Her fingers had been magical, and her meat-feast had been glorious. I did not want to leave her behind, but she'd forgotten us. We were on our own. I turned to give her a last sad look.

Alone on the stage again, Mila raised her arms. "All of the magic you've seen this evening has been leading to this moment! The object I am about to show you is so powerful that with it, I can make an invisible hole into another dimension and pull something special through!"

She pulled a piece of cloth from the table, sending the clear cellophane and the little crumples of paper skittering across the stage.

Of its own accord, my tail twitched again.

If I was tempted, though . . .

Oh no.

I looked over at Boppity, but it was too late. He soared through the air toward the twisting sheet of fabric brushing against the red velvet curtain beside us. With a joyful trill, Boop raced after him. There was nothing to do but follow close on their heels. After all, I was in charge. My family was my responsibility.

Boppity narrowly missed the corner of the fabric, landing behind it on the stage floor. Mila flicked the cloth into the air and it shot upward, vanishing, to reveal the room full of people on the other side.

A cooing roar rose from the sea of humans below us. Words drifted up from it.

Kittens!

Out of nowhere!

How cute!

Wow!

Awwwww!

Amazing!

They were smacking their hands together again.

Mila froze, eyes wide. Then she turned to her audience with a broad smile.

"That's right, friends, I can make kittens appear out of thin air! Magic is a wondrous thing!"

From the audience, a thunderous voice boomed, "Make them disappear again!"

"I . . . uh . . ." Mila's eyes were racing around the room. Her smile faltered as her gaze fixed on the audience. She cleared her throat, and her fingers began to tremble.

A lesser cat would never have understood the situation. My siblings certainly didn't. Boop was purring and staring into the lights, and Boppity was eyeing the hem of Mila's cape.

But our arrival had caused her a problem. It was something to do with the demand of the human with the nose-tails that she should make us disappear. For some reason, obeying him was important to her.

She started toward us, her cape swirling.

I watched Boop gazing at Mila, hindquarters quivering as he prepared to pounce, and I knew what I needed to do.

Squeezing my eyes halfway shut and twitching my tail in concentration, I shooed away all of the photons that were heading toward me and my siblings, just as Mila's cape swirled past us. Only our shining black pupils remained visible, absorbing the ambient light so we could see. It was enormously difficult but I was, after all, a very impressive kitten. No photon dared defy my will. I was Bippity, the Light-Bender!

Even I could no longer see myself or my siblings, save for their gleaming, iridescent pupils, and when the cape swirled past, neither could the humans.

Shrieks and high whistles sounded from the room of tables, and Mila leaped back, staring at the ground where we had been visible a moment before. Boppity was darting about like a comet, no doubt shouting with his invisible tail about how fierce and terrifying he was and how his enemies had better watch out.

The humans below were so noisy that I twitched my ears and nearly lost command of the photons. Boop meandered over and scaled Mila's fluttery gown, gazing fondly at her face. She whirled around, her mouth and eyes making three perfect O's.

For a moment, I thought she was going to scream, but as Boop perched beneath her left ear, purring, she seemed to grow surprisingly calm.

It was becoming incredibly difficult to keep shooing all of the photons from three different areas at once. Somehow, though, Mila seemed to sense that my grip was slipping. She raised a hand in the air.

"Are you ready for the kittens to return from another dimension?" she asked, her voice growing steadier and louder with each word.

The humans below hollered. "Bippity . . ." she intoned. "Boppity . . ."

Hearing his name, my brother hurtled himself at Mila's cape and began to climb, soon arriving on her right shoulder. I leaped up onto the table in front of her.

"Boop!" Mila shouted.

I released the photons, which leaped back to their usual paths of travel. The three of us reappeared abruptly.

Hearing their name, Boop reached out a paw and tapped Mila smartly on the nose.

The humans leaped to their feet, roaring and stomping.

I allowed myself to bask in the glory of my own incredible achievement as the exaltation of the seemingly endless ocean of humans crested all around me. Mila bowed, steadying Boppity and Boop with her hands as she lowered and raised her body. Then she lifted me from the table and raised me into the beam of light before her. Impossibly, the cheers grew even louder!

Just when I thought the noise of the humans couldn't get any louder, there was a massive crash behind us.

Mila jumped and spun, and the room went silent all at once.

On the floor behind Mila sprawled a human.

A dead one.

Chapter Seven
The Body

Boppity.

Mila's heart was hammering so hard I could feel her body pulsing beneath my paws. Her eyes were huge balls of white with only a little black dot ringed in green at their center. Her hands flew into the air, dropping Bippity to the floor with a soft *mmph* sound. Then a caterwaul higher and louder than anything I'd ever heard before filled the air around us.

It wasn't until Mila's wail finally stopped that I realized I had been yowling along with her. I curled my claws into the shoulder of her cape as she sunk to the floor, splaying out her palms. She was frozen. Staring.

So was I. The thing in front of us didn't look injured. It *looked* human. It looked like a shiny man with shiny golden hair in a shiny gray suit. It could have been sleeping, except its eyes were open.

And there was a massive silver knife protruding from its chest.

Its cloudy, unblinking gaze was horribly empty. It wasn't a person anymore. Just meat that still had a face. I told myself I wasn't afraid, but my stare scooted away from it and wouldn't go back.

Instead, I looked down at my sister. Her huge eyes darted. Something was repeating over and over in her body language. Something I didn't want to see. But I couldn't help it.

"Dead. He's dead."

Just like Mother.

A sharp, bitter howl filled my chest and throat. When I opened my mouth, it escaped, filling the room and drowning out Mila's soft sobs. She was repeating herself over and over, just like Bippity, except she was saying, "Brandon. No. Please. Brandon."

A man from the pit of humans leaped up the stairs and onto our stage. He knelt by the former human, settling his fingers beneath the jaw. His mouth tightened until his lips vanished completely.

After a moment, he shook his head. A metallic star gleamed on his beige shirt. "Sorry, Mila."

"I . . . I don't understand, Pete." Her words were broken into pieces and pushed out between gasping sobs. Her whole body had wilted like the floppy green nonsense humans stuck into a tuna sandwich. "Someone stabbed him? He was m-murdered? And why was he . . . Why was he up there? What possible reason could there be?" Mila was shaking so hard that Boop slid down from her left shoulder and dropped into her lap.

They stayed where they landed, sprawled on their side across Mila's thigh. I watched them stare at the dead Brandon with eyes so wide, the blue rims of their irises seemed to have vanished entirely.

"I don't know." The man shook his head again. "He's been dead a while. Based on his condition, I'm gonna guess about four hours. I'll have to get verification. Consult with someone on the mainland. I've nev—" His voice crumbled like loose gravel. He made a choking growl deep in his throat. "Never dealt with a murder before."

The crowd on the floor below us lurched and churned, voices rising in a noisy tangle.

The man with the gold star, Pete, put his fingers to his lips and made a sharp whistling sound. He scanned their faces with his eyes.

"Everyone, quiet," he ordered. "Deputy Chantelle, get everyone outside in an orderly fashion. Don't let anyone leave the premises until I get statements."

A curvy woman with blonde hair gave a determined nod.

"But I—" blustered the man with the tail-shaped decorations on his upper lip.

"Sorry, Mr. Cavendish." The deputy's tone was crisp. "You, too. Won't take long."

Sheriff Pete set a hand on Mila's shoulder. His voice got gentle and kind. "Are you okay?" When Mila nodded, he said, "Why don't I have your landlady take you home? Do you mind, Ms. Fi?"

"Of course not," said a woman with short, tight curls in a mix of white and black. Her complexion was the medium-beige shade of our home-box. She put a gentle hand on Mila's forearm.

"Thanks." Sheriff Pete gave Mila a worried smile. "Okay, try and get some rest. I'll come check on you and get your statement tomorrow morning."

Mugsy shuffled over from behind the fuzzy red curtain, holding the box Brutus had chewed open for us. It was hastily repaired with grayish tape.

We were stiff with shock as he scooped us up and deposited us inside. After some jostling, cool outdoor air drifted in around us. A gentle voice, gravelly yet sweet, said, "Let's get you home, dearest."

We watched through the slits in our box as we were loaded into Mila's car. Nobody made a sound. Not even Bippity, though she did start to shake. Boop tried to give her purrs, but they sounded weak and tinny. Mila's smell all around us was our only comfort. Eventually, the car stopped. The door opened, and the kind voice said, "Come on. I'll help you into the house."

Fresh air tinged with the scent of lilac washed over us. Ahead of us was a big house with a wide white porch like the ones I'd seen in the real estate pages. The blue wooden exterior had two front doors—number thirteen on the left and number fifteen on the right.

The half of the porch in front of fifteen was screened in. As I watched with wide eyes, a flap in its door opened, and the most beautiful cat I'd ever seen appeared. She had long, silky fur whose swirls of black, orange, and white made me think of stars and galaxies whirling through the clear night sky.

"Help!" Bippity shouted at her. "We're trapped in this box again and a man called Brandon is dead and everything is awful! Hellllllllp!"

When I heard her say *dead,* there was a terrible lurching sensation in my chest. I began to yowl. "Motherrrrrrr!"

Boop pressed their ears back against their neck. Their eyes went wide with desolation. "We are miserable! Miserrrrablllllle!" they cried.

"Desist that ruckus at once, catlings." Her voice was as strong and wise as an ancient mountain. Her tail twitched with irritation. "Mila is obviously in crisis. She needs you. Gather yourselves immediately."

My siblings and I quieted.

"Good." She flicked a tufted ear and sat, tucking her chin primly. "See to her for the night. Tomorrow, I will get my human to bring me to you for a visit."

Get her to? I wondered how this worked. As far as I could see, the humans couldn't understand our language at all.

There was some shuffling and jostling as we were brought through a dim room with a lumpy brown sofa and a low glass table set atop cream-colored carpet. We arrived in an equally dim room, smaller than the first, with a tiny dresser and a huge, fluffy bed. The human voice, the rumbly-sweet one, returned as our box was set onto the bed.

"Here you are, dearest. Let me just get your shoes off, and . . . that's right, into the covers, and here's a box of tissues." The lady shuffled away, returning after a moment with a pitcher, an empty glass, and a low, flat dish.

"Here's water for the kittens," she said, filling the dish and setting it down inside our box, "and three cans of food." She added three open tins of meat-feast, then tore away the tape holding the crushed portion of our box together.

Setting the pitcher and empty glass on a little table next to the bed, she said, "Here's water for you. Don't pour more than you can drink unless you want it on the floor."

"Thanks, Ms. Fi." Mila's voice was weak and quavery. But the other human was padding away again.

Hunger overrode all of the other instincts flooding through me. I shoved my face into the dark brown glop, gulping it down as fast as I could. I needed my strength if I was going to look after this human.

Ms. Fi returned with a low, flat rectangular box filled with grayish sand. She set it in the corner, then pushed a stool up against the bed so we could get down to it and back up again.

I bite-scooped another mouthful of food and looked at her face. She wore a soft, sad smile as she looked directly into my eyes.

"Take care of her," she told me.

I chomped a huge hunk of meat-feast. "I will," I assured her. I looked over at Mila.

She looked crumpled and ragged. "Thanks," she murmured again to Ms. Fi.

Ms. Fi nodded. "Always. I'll be back tomorrow morning to check on you."

She pulled the door to our room closed behind her. Bippity had only taken a few nibbles of her feast and a few licks of water, but she climbed out of the box and stalked up Mila's chest, inspecting her.

"You okay?" she asked. "You're leaking." Streams of water flowed from Mila's eyes and down her cheeks. Maybe something fragile had broken inside of her.

Boop took a last bite of their tuna-feast and joined Bippity. "Here," they offered with a deep, rumbly purr. "Let me help." They licked at the water on Mila's face.

She gave a half-hearted giggle, but her eyes were sad and her breath hitched.

Mila was my responsibility now. Ms. Fi had said so. Reluctantly, I turned away from my roast-feast and scaled her. I knew what she needed. Climbing right up to her face, I put my paws on her chin and gazed at her. I could see right away that her heartbreak mirrored my own. She needed to know she wasn't alone. I would cry with her.

I tucked myself up next to her cheek on the fluffy pillow and released my grip on the pain I had barely held at bay ever since the dead man fell from the sky. "Motherrrrrrrrr . . ." I cried silently. "Motherrrrrr."

Bippity and Boop smooshed in on either side of me. Mila's arms curled around us, and she buried her face in our fur.

Her soft sobs rocked us all to sleep.

Chapter Eight
The Big Cat

Boop.

It was lovely to have Mila in our snuggle pile. We were all exhausted, so we slept nice and hard. I woke up first. A few hopeful sniffs of the empty meat-feast cans did not cause them to refill themselves, so I decided to try out the new sandbox.

The ground inside had a sink-slippy texture I loved immediately. I paced around for a while, putting my pawprints everywhere. Making a little hole for my business and burying it was so much fun that I decided not to leave when I finished. I was twirling around, flinging pawfuls of sand through the air and singing a chirp-tune of joy, when a much louder bit of music eclipsed my own.

Ding-dong! it sang. Mila shifted in her sleep. I looked around, bewildered, before realizing that it was our new home that had sung to us. What a cheerful sound! I hoped it would do it again.

Then it did!

Ding-dong!

"No! Brandon!" Mila shouted. She bolted upright. "What? Oh. Uh . . . Coming!"

Bippity and Boppity tumbled into the pillow crater where her head had been. They made a wobble-eared heap and blinked bleary eyes. Mila was heading to the bedroom door, so I trotted after her, trilling hopefully.

"Meat-feast?" I sang. "Lovely tuna-feast for meeeeeee?"

She giggled and lifted me in her huge, warm hands. "Round face, short tail. You're Boop."

"And you're Mila," I told her, tapping her nose with my paw fondly.

"Hi, little love," she said.

"Hello," I purred.

Beneath me, Bippity was following up on my request. "Food?" she called out.

Boppity was less circumspect. "Feed us, human!" he hollered. "Feed—" he went silent midyell. "Intruders!" he hissed. "At the door. Battle formation!"

I wasn't interested in battle. Mila was giving my neck the loveliest little scratches. I watched through half-closed eyes as Bippity darted beneath the sofa. Boppity zoomed around the room, scouting for a good hiding place.

Mila was reaching for the doorknob when Boppity discovered a spot between the door and the open expanse of the big room. It was a large urn full of dirt with a whole miniature forest of grassy green stems growing up from it. How interesting. I wondered if it was a human snack. Boppity burrowed to the middle of the dense thicket.

As soon as he was in place, he grew completely still. Invisible. How impressive he was. I was lucky to have such a fierce brother.

When Mila pulled the door open, a delicious fragrance drifted into the room.

"Hello, dearest," said the woman at the door. I recognized her from last night. Ms. Fi, who'd brought us meat-feast and water and the wonderful box of sand. Maybe she had more food for us.

"*Trrrnow?*" I asked hopefully. "Yummies?"

Then I smelled something even more wonderful than food. I looked down.

It was the Queen cat from last night. The one who had told us to take care of Mila.

The shrubbery concealing Boppity jiggled ever so slightly. Preparing his hindquarters to launch, no doubt. But he was terribly fierce. If he pounced on the Queen, she might leave.

I didn't want her to leave.

I opened my mouth to warn her, but before I had a chance, the regal cat bopped my brother on the forehead with a paw. She didn't even have to look. As she strode past, Boppity tumbled from his hiding place and landed on the floor.

Bippity scooted out from beneath the sofa, hilarity fluffing out her whiskers and tail.

"What are *you* laughing at?" Boppity fizzed. His fur stuck out in crooked spikes, and there was a bit of green on his ear.

The muzzy sleep energy was fading from Mila, replaced by sharp spears of grief and fear. Ms. Fi smiled at her. "How are you today, dearest?"

Mila's shoulders tensed, but she said, "Hello, Ms. Fi. Hello, Hylia."

Now I knew the Queen cat's name. Hylia. It sounded magical.

"I'm alright." Mila smiled, but only her mouth looked happy. The rest of her was still sharp and sad.

I looked up at her. "You're not," I told her.

I guess I shouldn't have, because she set me down on the sofa and hugged Ms. Fi, who hadn't corrected her. Maybe humans didn't like to talk honestly about their emotions.

Boppity sniffed hopefully at the basket hooked over Ms. Fi's arm. Red and white checked fabric was draped across whatever lay inside. Fragrant steam escaped, drifting into the room. The basket made its way toward a slick-floored kitchen, where it settled itself gently on the table. Boppity stalked it, belly low to the ground, ears and tail flat.

I hopped down to join him, my belly plopping into the soft carpet.

But he was way ahead of me. He flung himself into the air and soared like a panther, splatting into the side of a chair and claw-scaling his way up its back. I couldn't help admiring his delicate, elegant grace. As soon as he'd scrabbled to its peak, he leaped again, organizing his paws after a brief sideways skid. What a nimble warrior he was.

I wondered if I could do all that. The smell from the basket made me eager to try. Picturing his impressive moves, I jumped at the chair.

I missed. Maybe I was better at plopping than soaring.

Boppity stood on his hind feet and pulled at the fabric with his front paws. He had almost uncovered the treasure inside when Hylia leaped up onto the sofa and settled herself neatly on its middle cushion.

"Come, catlings," she called out. Her meow was clear and musical. Boppity ignored her, intent on the basket. I padded toward her beautiful, fluffy fur. I wanted to nuzzle into it.

"Is Hylia going to be okay with the kittens?" Mila asked.

That gave me pause. What could Mila mean? What about us could possibly not be okay with Hylia?

Ms. Fi shrugged. "I guess we'll see. I trust her, though."

Hylia's voice rang out again. "Now."

This time, her command vibrated through my bones. My body softened into a freeze response just like the one that came when Mother grabbed me by the scruff. I pivoted and marched to her as if I was being propelled by her voice.

Bippity and Boppity arrived on either side of me.

As we approached, Hylia puffed out her sumptuous fur and lifted her tail, pinning her ears.

Wintery panic clenched my throat and froze the air around my siblings. She looked like she wanted to battle us. There was no way we could defeat someone so magnificent.

"Pretend we are enemies," she growled.

My siblings immediately copied her posture, hissing.

I looked from them to Hylia and started to purr. Her coat was so beautiful, and her energy was firm but friendly. I couldn't resist rubbing my whiskers against her foreleg, and once I felt how soft she was, I wrapped myself around her and purred even louder.

She flicked an ear at me in irritation. "Not good at following instructions, are you?" she muttered.

"I love you," I told her.

She sighed, then sat. "Well, I suppose you do need some tidying up. You're covered in the sharp, rude smells of the human world." She pried me from her foreleg and pinned me down, then bent and began to groom me.

Bippity and Boppity ran up and began to sniff attentively at her majestic ruff.

"Now listen closely," she said. "Mila may be in danger."

"Aw, look at them!" There was light in Mila's voice for the first time since Brandon's body fell.

"I've never seen the like," Ms. Fi responded. She didn't sound surprised, though. Her tone was laced with affection.

Ms. Fi guided Mila to a chair at the kitchen table, then fiddled with a machine on the counter. Soon, a bitter, tangy stink like burned dirt began to clog the air.

"Mmm . . ." Mila sounded pleased despite the poisonous stench. "Coffee smells good. Thank you, Ms. Fi. At times like this, I can almost believe the rumors that you have some sort of magical powers."

"Kids do love their spooky stories," Ms. Fi laughed. "But it's nothing more than coffee and the experience of my years. Even after shock and tragedy, life goes on."

Once she'd set a mug of hot, stinky beverage before Mila, she padded across the creamy fur-floor to us. She placed a dish in front of Hylia and stroked the cat's elegant head.

"Your favorite sage and Manchego biscuits, love," she murmured. The dish held two steaming, fluffy disks rich with the scent of purest heaven. Hylia's chin lifted in regal acknowledgement of her human's adulation. When her eyes squeezed briefly shut, her fondness for her human made my belly warm.

"Sit, kittens." Her whiskers twitched in satisfaction as we obeyed. She bent, pulling a dainty bite from the edge of one of the biscuits. My siblings stared with unabashed longing. "You are new to this world, and there are things you must understand. Let me tell you about your home, Corvin's Crossing. Then I will explain about humans and cats, and about humans and murder."

She took another neat bite. "First, imagine a cat racing toward the sunrise."

I liked this game. I pictured a cat just like Boppity, with big paws and a long tail.

"Now imagine that you lay the cat down flat and trace its shape onto paper."

Weird, but okay.

"If you were in the sky, floating with the clouds, and you looked down on Corvin's Crossing from a great height, our island would look a bit like the shape on the paper in your mind, surrounded by sea on all sides."

OooooOOOOoooo. "Then we would be the size of teeny tiny fleas?" Boppity asked.

Hylia twitched her whiskers, amused. "Correct. Sunrise is east and sunset is west. Toward the calm sea where the ferry boats land is north, and toward the raging ocean that breaks itself on the cliffs is south. The middle of the cat is the center of town. The tail, at the northwest, is Wilby's Woods, where the human hospital is located. It, along with the head and paws, are full of hazards."

"We are little cats on a big cat," I purred.

Boppity tilted his head. "Are we near the tail? I think I smell woods nearby."

Hylia's eyes softened with approval. "Yes, clever kitten. Just below the base."

Bippity paid close attention, even after Hylia nudged one of the biscuits toward us and we all began devouring it, so Boppity and I focused on our treat.

In the background, Ms. Fi said, "Tell me how you're really doing."

Mila sighed. "I don't know. Brandon's gone, and I'm sad and tired and . . ." She tapered off, then said in a small voice, "And angry, which doesn't make any sense. Nothing makes sense."

"Sometimes," Ms. Fi said gently, "I think we're so busy trying to do what we're supposed to do and feel what we're supposed to feel, we forget to just be ourselves. You'll figure it all out. Try to trust yourself. Even your anger makes sense to me. Brandon was no prince."

"What do you mean?" Mila sounded tense, like she was getting ready for battle. I couldn't imagine why. Maybe I should go over and cuddle her.

"Listen." Ms. Fi leaned closer. "Brandon's gone. Possibly murdered. You're the girlfriend, and that's going to make you a suspect. Especially because of what he was up to before he died."

Hylia's growl snapped my eyes to her.

"Pay attention, kittens. Mila is going to need your help."

"But how can we help her?" Bippity asked. "Humans are huge and strange and absolutely incompetent at communicating. They make good servants, and they're nice to sleep on, but how could we ever help them?"

Hylia tilted her head. "Mila is your responsibility, at least for now. You must use your abilities to help her discover who murdered her boyfriend."

"Our abilities?" Boppity asked.

Hylia's eyes narrowed. "Surely your mother taught you about cats and physics? What the humans call *magic*."

We were all quiet.

Mother had mentioned that cats could do special things, but had also said that we were too young to learn. She'd promised to teach us as our abilities began to appear. Even Bippity's most eager pleas, Boppity's fiercest pounces, and my deepest purrs had been unable to convince her to tell us more.

Boppity's eyes glazed over. "Mother," he whispered.

I glowered at Hylia, then abandoned the biscuit and crept over to him. Starting up a gentle purr, I licked his tail.

Bippity put herself between my now quivering brother and the big Queen. "We lost her before she could teach us." I was impressed by her calm demeanor, so at odds with her dark grief, as she described our mother's disappearance and our rescue from the brink of death. Boppity shuddered, sinking into himself.

My poor brother. So strong. So wounded. I licked his ears.

At the table, Mila dropped her face into her hands. "I don't know what I'm going to do," she whispered.

Ms. Fi's voice was a gentle murmur. "It's okay, dearest. Everything will be okay."

Hylia was eyeing each of us in turn, her expression heavy with pity. "Learning the ways of cats can be hard for the motherless," she said.

Boppity gave a great mournful yowl. I redoubled my licking, trying to give him huge swirls in his fur like Mother always had.

Why had Ms. Fi and Hylia come here? They were only making everything worse.

I couldn't do anything but fill the room with as much love as possible. I purred louder. Eventually, Mila's head lifted and Boppity's fear and sadness began to fade.

But then a sharp *knock* at the front door threw us all into the air. We landed with wide eyes and stiff tails, staring.

Hylia was the first to relax. "Sheriff Pete," she said.

Ms. Fi opened the door, and sure enough, the beige-clad man with the shiny star on his shirt stood outside. He had been useful, especially when he'd taken charge of the raucous human crowd. Maybe he would help Mila.

"Morning, Ms. Fi." His voice was deep and friendly, but he had a calm, battle-ready air to him. "May I have a word alone with Mila, please?"

Ms. Fi nodded, then crossed the room to hug Mila, who sat cradling her steaming drink. "Remember," Ms. Fi whispered. "Be careful what you say."

Mila's posture stiffened. Cold fear tightened her face. I turned to ask Hylia what it all meant. Why did Mila have to be careful? And how could we help Mila? But the elegant Queen was already following Ms. Fi out the door.

Chapter Nine
The Confrontation

Mila.

"How you doing? You okay?" Pete asked. Why did everyone keep asking her that? It seemed perfectly obvious that she wasn't okay at all. Nobody would be, after watching their murdered boyfriend plummet to the floor like that.

"What do you need, Pete?" she asked. Ms. Fi's warning rang in her mind. But Pete wouldn't suspect her of malice. Ms. Fi had to be wrong.

Pete and Becca had taken Mila out for margaritas on her first night in Corvin's Crossing, nine years ago. She'd been friends with them both ever since. Nine years was longer than she'd ever been friends with anyone before.

"Could I sit for a minute?" He reached for a kitchen chair, tilting his head questioningly.

Mila nodded. "Sure. Let me just feed the kittens and grab you a cup of coffee."

She opened three cans of food and scooped them onto saucers. A little glow of warmth lit in her chest when she set the food on the floor and the kittens galloped toward their breakfast, emitting tiny peeps and mews of glee.

How simple it must be, living life as a kitten. She wished for that simplicity with all her might as she grabbed a mug and filled it from the pot Ms. Fi had made.

"I'm sure this must be hard for you, Mila," Pete started, "but I—thank you." He took a sip as Mila pushed Ms. Fi's biscuits toward him. "I've got to ask you a few questions."

"Okay." Her voice sounded far hollower than she would have preferred.

There was a scrabbling sound on the back of her chair. She bent over to see little ball of black fur clinging tenaciously to the upholstery. An aquiline face with huge eyes peered up at her. Bippity.

"*Yew*," the kitten said in a tone that brooked no argument. Her eyes widened even more, which didn't seem like it should have been possible.

Mila carefully unhooked her claws and set her atop the chair-back.

"Okay," she said to Pete. "So what did you need to ask me?"

Before he had a chance to respond, Bippity climbed up onto Mila's shoulder, huffing into her ear with a cold little snort. Mila giggled, a moment of buoyancy breaking through the crushing weight of reality. Her hand went to the kitten's soft back.

"He's a cute li'l guy," Pete said, pointing to Bippity. "Which one is that? Boppity?"

"She. It's Bippity," Mila responded. Her tone was colder than she'd intended. Nothing about this situation was Pete's fault. No need to take it out on him. "Can you just ask whatever it is you need to so I can get back to staring into my coffee and trying to come to terms with this nightmare?"

Sheriff Pete cleared his throat. "Uh . . . If this is a bad time, I can . . ." He shifted awkwardly.

"No. Sorry." Shame heated Mila's cheeks. "I'll try not to be so rude. I just . . ."

"Hey. It's okay, Mila." Pete gave her a gentle smile. "I'm having a hard time dealing with what happened, too, and I wasn't close with Brandon. Nothing about this situation is easy. I'm just going to ask what I have to for the investigation, so I can get out of your hair."

Mila nodded. She was sure his questions would be routine, which was good. She was full up on feelings she couldn't sort out. She didn't need any more.

"Your argument in the alley with Brandon yesterday. Could you tell me what it was about?"

"You heard the whole thing," Mila said. "Didn't you? It was just . . . Brandon told me he might not make it to my show. I told him I needed him. He called me melodramatic. That was it."

Pain lanced through her as she realized that was the last time she'd seen Brandon alive. The last words she'd spoken to him had been words of anger.

"Did he tell you why he couldn't be there?"

Mila blinked. Pete's face was carefully blank. What was he getting at?

"No. Did it have something to do with why he was mur—" She squeezed her eyes shut and clenched her jaw so her lips wouldn't tremble. "Why he was murdered?"

Pete searched her face. "Did you know he was meeting up with Becca last night?"

Mila's eyebrows lifted. "How did you know about Becca and Brandon?"

"She told me when I got her statement." Pete tilted his head, his gaze suddenly piercing. "How did *you* know about them?"

"Jenny told me when I was at the vet's office yesterday." Mila pursed her lips. "But if they met up during the show, Becca must have snuck out after I started my act. Wait, was that why he didn't come to the show? That jerk!"

Pete's mouth was tight. "So you already knew that Brandon was cheating on you with your best friend."

"I did. But I—" Mila leaped to her feet. Bippity scrabbled painfully for purchase atop her shoulder. "What are you implying, Pete?"

The sheriff watched her closely. "You found out about Brandon and Becca yesterday afternoon, and then last night, Brandon's murdered body turned up on your stage with your knife through his heart." He cleared his throat. "Have I got that right?"

"No! I mean, yes, but Pete, you don't think that I . . ." Mila swallowed. Could he really believe she was capable of murder?

"I'm not ready to jump to any conclusions yet, Mila. I just need to go where the evidence takes me."

Mila's hands were shaking. She curled them into fists. "Okay. I want to get to the truth as much as you do. What else do you need to know?"

"Did you see Becca leave during your show? Or did you see her at the bar or in the audience when you were performing?"

"The house lights are too bright. I can't . . ." Her throat was dry. She swallowed. "I don't . . ." This was all too much. Her head spun and her knees wavered.

"Mila!" Pete's voice was sharp with alarm. He lunged to his feet, reaching out to steady her.

Seemingly out of nowhere, an empty cat food can shot through the air and hit his stomach with a tinny *whack*, stopping him in his tracks. He looked around, confused.

Boppity sat in the middle of the carpet, a little pink toy mouse in his mouth. Boop was over by the two remaining food cans, sniffing them curiously.

Mila probably would have laughed, except that her initial shock was building into a boiling rage. It was bad enough that Brandon and Becca had been sneaking around behind her back. Now Brandon was dead and the suspects seemed to be her and Becca.

"Look." She rubbed her forehead. "I know you're just doing your job, but unless there's anything else you want to say, I need you to leave."

"Okay, fair enough." He stood to leave, opened the door, then looked back over his shoulder. "I . . . Sorry, Mila."

He pulled the door shut behind him and Mila collapsed to the sofa, emotions burning through her like wildfire. A soft nudge against her neck had her raising her palm to pet Bippity, who still clung to her shoulder. Boop was already clambering up into her lap, and Boppity abandoned his mouse to join them.

As Boop's rumbling purr soothed her jangling nerves, she let out a long, shuddering sigh.

"Good kittens," she said. "I'm so glad I found you when I did."

Chapter Ten
The Farm

Bippity.

I didn't know what an affair was or why it mattered, but one thing was clear. Mila was in some kind of trouble because of Brandon's murder. She needed to calm down and think, so I thought with her. She tried again to eat Ms. Fi's biscuit. I helped by trying to bury her coffee. It smelled like it belonged in the sandbox.

But she couldn't seem to quiet her anger. She leaped up and began to pace, frantically scribbling notes into a little notebook covered in purple rhinestones. "Is that why he . . ." she whispered, but then she interrupted herself. "No, that doesn't make any sense. Maybe Becca knows."

If there was meaning or value in this argument she was having with herself, I couldn't discern it. Perhaps it was intended to calm her, but it had the opposite effect. She grew more and more agitated as she stalked back and forth across the big room.

Finally, she unhooked a floppy gray backpack from the shoulder of a kitchen chair. She put it on backwards, snapping it to her front, and unzipped it.

"I look like a kangaroo now, right, Bippity?" she asked me.

She was neither furry nor brown, and lacked a tail. Her legs were long, but by no means ferocious. However, I didn't want to hurt her feelings by pointing out her deficits, so instead of answering, I rubbed myself along her ankle.

"Good kitty," she said, scooping me up and depositing me in the backpack. "Ms. Fi gave this to me. It used to be Hylia's when she was a kitten."

She set my siblings into the pouch on either side of me, then zipped it closed. We were swallowed in darkness. I opened my mouth to shout in protest, but then there was another zipping sound, shallower in pitch than the first.

We were still enclosed, but now there was only a sheer mesh barrier between us and the world.

"What do you think?" she asked. "You're so little, I don't feel safe leaving you here all alone. You could get stuck somewhere, or chew an electrical cord, or . . ." She shook her head. "I can't take any more calamity right now. So you're coming with me. Okay?"

I supposed this new conveyance would do, and said as much. Boppity grumbled about being unable to attack from here. Boop was elated. "I love it!" they crowed.

I rooted around a bit, investigating. The kangaroo pouch was less roomy than our box, but far cozier. We could hear Mila's comforting voice, feel her breathing, and lean into the warm cush of her belly through the thin layer of gray fabric. The floor was lined with fleece, and Boop was already kneading it and purring, a contented look on their round face.

Boppity was chirping to himself about how he'd shown that Sheriff Pete a thing or two with his amazing powers. I rolled my eyes. I hadn't seen him do anything but sit there with his toy.

"Here we go," Mila said. "I need to figure out who killed Brandon and why. Which means I'm going to have to talk to Becca." She grabbed her keys. Soon we were outside, smelling the fresh spring breeze.

A growl caught my attention as we descended the porch steps. I turned to look out the side window of the kangaroo pouch. Hylia sat in her screened-in porch.

Her spine was rigid with anger. Her narrowed eyes looked past me to Boppity, who went stiff under the weight of her furious stare and began to shake.

"I know what you did." Threat coiled through her body-language, silent and terrifying. Boppity clambered over me and Boop to keep his eyes locked onto her until she was no longer in sight. Once he was beyond range of her fury, he shook himself.

"She's not in charge," he grumbled. "Mila is *my* responsibility. *I* have to protect her." Obviously, he needed to be reminded that we were all responsible for the hapless human. Before I could correct him, though, I realized where we were going.

"Not the car again!" I hollered. Every time we rode in it, I felt like my stomach was trying to escape from my body and hop away like a clumsy frog. But my shouts were to no avail. The door clanked shut and the engine rumbled to life.

"Watch out for enemies, Mila," Boppity called. "They come from all sides! Here's one now, coming right at you!"

I fought to master my terror.

Unfortunately, I lost. "We're all going to diiiiiiiiiie!" I screamed.

Boop pushed themself into my back, knocking me flat against the fluffy floor, and wrapped their forearms around me, purring. I dug my back claws into the fleece, preparing to flip them off me. But their rumbling was a comfort, and their weight was not entirely unpleasant.

"Concentrate on me," they said. "Feel me smooshing into you. Listen to the beat of my heart and hear my love and caring."

"My stomach," I heard myself scream. "It's getting away!"

"Breathe through your whiskers," Boop murmured.

"What . . . ?" I bucked, trying to dislodge them so I could glower at them. "What in creation does that even mean?"

"Shhhh . . ." they soothed, cracking their mouth open so that their purrs took on that slobbery, echoing tone.

I rolled onto my side and struck their ear with my forepaw.

They purred even louder.

"Let your tail be an antenna to the sky gods," they intoned. "Vibrate your underfluff in harmony with the great question that rules all questions."

What utter nonsense. "I hate you," I grumbled. But the fight was going out of me, and I was growing inexplicably languid. My whiskers drooped.

At that moment, the car stilled, and its rumble went quiet.

"We're heeeeere!" Boop leaped off of me. "See? That wasn't so bad, was it?"

"Ahem. Right. Well." I twitched my left ear and licked my shoulder twice to gather my dignity. Time to see where Mila had brought us.

There was a boxy gold two-door car next to Mila's, decorated with a winged human halfway through taking a bow. "A Rolls," Mila muttered. "Mr. Cavendish must be here."

The air smelled wildly different than anywhere we'd been before. The salty tang of the sea was stronger, and over it was a rich blend of animal and plant scents. Ahead was a huge mauve farmhouse with lacy white trim dripping from its eaves like cookie icing. In its front yard stood a wooden sign painted with elaborate, curly letters.

Scarborough Farms Bed & Breakfast

A white picket fence surrounded the house. To its right, a little red barn sat inside of a taller fence, also painted white. In the field were three magnificent horses and two floppy-eared goats. I tried to introduce myself, but they must not have been able to see me through the mesh screen of the kangaroo pouch.

On the left side of the house was a field surrounded by a wire-mesh fence. Neat rows of little plants grew in its rich black soil. I couldn't tell what they were, but I was certain they had been planted by humans. The whole thing was far too orderly for the grand, riotous chaos of nature.

A rooster and half a dozen hens meandered around the field, scratching at the bases of the plants and dropping their business everywhere. None of them even had the self-respect to bury it. I looked away, embarrassed to witness their shameful behavior.

A tiny cottage, painted to match the barn, overlooked the neat rows of plants. It was exactly the right size for a pride of cats. But I didn't see any cats anywhere, nor could I smell any on the cacophonous breeze. As I watched, another hen emerged from the front door of the little cottage.

Who would go to the trouble of building such a beautiful house for a bunch of puffy, wayward-pooping birds? My tail twitched. Humans were ridiculous.

Mila opened a gate in the picket fence, and it closed behind us with a satisfying *clack.* A path of stepping stones led us up to the front porch of the main house. Instead of grass on either side of it, there was a sweep of low-growing herbs blooming in pinks and purples. Behind them, taller plants rose in a tangle of textures and colors and fragrances. Fat bees bumbled from blossom to blossom. Twittering birds sang out the weather report—sunny today, raining tomorrow—and announced our presence to one another.

When Mila pulled open the front door, a bell tinkled and a warm, delicious smell filled the air. Before I had a chance to look around, our kangaroo pouch was crushed between Mila's soft belly and another. The hugger had a soft pad of fat, too, but beneath it was hard, flat muscle. They smelled of hay and herbs and leather polish.

"Mflm Mf Ffmrmfm," said Mila.

The other voice was delicate, yet musical, with a wiry core. "Mflm, Mllmf," it said. "Ffm fll lmm fmfmmllm?"

"Hugs are nice," Boop told them.

I was more acerbic. "You're squashing us."

"Murderer! Release us at once!" shouted Boppity. He yowled a ferocious battle cry, and the hugger jumped back, releasing Mila.

"Are the kittens in there? I'm so sorry!" The new voice came from a white-haired lady I remembered from the magic show. She'd been the one with the card under her seat. I closed my eyes, thinking hard. Mother had said it was wise to pay attention to the names and ways of humans. I was nothing if not wise. I knew I'd heard this one's name before.

Ms. Scarborough, Mila had called her. I looked for a scar, but couldn't see one. *How did she earn her name?* I wondered.

She was a small woman with a sturdy build, draped in a neatly stitched calico dress printed with tiny purple flowers. Spectacles of gold wire perched on her round nose. She stood before Mila in a small room with a little writing desk beside the door. A faded photo of a man in a straw hat and overalls whose smile did not reach his eyes hung above it in a simple black frame inscribed, "Vernon Scarborough. Gone but not forgotten." I shuddered. He looked dour and unpleasant.

A mauve floral runner rug ran through the center of the hardwood floor. Plates painted with detailed enamel portraits of plump, colorful chickens dotted the rose-printed wallpaper, punctuated with brackets holding strangely elaborate spoons. There was a staircase in a hallway directly ahead of us.

To the left was a large room nearly filled by a massive cherrywood table adorned with candlesticks and lacy mats. On the walls around it were portraits of tragic looking humans standing on cliffs above crashing waves or framed by melodramatically flailing trees. Some of them had dour-looking dogs with embroidered collars and pointy faces lying at their feet.

To the right, behind the writing desk, was a room filled with windows that let in dusty rays of sun through cream-colored filigree curtains. Velveteen wingback chairs in varying hues of green were tucked into corners between bookcases crammed with books of every description, including an entire shelf of books by someone called Agatha Christie, many of which had the word *murder* in the title. A glass case held dozens of flat boxes labeled with mysterious names such as Jigsaw Puzzle, Trivial Pursuit, and Clue.

The man from the magic show, the one with the nose-tails, sat in one of the chairs, folding and unfolding a newspaper. What had his name been? Ah, yes. Mr. Cavendish. Remembering these humans was a lot of work. My family was lucky to have such a clever leader.

Ms. Scarborough hurried over to Mr. Cavendish and set a plate covered with a delicate ceramic dome onto a little table near his elbow. A pot of tea and a tiny teacup already sat behind it. She lifted the dome to reveal a white ramekin with ridged sides. A fluffy concoction the color of gold rose from it, filling the air with a bright, hearty fragrance. "Our house-made soufflé of parsley, sage, rosemary, and thyme with aged goat milk gouda and my fresh venison sausage. Every ingredient is made from scratch right here on my little farm."

"Thank you, Ms. Scarborough." His voice was as deep as thunder even when he talked quietly. "You're quite an impressive lady. Farmer, hunter, horsewoman, baker, chef, hotelier . . . is there anything you can't do?"

"Flatterer." Ms. Scarborough laughed and batted at his shoulder. Even though he made no effort to dodge, she missed him completely. I was not nearly as impressed as Mr. Cavendish.

She leaned forward, giving him a little smile. "I'm sure it's nothing like the elegance you're used to, but nevertheless, *bon appétit*!"

"It's lovely," he told her. "Your little bed and breakfast is charming, and your food is delicious."

"I'm so glad you enjoy it." She interlaced her fingers at her waist. "There aren't many places like this left in the world, you know. Little unspoiled towns where everyone knows one another by name. Old-fashioned establishments like mine, still doing everything by hand."

"I know, Ms. Scarborough. That's why I chose your Corvin's Crossing for my new Luxe Hotel and Resort. It's a special place. High-end tourists are going to love it. Maybe not as much now that there's a murderer on the loose."

"Maybe not, Mr. Cavendish. Although, some of us don't worry so much about what tourists think."

He gave her a noncommittal grunt as he turned to his soufflé.

Ms. Scarborough hurried back over and patted Mila's forearm. "Sorry about that, my dear. It wouldn't do to serve our esteemed guest a cold brunch, you know." She squatted down and peered into the window of our pouch.

"Hello there, dearies." She gave us a sweet little smile, then straightened. "They're beautiful," she told Mila. "How are you holding up?"

"I'm okay." Mila's voice was tight. "I really need to talk to Becca, though." As she spoke her friend's name aloud, Mila stiffened. "She's here ten to two, six days a week, right? Is she out in the barn doing stalls?"

"Right, plus she comes by most nights to spend time with the horses. But right now, she's upstairs clean—"

A thud from the staircase stopped Ms. Scarborough's words. Becca appeared, hauling a vacuum cleaner and a wide cart laden with cleaning supplies down the stairs. On the walls behind her were elaborate silhouettes of human faces cut out of black paper and set atop dainty lace doilies, framed in golden ovals.

"Becca, dear. Good." Ms. Scarborough reached up to help her with the cart. "I need you to clean out the hayloft this afternoon. Something died up there. I had to bring down three different bales this morning to find one that was fresh."

Becca nodded. "I haven't smelled anything, but then again, Mr. Scarborough always used to say warm air rises up through the barn and carries odors out the eaves."

Ms. Scarborough stiffened briefly, then curled her mouth in a sweet smile. "Of course, dear. He did, at that. Will you see to it for me?"

"Sure thing, Ms. Scarborough, absol—"

Becca spotted Mila and broke off. A complicated series of expressions washed over her face too quickly for me to read them. "Mila. What are you doing here? How are you holding up?"

Mila heaved out a sigh, half anger and half fear. "Sheriff Pete was just over at my house, and . . ." her voice cracked. "We need to talk about your affair with Brandon."

Becca's face went slack. Her wide eyes darted.

Ms. Scarborough glanced between the two younger women, her lips pressed together, and quietly cut through the dining room to disappear into the door on its far side. Mr. Cavendish cleared his throat and hid behind his newspaper.

"I don't understand. How could you do it?" Mila's body was rigid behind the kangaroo pouch. "You're my best friend."

Becca grabbed Mila's wrist and led her outside, to a bench beneath an arbor covered in thorny green brambles dotted with pink buds.

"Listen . . ." She swallowed hard, her brown eyes glassy in the sunlight.

"No." Mila held up her palm as if to push Becca away. She was shaking like a cold winter kitten now. "I know Brandon and I had our problems, but that's no excuse for what you did."

Tears welled in Becca's eyes. "Mila, I . . ."

A low growl started in Boppity's throat. I told him to hush, and he spun to face me, fur stiffening along his spine. "Ms. Fi told *me* to take care of Mila. She's *my* responsibility. That means *I'm* in charge here. Don't you hush me when I'm defending her."

"You're not in charge," I told him. "*I'm* the head of this family." Mother had reminded me to look after my siblings before she left for the last time. I intended to live up to her expectations. Boppity needed to be put in his place. "You nearly ruined everything at Mila's magic show, leaping out onto the stage like some clueless puppy. I'm in charge." I arched my back to cement my point, showing him how impressive and big I was.

"But you didn't raise a single paw when that Sheriff Pete upset Mila with his words, any more than you're defending her now. I'm the one who made a quantum entanglement between my Mousie and that meat-feast can."

I had no idea what that meant, but before I could ask, he continued.

"*I* used Mousie to hit that rude Sheriff with the can and sent him away. *I'm* the warrior here. *I'm* in charge. So *there!*" He slapped me hard with his broad paw. "Ha! Right in your self-important nose!" he shouted.

His strike and his words stung, but I couldn't let him know that. I tossed him a disdainful look. "You could *never* be in charge. Mother even said—"

Before I could finish, he hooked his paw around my neck and yanked, pulling me over so my shoulder landed in Boop's ribcage. We all tumbled into a yowling, fizzing, writhing pile of tangled paws and glaring eyes.

"Kittens!" Mila's voice was sharp and quavery. "Stop it! I'm . . . I . . ." her voice was crackling with misery. We froze, ashamed.

"I'm so sorry, Mila," Becca said. "I never meant to . . . I was in love with him. I wanted to tell you, but he told me to wait. I was supposed to meet him during your show to talk about what to do, but he never came."

"So you didn't see him yesterday before the show?" Mila asked.

"I didn't see him at all yesterday." Becca's voice was pleading. "I was working here until two, and then he had meetings right up until the show. His only window was while you were performing."

"Do you know what the meetings were about?" Mila asked.

"No." Becca shook her head. "Why do you ask?"

"It was my prop knife in his chest. My stage he fell onto. I need to know who did this and why."

"Maybe I could help?" Becca asked hopefully.

Mila stood. "How could *you* help? I can't even trust you. You're a liar and a cheat." She spun and stormed toward the car. Behind us, a choking sob rose into the air.

I turned to Boppity. His face was millimeters from mine, and I could see the hurt hidden behind the fury in his eyes. The verbal barbs I'd flung at my brother echoed in my mind. Remorse rose up in my chest and tightened my throat.

Maybe I didn't deserve to be in charge after all.

Mila flung herself into her car, closing the door with a thud. Her breaths were fast and ragged. I stared into my brother's eyes, feeling lost and hopeless.

Boop clambered on top of us and began to lick in broad strokes that started on Boppity's shoulder and ended on my spine. Their purrs reverberated through us.

Mila wrapped her arms around the kangaroo pouch. "Thanks, Boop," she murmured.

My mind raced. Mila really did need our help. These humans all seemed to care about her, but every time she talked to them, she ended up hurt and alone.

Chapter Eleven
The Law

Boppity.

"But why was Hylia mad? What did you do?" Boop asked. They rolled over on the living room carpet, showing their belly to the sun streaming through the window.

"All I did is . . ." I paused, turning my back to the door. There was a beautiful, angry cat out there. I didn't want to think about her, though. "It was easy." My eyes flitted from Bippity's fascinated face to Boop's drowsy one. "I just tangled up the qubits of—"

I was interrupted by a buzz at Mila's hip. She pulled her quivering phone from her pocket and put it to her ear. My sister, perched on her shoulder, was suddenly shrouded in magnificent shadow as the human's silky hair fell around her like a curtain.

"What are qubits?" Boop yawned, scootching toward a patch of sunlight on Mila's slipper-clad foot and draping themself across it. "Are they delicious?"

Bippity flicked her ear toward our sibling as if to scoff at their nonsense, then glanced at Mila, who lowered herself onto the cushy sofa.

"No, it's a good time. I'm glad you called, Mugsy. I don't know what to do. I can't believe Becca would do that to me. I really . . ."

As Mila's voice faltered, my sibling started to purr. "Well?" Boop coaxed. "Are they?"

I tilted my head. "Are what?"

Boop cocked their chin to the side. "Are qubits delicious?"

I stared at them. How could they be so clueless?

"No, silly," I sniffed. "You don't eat them."

"So . . . what are they?" This time, it was my sister asking.

I loved knowing things she didn't, so I considered refusing to explain. But then again, how would she *realize* how impressive I was, unless I told her?

"Yeah," Mila said. "I guess it takes two to tango. But Becca was my best friend, so . . ." She shook her head. "Well, I'm upset about all of it, obviously. Brandon's death, and the betrayal, too."

"You know." I shrugged casually. "Qubits. Units of quantum information?" I looked back and forth between Bippity and Boop, amused by their confusion. "Subatomic particles, like electrons or photons?"

At the word *photons*, Bippity's eyes lit with understanding. Not wanting to lose the upper paw, I continued. "I just entangled a bunch of the qubits in my toy Mousie with mates at corresponding locations in the can. Then, when I tossed Mousie into the air, the can had no choice but to mimic her."

"Of course," Bippity murmured. But the way she licked her shoulder, I knew she didn't understand what I was talking about.

She turned to watch Mila, who was talking again. "You did? No. I hadn't even thought about a service. Thanks, Mugsy. And please thank Q and Ms. Fi and Reverend Bak for me too. I don't know what I'd do without all of you. I just wish Becca hadn't . . ."

Boop walked over and poked Mousie.

Across the room, the meat-feast can rattled against the inside of the kitchen wastebasket, knocking it over. Trash spilled across the floor.

Huh. They'd stayed entangled. Neat.

"Aha!" Bippity shouted. "That's why Hylia is mad at you!"

I scowled. "What do you mean?"

"Weren't you paying attention to her when she told us about cats and physics?"

I shifted my eyes. If I was being honest, I'd been paying closer attention to the delicious biscuit. Hylia's lecture hadn't held my interest, once I'd figured out she wasn't going to teach us anything useful.

"See, this is why I'm in charge." Bippity's nose lifted pertly. "Hylia said that the first and most important Law of Cats is that we can never let humans know about our abilities."

"I didn't," I told her with a sour twitch of my whiskers. "The humans thought Boop whacked the can into him." I didn't love that I hadn't received credit for my fierce attack, but maybe it was a good thing after all.

"But if things are flying around all willy nilly, the humans are going to figure it out," Bippity said. "So no more Physics in front of them."

I glowered at her. She wasn't the boss of me.

"I don't know about *better off* without him," Mila was saying. "But I think I understand what you mean. He wasn't the kindest guy, sometimes. And now that the shock and horror of it all is starting to wear off, I'm weirdly not as sad as I thought I'd be? I'm more upset that I don't have Becca anymore, which . . ."

Mila lifted her hand to Bippity idly, stroking her back. "It wasn't all rainbows and unicorns, that's for sure, but it was familiar. Comfortable. It never occurred to me that I might not actually be . . ."

Unicorns and rainbows? What did that even mean? Humans were overly fond of nonsense.

Mila laughed. "That's not what I meant by rainbows, but I guess . . . I don't know. Maybe?" My sister butted her forehead against Mila's palm and shot me a self-satisfied look.

Whatever. I had more important things to do than be petted.

Being a tidy fellow, I figured I should disentangle the qubits. I stared at them sharply, finding the mated pairs and freeing them of their bonds. I didn't want to forget about an object pair I'd entangled and get thwacked. It had looked pretty painful when it happened to the human.

Painful . . . and hilarious.

I laughed, remembering the expression on his face. "Physics is my obedient soldier!" I announced. "I, Boppity the Great, World's Fiercest Warrior, have the universe itself at my command!"

Not to be outdone, Bippity leaned into Mila's hand again and chimed in. "I can command the universe, too," she preened. "I can shoo photons around!"

She lifted her whiskers and fanned them out. Vain creature. I tried to ignore how pretty she was, cloaked in the shadow of Mila's hair, eyes gleaming bright and blue as the sky. "Watch." She gazed at the patch of light Boop had just settled into. I stiffened in annoyed surprise as it slithered across the floor toward me.

"Awww," Boop grumbled. "Give that back."

"Hey! Mila could notice! You said . . . Ahhhhh . . ." The beam of sun settled on me, and I sighed in delight.

"That's actually a good point." Bippity blinked and the light vanished from my back and reappeared on Boop. I pondered pouncing on them and stealing it away.

"So Boppity can entangle qubits and move objects. I can command the light. What can you do, Boop?" Bippity asked.

"Me? I can purr." They demonstrated, starting up a warming rumble.

"Every cat can purr," my sister scoffed.

Boop squeezed their eyes half-shut, unbothered by her rudeness.

I had been creeping toward them, but it occurred to me that the sun might be even more cozy if I smooshed up against them instead of batting them away.

I gave it a try, savoring the warm sunlight and Boop's thrumming purr. As the twin comforts soaked into me, my irritation melted away. I suddenly felt calm. *Safe.*

Boop licked my ear fondly.

Everything was lovely. Perhaps it was time for a nap.

My eyes were growing heavy when there was a tap at the door.

I leaped into the air, hissing. I landed on Boop, who also leaped, their claws scrabbling at Mila's bare ankle for purchase. This caused Mila to yelp and leap to *her* feet, and Bippity tumbled from her shoulder. She let out a terrified, primal scream that cut off abruptly when she bounced to the sofa with a grunt.

Heh. Where was her precious dignity now?

"No," Mila said into her phone. "Just a bit of a kitten cataclysm. Listen, I have to go. Someone's here. Okay. See you there. And Mugsy? Thanks again." Mila slid her phone into her pocket and hobbled over to the door.

On the other side stood Sheriff Pete.

Not again. A low growl started in my throat. I'd fight him if I had to. I was half-tempted to entangle Mousie with something big. A *real* weapon. That way, I could teach that Sheriff a lesson he wouldn't forget. But then Hylia would be even angrier at me. I shuddered, chilled by the thought.

Mila gave Sheriff Pete a hug. I supposed that must mean he wasn't an enemy. Unless she was engaging in some sneaky warfare tactics I wasn't aware of. I narrowed my eyes. This situation required close monitoring.

"Hi, Mila. How are you doing?"

"I'm wishing people would stop asking me that," she snapped. "Sorry. I'm okay. What's that?" Mila pointed at a bundle of papers in his hand.

"Well, I need to fill you in on a few things," he said. He sounded tense. "Firstly, since all of Brandon's biological family are deceased, he had you on record as his next of kin. That means you're the one I give updates to. A medical examiner and a forensics expert from the mainland examined Mugsy's Club and the . . . er . . . body. We'll see what their findings are, but they said it's all pretty straightforward. I'll have their report tomorrow. Meanwhile, they cleared the crime scene so Mugsy can reopen, and they've released Brandon for burial, which—"

"Which you already told Mugsy, and he and Ms. Fi organized the service and the reception," Mila interrupted. "I know. Mugsy called and told me."

"Hope you don't mind." Pete gave her an anxious smile. "I just figured . . ."

"It's fine. I appreciate it. What else?" Her tone was clipped. "You said, 'firstly.'"

"Right," The sheriff shuffled his feet for a moment. "Since you're next of kin, you also need to handle all of Brandon's possessions."

"Wait, *what?*" Mila's face was white with shock.

Sheriff Pete's brow scrunched in confusion. "Come on, Mila, you must remember signing the paperwork. It's not like it was a birthday card or something. This is pretty important stuff."

"I've signed hundreds of 'pretty important' things," she said. "He was my business manager. I didn't pay attention when he put something in front of me and asked me to sign it. I trusted him."

"Really?" The way the sheriff pressed his lips together and lifted his eyebrows, he was obviously challenging Mila's honor. I grabbed Mousie, preparing to teach him a lesson, but Bippity slapped her out of my mouth.

"Don't you *dare,*" she hissed.

I was rearing up to tackle her when a jingling sound caught my attention. Sheriff Pete pulled something shiny from his pocket.

"Here are the keys to his car and loft. Seems his money is all tied up in some sort of investment or holding or something, which the bank is working on sorting through. Same down at town hall. Hopefully, the various departments can make sense of his holdings. Anyway, here you go." He dropped Brandon's keychain into her palm.

"Listen, Mila," he said. "All of this obviously gives you even more motive. We're still investigating, but the weapon was your trick knife and the crime scene was your stage. I need to formally instruct you at this point that you're not to leave town. You should probably hire a lawyer."

"But Brandon was the only lawyer in Corvin's Crossing. He . . . Wait. What are you saying? You're telling me I'm . . ." She shook her head. "Am I a suspect?"

Sheriff Pete rolled his lips into a tight line. "You're not *a* suspect," he said. "You're *the* suspect."

Chapter Twelve
The Glow

Boop.

Mila's hair flew out behind her as she wheeled and stormed back and forth across Brandon's shiny loft. Poor Mila. Her feelings got really big, really fast. I offered her a supportive purr as I gulp-chomped some water from a clear glass dish she'd set on the white marble floor.

Everything about Brandon's home was hard and slick and cold. Even the black leather sofa with the chrome frame. One wall held a massive portrait of a man with peachy skin, dressed in an old-fashioned suit. Huge strips of fluffy white fur billowed from his balding head down past his ears to his jawline, framing his face like a lion's mane. His sneer was oddly suited to the elegant, unwelcoming space.

The other walls of the loft were made mostly of glass. Stark cliffs below us were unconcerned with the raging sea smashing up against them again and again.

Bippity tucked her chin and gazed from the furious drama of the fiery sunset ocean to the tiny humans entering and exiting the tall apartment building far below. The entire top floor, and the views that went along with it, had belonged to Brandon and now belonged to us. My sister gave off a solemn, noble air, catly and benevolent, as she surveyed the teeming world of mortals. She would have made a very convincing sky god.

Boppity was glorious in an entirely different way. My brother zoomed around the apartment with his tail arched high and his back all afloof, shouting, *fyoo fyoo fyoo!* It wasn't clear what he was battling, exactly, but he was obviously winning. He had already mastered the graceful skid-and-scrabble maneuver, changing directions with the most precise flailing I had ever seen. Now, he appeared to be working on a new move where he ricocheted off of the walls to give himself even more speed. He was magnificent to behold.

I appreciated that my siblings were enjoying this new space, but I was worried about Mila. I poked my claws into the leather sofa so that I could scale its slick cushions, and when I reached its summit, I opened my mouth and gave her my loudest purrs.

"*Traaanoooun*?" I rumbled, adding the meaningless sound into the middle of my purr so that it took on a lovely, reverberating trill.

Mila stopped midstride and turned to look at me. For some reason, she burst out laughing. "Oh, my goodness, Boop!" She reached for me, a grin breaking across her features like a sunrise and clearing away the storm.

"You're so upset. What are we going to do?" I asked her as she lifted me to her chest, nuzzling my back. I rolled in her hands to give her easier access to my soft belly-fur.

"I can't believe this is happening. What am I going to do?" she asked me. Humans were not very good listeners.

She buried her nose in my tummy, and I stroked her cheek with my paws. "You're not alone," I told her. "Whatever it is, we can do it together."

"At least I'm not alone," she sighed. "Thank goodness I have you and your siblings."

"You sure do," I agreed.

"Someone murdered Brandon, and I need to know who. Which means I need to know why." She sighed, frustrated. "What do you think, Boop? I already looked through the files in his home office, but I can't find anything about this mysterious business of his. But he must have been up to something. Something that made someone want to kill him. If I don't figure it out, I could to end up in jail."

I wondered what jail was. Judging by her spiky, anxious intensity, it wasn't anything good. "Maybe we should make a nice comforting nest for some snuggles," I suggested.

"Maybe I should search the bedroom," Mila told me.

"Okay," I agreed. "We can search and make a nest at the same time. I believe in us."

Brandon's sleeping area, tucked behind a wall of frosted glass bricks, was just as flat and hard as the rest of his loft. The thick glass wall back here looked out over the forests and hills of Corvin's Crossing, striped with roads and dotted with shops and houses that glowed with warm and hopeful light against the rapidly darkening sky. A wide, low bed covered in gray silk was framed with tall chrome lamps. At the foot of the bed, a dresser made of the shiniest substance I'd ever seen held a huge flat-screen TV.

Mila set me down, which was disappointing until I saw the most charming, zestiest little kitten right in front of me. They looked so similar to my siblings, we could almost have been related. I lifted my tail in greeting, and they did too. So they were friendly!

Above me, Mila opened a drawer and rooted around inside. "Nothing good in here."

"*Trrrn?*" I asked the delightful kitten, who was looking right at me. "Play?"

They asked the same question at the exact same moment. Our voices overlapped so precisely that I either didn't hear myself, or didn't hear them. I took a step forward, closing my eyes halfway for a moment to signal affection, and so did they.

Yes! I was navigating my first new friendship perfectly! I raced toward them, eager to sniff noses and begin a friendly game of wrestle-chase.

Bonk! I crashed into something hard and bounced backward, dazed.

"Poor little Boop!" Mila's voice was concerned, but mirth flowed out of her in buoyant waves. I wondered what was funny. "It's just a reflection. See?"

She reached toward the dazed kitten in front of me, and a copy of her hand appeared in reverse. When the two touched, she pulled, and a drawer opened.

What trickery was this?

"You're going to need to get used to mirrors, sweetheart," she told me. "We magicians use them all the time." She picked me up, depositing me in a mound of soft-looking balls of fabric. "See? No kitten in here. Just socks."

I quelled my disappointment that my friend had been an illusion by getting down to the business of building a truly perfect nest. I could tell Mila really needed the comfort.

The first step, obviously, was to root around and fluff everything up. It was great fun, despite the sock bundles smelling like Brandon's copper and slate musk as opposed to Mila's hopeful petrichor and honey fragrance.

I was nudging mooshy lumps of viscose and cotton aside when one of my claws caught on something thin and flat and flexible. I peeled at it, trying to get it out of the way, but it was big. When I sniffed, it smelled like a mix of strange things, but pine tree pulp was one of them.

Paper! But this wasn't like the soft, crumbly newspapers Mother had brought us in our box. It was coarse and flat and no use at all for nesting. And rudely, it wasn't moving out of my way, no matter how much I batted at it.

The best solution was probably to eat it.

After all, if you ate the newspapers with boring stuff on them while Bippity wasn't looking, Mother would bring new ones. Then there would be new things to look at. Things that were full of facts and stories and emotions. This junk was mostly numbers.

I took a bite. It got melty in my mouth almost immediately, smashing into a wad that clung to my teeth. It was sticky and slimy and a little sweet. I chewed and chewed, making smacking sounds as I produced extra saliva to help me. Eventually, I got it soggy enough to swallow. The experience wasn't so nice, but I wanted a soft, tidy nest. I took another bite and began to chew as wetly as possible.

"What are you getting yourself into down there?" Mila asked. She must have heard my nom sounds and decided to help.

When she spotted the obnoxious paper that was stymieing my nest-building, she reached down and tugged at it. An entire book of the stuff came free.

"Aha!" she exclaimed. "This must be it!"

"Thank you for helping!" I said to her, but she didn't take a bite like I expected. She was tense. Angry. Her focus was on the nonsense written on the page.

"This is gibberish," she said. "I don't know how to . . ."

"Could you start chewing that one up?" I instructed patiently. "There's more down here." She didn't notice, so I added a "*mrrrrrt?*" sound to get her attention.

She didn't follow my directions, but her hand reached down again. This time, she rooted around, even unseating me with her fingers. She pulled out another book and a strange wooden spool with letters and numbers on it.

"Can you *believe* this, Boop?" she shouted in a battle voice. I could tell from the direction of her fierceness that the enemies were the books and the spool. "These books are in some sort of code, and this must be a codex! What kind of person has to *encode* their financials?"

Boppity came racing in, Bippity close behind.

"Where's the bad guy?" Boppity demanded. "Let me at 'em!"

Bippity was much calmer. "What's going on?"

Before I could answer, Mila's phone began to buzz. She looked at it and made an aggravated grunt in the back of her throat.

"Ugh. Becca. Leave me alone." She silenced the phone and put it away. "The more I learn about Brandon, the more obvious it becomes that I didn't know him at all. He was lying, keeping secrets, cheating . . . And who even knows what *this* is all about." She lifted the spool and the books.

Shaking her head, she scooped me and my siblings up, and deposited us into the kangaroo pouch. She slid the books into a mesh pocket in the back wall. Anger and hurt were sheeting off of her in hot waves. "I don't want to go to his memorial service. I just want to go home. I have to think. But Pete is already half-convinced that I killed Brandon. Maybe more than half. I can't be acting suspicious. I have to go."

I was prepared to help Bippity cope with the car ride again, but she was so busy staring at the nonsense-books that she barely even noticed.

* * *

When we parked and Mila climbed out of the car, I saw a spectacular building of glowing white wood whose roof rose toward the sky in an impossibly tall, impossibly straight spire like the tail of the proudest cat ever to have lived. It was lit from inside with a gentle, glowing radiance that shone down on us through a strange, beautiful window.

Instead of being plain, this window was made of colorful little shards, each outlined in black, which came together in the shape of a huge, flying bird in a patchwork array of lively hues that called to mind the boggling diversity of human emotions. Beneath it were two very grand doors that rose to an arched peak where the met, like the shape of a cat's ear.

I could feel Mila settling, her breath slowing. As she approached the building, I thought I felt a kind of glow coming from it that had nothing to do with the light. Mila turned away from the grand cat-ear doors and walked around the corner. There, she pulled open a gate in a wrought iron fence and followed a curving path through a tidy garden to a door that was far plainer. I was a little disappointed, until I realized that it was the same building, warm and welcoming.

The door creaked as Mila stepped in through the unassuming side door. If a room could give a hug, this one would've been golden and soft. My pupils constricted as I gazed around.

The big space was filled with long wooden benches, each topped with an equally long cushion that looked so fluffy that I found myself yawning and stretching, just in case this was a napping-house. The benches all faced a sort of stage to our right, with a tall, thin booth in its center.

Maybe this was a place for magic shows!

Little tables in the back corners contained flickering candles and neat stacks of books. A basket near the stage held an array of cans that reminded me of the ones Mila fed us meat-feast from, but much larger and with pictures of colorful human foods on them.

Around the room, the walls were hung with a variety of decorations, all equally spaced from one another. They ranged from plain to elaborate, but each was made in the shape of a lowercase *t*. Some had a man with brown or beige or white skin draped over them. Even though the men all looked vastly different, I thought they must somehow be the same human, because they all had the same expression of sadness and love on their faces.

Mila sucked in a breath and I stopped looking at the pretty Ts and glanced around to see what had caught her attention.

A slight figure was walking toward us. The magician, perhaps? He had short gray hair and a weathered face. His kind eyes were nearly the same shade of golden beige as his skin.

"Shoot," Mila whispered. "I'm not sure you guys are allowed in here. I'm going to zip you shut. Stay quiet."

"Mila," the magician said, his voice soft but full of kindness.

"Reverend Bak," she responded. "It seems I'm early." Uncertainty was building behind her ribs. *Reverend* must be a fancy word for a magician. "I guess Mugsy built in a buffer so I wouldn't be late. He knows me too well."

"It's okay," Reverend Bak murmured. His voice was so soothing, I felt myself yawn. "I'm glad to have a moment alone with you. I'm sure everyone is asking you how you're doing, but what I really want to know is how I can help."

Mila sighed. "I don't know. Everything is completely out of control. I keep thinking it can't get worse, and then it does."

"Perhaps we could pray together?" Reverend Bak suggested. "Would that be a comfort?"

Mila's lips tightened. "I . . . I don't think . . . That is, I'm not Christian anymore, Reverend Bak."

"I know. I'm glad you're walking down your own path. There's no pressure to, of course." His footfalls were soft as he came up beside her. "But there's no reason not to, unless it makes you uncomfortable. I've come, over the years, to think of faith like an enormous crystal. We all get to find our own way to connect with the truth at its center. We're gazing at the same Light, but each of us is pressing our faces to a different facet, trying to understand what we see. Why should we not pray together? Perhaps we'll each come away a little wiser than before."

He sneezed, which was an excellent way to punctuate his important message. I would try to remember it.

The tension faded from Mila's frame. "Okay," she said quietly.

They sat and began to whisper. She was talking to *Goddess* and he was talking to *Lord,* but that radiance I'd picked up from the building when we were outside began to build within them. Between them.

It grew until it reached a certain fullness. I heard the magician whisper *amen* and Mila chant *so mote it be*. They stood.

"Thanks, Reverend Bak." Mila's voice was warm and calm. "I hadn't realized how much I needed that."

Abruptly, we were smooshed between their bellies, surrounded by her smell, like golden light on wet earth, and his, like incense smoke and fresh garden herbs.

"Oof," Bippity complained.

"Rawrrrrr!" Boppity shouted. "You'll never crush us!"

I was in bliss.

The magician leaped backward. "Did . . . did your satchel just *move?*"

"Um . . . It's my kittens—"

He sneezed again.

"Oh." She sounded chagrined, but the magician burst out laughing.

"I do believe I would be a cat person, if only—" *Achoo!* "I weren't allergic. They're so wonderfully pensive, as if they had secrets." *Achoo!* "I believe they know things we can't even hope to imagine."

"Very sensible," Bippity agreed.

"Too loud, though," Boppity grumbled, flattening his ears as Reverend Bak sneezed again.

"I like him," I announced.

"I'm so sorry!" Mila stepped backward. "I should never—"

"No." The magician shook his head gently. "You should *always*. I'm here whenever I can be of comfort. Just—" *Achoo!* "Let me know if you're going to bring them, so I can take an allergy pill."

He put a hand on her forearm. "It's time, Mila. Are you ready for me to open the main doors?"

He watched her face carefully.

"Ready as I'll ever be," she said.

Reverend Bak gave her a gentle smile as he offered her a seat in the front row of benches, then turned to the doors.

Chapter Thirteen
The Service

Mila.

Her head swam as she listened to Reverend Bak go on and on about Brandon. He'd been a pillar of Corvin's Crossing. His little one-man firm, Jameson Law, had helped nearly everyone in town, from wealth management and probate law to real estate deals and environmental protections to weddings and even the occasional criminal case. He'd always shown up for his friends and neighbors, like the time he spearheaded hurricane cleanup and set up a repair committee back when he was just starting his practice, or the way he covered the cost of the free self-defense class Sheriff Pete and Mayor Quincy Adams taught every summer. He'd touched the lives of everyone in town, and his memory would live on in the fond and grateful hearts of all who'd known him.

A bitter taste coated Mila's tongue. Brandon had been a master at showing a polished veneer to the world, but the more she learned about him, the clearer it became that his golden reputation had been built on lies. Her growing fury was interrupted by a tiny snore rising from the gray satchel on her belly. She pressed her hand to her mouth, desperate to trap in the wildly inappropriate giggle suddenly trying to escape.

"In lieu of inviting loved ones to the lectern to speak," Reverend Bak said, "I have been asked to do a reading from the Bible."

Mila turned to give Mugsy and Ms. Fi a grateful smile. They really had thought of everything.

"Psalm thirty-four, verses fifteen to eighteen." The minister raised his hands to the sky and brought them down to his chest in prayer. Opening them as if offering something to the mourners, he moved his gaze from face to face among the pews. "The eyes of the Lord are on the righteous, and his ears are open to their cry. The face of the Lord is against evildoers, to cut off the remembrance of them from the earth."

He smiled gently at Mila. "When the righteous cry for help, the Lord hears and rescues them from all their troubles. The Lord is near to the brokenhearted and saves the crushed in spirit. Amen."

"Amen," murmured the congregants.

Reverend Bak walked to the doors, opening them wide. "Now please join us for a reception at Q Tea Pie."

Mila was swept up in what felt like a river of people flowing down the aisle toward the doors. Mugsy and Ms. Fi were at her elbows like buffers, smiling at people who approached and somehow gently redirecting them. The crowd washed down the church steps and along the sidewalk, past the herb garden Q and Reverend Bak shared, and into Q Tea Pie, the bakery that always felt to Mila like the warm and comforting soul of Corvin's Crossing.

Golden light flowed over the cozy room, which was filled with clusters of comfortable chairs and low tables set up for long, meandering conversations over hot drinks and sweet treats. The mixture of button-tufted brocade Victorian parlor chairs, brandy-hued leather gentlemen's armchairs, and fat velvety sofas should have felt like a chaotic muddle. Yet somehow, they all went together perfectly. On the wall beside each grouping of table and chairs was a selection of work from a different local artist. Prices and contact information were discreetly displayed beneath each piece.

Becca was sitting in a purple and gray wingback chair near the entrance when Mila walked in. She stood, lifting a hand in greeting, but Mila couldn't deal with her and the tornado of emotions that came along with her. She hardened her features and turned toward the center of the shop, where an enormous island of glass cases bore a framed placard in curlicued script. It read:

Eating too much may be the sin of gluttony . . .
but please eat all the pie you want.
The sin of pi is always zero.

Beneath the sign were oversized, flaky pies with wedges missing and red, orange, and purple fruit fillings peeking out from between their crusts. Glazed tarts and elegant galettes on little silver doilies sat beside rustic crocks of cobbler and crisp. Mountainous billows of cream topped shortbread crusts filled with satiny custard or fruit chiffon.

Smaller cases forming a nearly complete ring contained cookies, muffins, cupcakes, scones, and tea breads on one side. On the other, loaves of rustic rye, light focaccia, and crusty baguette nestled between platters of tuna salad, chickpea-artichoke salad, liverwurst, hummus, smoked salmon, and more.

The entire back wall was filled with brushed steel canisters, each bearing a plaque with a name like *birthday cake rooibos*, *melba fruit blend*, *temple of heaven pinhead gunpowder*, or *organic Irish breakfast* written in Q's even, blocky handwriting.

Mila's phone vibrated. She pulled it out to find a text from Becca. *I'm so sorry. Please forgive me,* it read. A crying emoji and a prayer hands emoji followed the words. Blowing out an irritated breath, Mila shoved the phone back into her bag.

Squaring her shoulders, she fixed her attention on Q, tall and stout and round-faced, with their huge black eyes behind oversized rainbow glasses, their tousled asymmetrical quiff, and their vine-handled rosewood cane. They had already set out platters of finger sandwiches on trays labeled *omnivore* and *vegan*, dishes of raspberry saffron poundcake and coconut melba cobbler, and massive carafes of ginger peach rooibos and honey jade bitten oolong.

Mila's eyes filled when she saw the spread. Q had prepared all of her favorite things. She gave the baker a heartfelt nod of thanks. Q pressed their hands against their chest, their eyes full of empathetic kindness.

Mugsy led Mila to a high-backed chair in the corner while Ms. Fi helped Q carry over a selection of treats and two steaming pots of tea.

Q's dark eyes looked into Mila's. "I know how overwhelming times like this can be," they said. "I'm here for anything you need. Anytime." They gave a little half-bow and departed to move between tables, checking on guests.

"How can I help, kid?" Mugsy asked.

"I don't know." She took a sip of hot oolong, savoring its smoky flavor and sweet finish, hoping it would give her strength. "I'm not sure what to do. I'm exhausted, and my mind is racing. I just don't know who killed Brandon or why."

"Maybe it's something to do with business?" Mugsy asked. A look passed between him and Ms. Fi. He glowered.

"Maybe, unless it was Becca." The name stuck in Mila's throat. "She said she didn't see him earlier in the day, but maybe she did. Maybe they fought."

"But what would they have fought about?" Ms. Fi asked.

Mila tilted her head, considering. "Becca said that Brandon didn't want her to tell me about them. Maybe she insisted, and he told her she was just a one-night stand."

"That wouldn't surprise me, actually." Ms. Fi nodded.

"So then Becca got angry and killed him?" Mugsy asked. "But how did she get your prop knife? And why?"

"Not to mention, why would she put Brandon's body up on the catwalk? And how?"

Mila tilted her head. "I don't know about the why. It sure seems like the killer was trying to frame me. But as for how, you left the back door to the club open for me. Were you and Brutus inside?"

Mugsy shook his head. "We went upstairs to get a nap. It didn't occur to me to worry about leaving the door unlocked. Crime's not really an issue around here."

"Or it wasn't, anyway," Ms. Fi muttered.

"Okay," Mila nodded. "So Becca and Brandon could have met up in the alley while I was at the vet, and when things started to get heated, maybe they ducked into the club to get some privacy. The back window of the sheriff's office is nearby, after all. If the alley gets noisy, he goes over and sticks his head out. Brandon knew I was preparing today, so he would have known the club would be open, and he wouldn't have wanted to be spotted fighting with Becca if he wanted their affair to stay secret."

"Yep," Mugsy agreed. "That does make sense, I suppose."

"But we don't have any proof." Mila sighed.

Ms. Fi's eyebrows lifted. "Mila, dearest, do you really believe Becca is capable of murdering someone?"

Mila felt the weight of Becca's betrayal as if it were crushing her. "Maybe. I wouldn't have believed her capable of having an affair with Brandon behind my back." She sighed. "I don't know. Maybe it has nothing to do with the affair. I need to find out what the deal is with his mysterious business holdings."

"I heard something about that," Mugsy said. "Larissa was at the bank when I dropped off my deposits."

"The mayor's assistant?" Mila scowled. "She was gossiping about Brandon's investigation?"

"No. She was getting an update on the investigation into Brandon's financials." Mugsy shrugged. "I just overheard part of it. It all seemed pretty routine."

"Word spreads fast in a small town," Mila grumbled.

"I'm sorry, dearest," Ms. Fi murmured. "Would you rather we didn't know?"

"It's just weird that *everyone* probably knows." Mila had been taught growing up that you mind your own business, you respect the family's honor, and you always hide the dirty laundry. But here, caring meant being up in each other's drama, and yet at least two people had been hiding lies and worse behind their friendly smiles: Brandon and whoever had killed him.

"Any idea what they've turned up so far?" Mila asked. "I found his books, but they're in some sort of code. Then there's this." Giving her wrist a sharp twist as she tucked her hair behind her ear, Mila dislodged the strange spool she'd found in

Brandon's drawer from a hidden pocket sewn to the inside of her right sleeve. She'd tucked it there for safekeeping before heading to the funeral, rather than giving the kittens an opportunity to gnaw on it.

She lowered her arm and the spool slid into her palm.

Should she show it to Ms. Fi and Mugsy? If she was going to trust anyone, it had to be them. She wished she could show it to Pete, but she didn't know what it meant, and she knew he had to conduct his investigation by the book. She couldn't afford to give him anything that might end up making her look guilty.

Maybe Mugsy and Ms. Fi would help her figure out how the thing worked. She was sure it was the key to decoding Brandon's books.

She was just uncurling her hand when Mayor Adams leaned over her shoulder. "Did I overhear you talking about Brandon's business records? That's a real tangle. What have you got there?"

With a flick of her fingers, Mila sent the spool back up her sleeve, rolling her arms open to settle it in place and displaying her empty palms. "What? Nothing." She adopted an innocent expression, tinged with grief. A good magician had to be a good actor, too. She wasn't ready to trust anyone other than Mugsy and Ms. Fi. If the mayor felt bad about bothering her at Brandon's memorial, he wouldn't prod.

Besides, the chaos of the day was wearing her down. She was having a difficult time getting a read on whether the mayor was acting strangely or just being nosy like everyone else in town. Mila gritted her teeth. She hated all of this uncertainty. She just wanted to go home and have some time alone with the kittens. To think.

"Do you guys think it's okay for me to leave?" she asked. "Would that be suspicious? I don't want Pete to think I don't care about Brandon's service. But I've got a lot of mixed emotions I need to sort out."

"You're being so brave, dearest." Ms. Fi patted Mila's wrist. "It's true the sheriff left, but you may want to stay a touch longer. It's only been about half an hour, and leaving too soon could turn heads. Let's talk about something soothing. How are those kittens doing?"

Mila smiled. "They're adorable. A little wild, especially at night. But so cute."

"They're not making a peep in there." Ms. Fi ducked to look into the kangaroo pouch. "Oh! Sound asleep, bless them!"

Mr. Cavendish settled himself into the chair across from Mila. "Hello, Mila. I'm sorry for your loss," he boomed. He stroked his slick black mustache with his thumb and forefinger. Mila's gaze flitted from his tailored linen suit to the $50,000 Patek Philippe Gondolo watch peeking out from beneath his monogrammed cufflink, then back to his prim face. His expression of polite detachment fractured just a touch as his eyes met hers. "I can't imagine . . . that is, losing someone you're in love with . . ." He cleared his throat.

"Um . . . thank you." Mila glanced at Mugsy, who was watching Mr. Cavendish closely. It seemed strange for him to be here. After all, he was just a visitor to Corvin's Crossing, virtually a stranger.

"Did you know Brandon well?" Mugsy's voice was halfway to a growl.

Mr. Cavendish's lips pursed as he considered. "Well enough, I suppose. He was managing the legal side of development for the Luxe Hotel and Resort. Seeing to permits, handling the subcontracts, dealing with inspections, that sort of thing. He seemed like a . . . er . . . charming fellow."

That was certainly true, Mila thought. He'd charmed everyone right into believing he was a good person. A flare of anger lit behind her breastbone.

"He also invited me to your magic show, which I quite enjoyed," Mr. Cavendish continued. "Is it a bad time to talk business?"

A surge of hope quelled the heat of her anger. Was something good going to happen? She'd almost forgotten what that felt like.

"I don't think . . ." Ms. Fi started.

"Sure," Mila cut in. "A change of subject would be a relief, actually."

"Excellent." Mr. Cavendish grinned, a strangely feral expression. "Your Brandon told me you were a rare talent. I figured he was exaggerating, but I must say I have to agree."

Dizzy elation buzzed through Mila. "Thank you!"

He nodded. "You're a real diamond in the rough. Your opening was amateurish, and your banter is terrible. To be honest, I would have walked out if you hadn't called me up on stage."

Mugsy growled low in his chest. He opened his mouth, but Mila put a hand on his forearm, and he closed it reluctantly.

"But your card trick was very solid," Mr. Cavendish continued, "and that finale with the kittens was stellar. Do you think you could put together a more polished act? Lean into the clean, elegant tricks and vanishes? More high-quality illusionist and less high school magic club?"

Mugsy bristled. Even kind old Ms. Fi was scowling. But Mila beamed. The sharp darts of Mr. Cavendish's critiques barely dented her joy. It didn't matter that she had no idea how the kittens had vanished and reappeared. It had certainly been a combination of lighting, instinctive improvisation, and luck.

But she was a magician. She knew she'd work it out eventually. She always did. "Absolutely!"

"Terrific!" Mr. Cavendish extended a long, elegantly manicured hand. "In that case, I've found my headliner for Luxe's grand opening!"

Mila clasped his hand and shook it, placing her other palm over the back of his fist to distract him as she unbuckled the custom clasp on his watch and smoothly slid it into the concealed pocket in her left sleeve.

"Thank you so much for this opportunity!" she said, giving him her brightest smile.

He nodded. "I look forward to working with you."

Turning to Ms. Fi and Mugsy, Mila squealed, then clapped her hands over her mouth. They congratulated her, patting her on the back and grinning warmly. The kittens jolted awake in her pouch and began scrabbling and yowling.

"Well," she said cheerfully," I'd better get these kittens home and fed. I'm not going to be able to maintain a somber expression after that, anyway." She turned to leave, then paused, calling out, "Oh, Mr. Cavendish? One more thing."

"Yes?"

Mila held out her two empty palms, then clapped them together and revealed his watch cupped between them. "Did you drop something?"

"What the devil? How did you do that?" He strode to her, and she handed him the expensive timepiece.

Mila let her lips curl up in a mysterious half-smile. "Is that the kind of polish you're looking for, sir?"

Another canny grin stretched beneath his curled mustache. "Talented and honest to boot. I'd say I've picked the right young lady for the job."

Chapter Fourteen
The Lecture

Bippity.

Mila had spent hours staring at Brandon's books, jotting in her little purple notebook, and fiddling with the strange cylinder she and Boop had found alongside them. It was a human puzzle, apparently. About the length of Mila's index finger and a bit wider than Boppity's Mousie, its body was made up of stacked rings, each engraved with randomly ordered letters and numbers. There were twelve rings in total. A great deal of Mila's energy had been spent spinning those rings so that the characters between the two carved arrows spelled out various names and dates.

She had started with her name, his name, and their names together in every permutation she could think of. She'd tried dates, the kind of car he drove, his mother's maiden name, his place of birth. Heaving a sigh, she'd flipped open the front covers of the two books.

"Look at these, Bippity," she told me.

I jumped up beside her, gazing at the books.

One was inscribed with the quotation, "The law, as I view it, goes too slow for me when I have the remedy in my own hands." The other said, "The tossing of money into the air as I throw balls in a tenpin alley gives me the greatest enjoyment that I have ever found."

"Aha!" She snatched up the spool, her face lighting up. "I know the answer! Both of these quotes are from Brandon's hero, Cornelius Vanderbilt. He was born poor, but used his boldness and ingenuity and determination to build himself up to the second richest man ever to live in America. Or so Brandon always said." She twisted the rings of the spool feverishly, lining up the letters: *V-A-N-D-E-R-B . . .*

"There's a problem, Mila." I tried to tell her. But she couldn't understand my flicking ear and my twitching tail. I sighed. She'd figure it out herself soon enough.

"Rats!" she exclaimed. "It's only ten letters, and I need twelve."

"Poor human," Boop purred. "Try to remember that the best solution to any problem is always a snuggle pile."

They had a point. Mila yawned and stretched. "I'm so tired my brain feels like mush." She went to the water room, where our sandbox now lived, to scrub her teeth with stinky mint and use the human toilet, which turned out to be a big white seat-beast that made a terrifying roaring sound each time it was fed human business.

Boop raced to the bed so quickly they were little more than a black, floofy blur. Boppity flew into me, tackling me to the floor. "Way to go, sis," he growled as the air was crushed from my lungs. "Pushing Mila until her brain is mush. Great way to take care of her. Lucky thing *you're* in charge." His long tail quirked sarcastically.

He leaped off of me and trotted toward the bed. I pinned my ears and flung myself after him, knocking him flat. "At least I'm helping," I said. "You're just racing around yelling at invisible bad guys." I thwapped his ear for good measure. But deep down inside, I felt my doubt growing. Maybe I wasn't a good leader after all. Maybe Mother would be disappointed if she could see me.

I clambered up to Boop, who was snuggled on Mila's pillow, and Boppity tried to stalk me but wobbled and sank into the purr-pile with exhausted ears. Mila let her fingers run over all three of us. "I'm not cut out for this," she said. "Performing on stage, I get to be everything I'm not in real life. Powerful. Clever. Confident."

I knew exactly how she felt. I, too, was pretending to be everything I wasn't.

She nestled into her pillow. Boop padded over and put their paw on her nose, purring. "I like you just the way you are," they told her.

"I'll teach you to be fierce and bold, human," Boppity said, climbing atop Boop and pressing his back against her cheek.

But I didn't have any words of wisdom for her. I tucked myself between her shoulder and her ear, trying to purr but failing. Eventually, I worried myself to sleep.

* * *

After breakfast, Mila packed us up in the kangaroo pouch and spent hours poring over the mysterious books with Mayor Adams. He was a tall, lean man with hair humans called "salt and pepper." He smelled like ocean and wool and cologne. There were smile lines at the corners of his eyes, which were a mix of blue and brown. His office was shiny like Brandon's loft, but the colors were warmer. There was a lot of reddish-gold wood, grand white pillars, and burgundy velvet everywhere.

I supposed it made sense for Mila to ask for his help. He was the leader of this human town, and thus a natural helper. Beyond that, a leader should always be knowledgeable, so he was probably an expert in the humans' odd obsession with imaginary resources such as money and property. She showed him the books, but not the spool. Perhaps she didn't trust him entirely, although a leader should also be worthy of trust.

Unfortunately, this Mayor Adams proved to be absolutely useless, and the whole thing was as dull as rocks.

The most interesting part was when Mila donated Brandon's car to the town. Mayor Adams looked at the paperwork. "I didn't know Brandon was a fellow Navy man," he said. For some reason, he smiled. I didn't know what he meant. Brandon had been a pale beige color, not dark blue, and the mayor was a similar hue.

"What?" Mila looked as confused as I felt. "He wasn't. At least not that I know of. Why do you say that?"

"Well, this vanity plate of his." The mayor tapped the paperwork with his index finger. "Commodore is a naval title. A pretty impressive one, actually. Odd that Brandon would use it for his license plate if it's not a title he held."

More nonsense. I wasn't surprised to learn that Brandon had been vain, but I couldn't imagine what his belly button had to do with anything, no matter how impressive it was.

"One more mystery, I guess." Mila sighed. "I wish you'd take the loft, too."

"No." The mayor shook his head. "The mortgage is all paid off. Whether you decide to sell it or keep it, I can't let you just give it away. You'd end up regretting that when the dust settles."

After that, there was more paperwork, and more poring over Brandon's books. Mila got quite upset when Mayor Adams told her that Brandon had already started the process of filing for bankruptcy on Luxe's behalf, but I didn't know how that was relevant, either. It was just more imaginary human nonsense.

To pass the time, I decided to reinforce my own value as a leader by lecturing Boppity and Boop about the importance of Mila's investigation. I knew I was in charge, but I was tired of feeling like I was the only one who cared about figuring out who had murdered Brandon.

"The sheriff is preparing to send Mila to the human pound," I told them.

"Ha!" Boppity thrust his tail in the air and lifted his chin. "You're wrong, little miss smarty-paws! Sheriff Pete is going to send Mila to *jail!*"

I sniffed, tossing him an irritated look. "Jail *is* the human pound."

Boppity and Boop gasped. We knew about the pound from Mother. They put cats and dogs into little cages there, and sometimes they killed them with poisonous gas.

"But going to the pound means nobody wants you," Boop protested. "We want Mila!"

I nodded sagely. "True. But humans are more complicated. Hylia says you can also get sent to the human pound if you're too much trouble to other humans and of too little value. Value has something to do with money."

Boppity stiffened. "If they send Mila to the pound, we'll be homeless and unwanted! We'll end up at the pound, too!"

"Precisely," I told him. "This is why we must become kitten detectives! Mila needs us!"

"Yes! And we should use our physics to help her, no matter what Hylia says," Boppity puffed out his coat, challenging me to a duel if I disagreed.

I didn't need to wrestle to make my point, though. "We can't. Not just because of Cat Law, though Hylia insists that should be reason enough. But if the humans discover that we have intelligence or abilities that rival their own, they'll send us somewhere even worse than the pound."

"No, but . . ." Boop's purr sputtered and died. "The pound is the worst place in the world." Their eyes grew wide with fear. "Mother always said so."

"She did, but Hylia taught me about someplace worse." I took a steadying breath. I needed to seem brave, even if what I was about to say frightened me to my core. Above all things, a leader should be brave. "It's called the lab. Humans do all sorts of strange and awful things to animals there, and then they take you apart piece by piece and show your guts to the other humans."

"What?" Boppity's whiskers quivered in horror. "Why in the world would they do something like that?"

I used my calmest big cat body language. "I don't know. But Hylia assured me that it's true."

I looked back and forth between them. I'd made my point, but now they were terrified. That wouldn't do, either. "It's okay, siblings. I'm going to keep us safe. We just need to help Mila figure out who killed Brandon. Then Sheriff Pete will put that person in the human pound, and Mila will be safe, and everything will be alright."

Boop looked deep into my eyes, and then rumbled up a purr. It started out weak and tinny, but it got stronger with each breath they took. "I believe in you, sis," they said.

"Yeah, well." Boppity added. "We have me, the most fearsome warrior ever born, so you're right. We'll be okay."

Against the looming danger we were facing down with Mila, I felt tiny and vulnerable. But the encouragement of my siblings gave me strength. I would be the best leader I could be. Maybe I would manage to live up to the responsibility Mother had given me.

Chapter Fifteen
The Horse

Boppity.

Mila parked in front of Scarborough Farms Bed & Breakfast. My teeth began to chitter. Soon, I'd see all those lovely fat birds wandering around the yard, just begging to be pounced on. Pushing my nose into the spot where the kangaroo pouch zipper closed, I nudge-shoved vigorously, digging with my front paws. I wondered what a mouthful of feathers was like. It was probably *delicious!*

By some terrible injustice, the chickens apparently got locked into their little house at night. The yard was empty. The horses and goats were shut away, too. I gave up on my attempt to escape. It was pointless, now. My chittering faded away. Along with it went any hope for the glee of the pounce.

"Perfect." Mila gestured toward Mr. Cavendish's boxy gold car. "He must be here."

A bell tinkled as we entered the Bed & Breakfast. Ms. Scarborough appeared from the door behind the dining room, carrying a tray piled with cookies that smelled buttery and bittersweet. They were dotted with little red berries and melty chunks of dark brown.

"Mila!" She glanced down at a sturdy watch on her wrist. "It's pretty late for a visit. Do you need something?"

"I just need to talk to Mr. Cavendish." Mila turned toward the library. "And there he is."

She strode into the plush green and gold room and stood over him. He was sipping from a delicate teacup. He glanced up at her questioningly.

"You're broke!" Her announcement had the vigor and sharpness of an attack. Mr. Cavendish choked on his tea. The cup rattled as he set it into the saucer.

"That was a good surprise assault!" I told her. "Now smack his face before he gets his bearings!"

"Don't bother denying it, Mr. Cavendish." She leaned toward him. "I saw the bankruptcy paperwork myself. You had no business hiring me when you knew there wasn't going to be a grand opening at your resort."

Not as good as a solid whack to the chops, but better than nothing.

Ms. Scarborough cleared a small hairball from her throat and set the plate of cookies on his table.

Mr. Cavendish pressed his lips together beneath his nose-tails in displeasure. "I'm not personally broke. Far from it. But it's true that the Luxe development project was in trouble." He selected a cookie. "It no longer is, however."

He eyed her. "You're a fiery young woman. I can respect that. But please." He gestured to a nearby chair. "Have a seat. Help yourself to a cookie. Let's be civil, shall we?"

"No!" I shouted. It was the oldest trick in the book. "Don't be disarmed!"

But she wavered and sat in the chair he'd indicated, reaching for a cookie. "Sorry," she mumbled.

"Never apologize for looking after your own interests," he told her. "You're quite right to question me. You deserve an explanation, and so you shall have one."

He set his cookie on his tea saucer and leaned back, interlacing his fingers. "From day one, the Luxe Hotel and Resort project was nothing but trouble. There were materials and code issues first, and then after we'd already broken ground, we got a notification that we had invalid permits. All of that was a big drain on our development budget."

He shook his head. "Then it turned out that one of the subcontractors needed a certification they didn't have, so that was another delay and more expense. Just as it seemed like those were about to finally be resolved, an EPA claim was filed for some sort of environmental infraction."

He sighed and took a neat bite of cookie. "I was over budget with no way to make up the lost revenue. Pouring any more money into Luxe would have opened my own private finances to liability, so I told Brandon to file bankruptcy paperwork for the single-owner holding company he'd made to shield me if Luxe failed."

Mila jotted some notes in her little notebook. I was pleased. Even though she'd given up her combat advantage by sitting, Mr. Cavendish's tone and posture were defeated.

That meant she was winning the battle.

"So development of Luxe was cancelled." Mila sounded angry. As she should. "Then why did you approach me at the reception yesterday?"

"Because everything changed overnight. The EPA complaint fell through, and—thank you, Ms. Scarborough." He nodded as she picked up his teapot, replacing it with a fresh one. "I love how friendly this little evening ritual is. I'll have to add a complimentary tray of tea and biscuits to the evening turn-down service at Luxe."

Ms. Scarborough chucked him gently on the shoulder. "Oh, Mr. Cavendish." She gave him a warm smile. "You're too kind. Just don't put me out of business!" She winked as she carried the old teapot away.

He turned back to Mila. "The mayor called me late this afternoon to tell me that everything was all set. Construction resumes tomorrow morning. So our grand opening is delayed, but we're back on track and looking forward to your performance, young lady."

Mila let out a huge lungful of air. "Oh, what a relief! I'm so glad to hear that!"

Obviously, this meant that Mila had won the battle. Mr. Cavendish had been subdued.

"Thank you for bringing your concerns to me directly." He patted her hand. "That's all too rare in this day and age. Now if you don't mind," he pushed himself up to standing with a courtly little nod, "I'm going to see myself off to bed. It's getting late, and as the great Richard Whately once said, 'Lose an hour in the morning, and you will spend all day looking for it.'"

What ridiculous human nonsense. Unless he was talking about losing track of your sun-patch when you were having a morning snooze. I'd had that unfortunate experience more than once already. I didn't care to repeat it.

Perhaps he was a sensible fellow after all.

Mila was nearly back in her car when a voice called out from the darkness.

"Hey!"

Mila stiffened. "Becca, I—"

"You haven't been returning my calls or texts. You avoided me at the memorial service, and at Q's afterward." Becca's form emerged from the shadowy barn. "I get that you might need space, and if that's what's going on, I'll respect it, but—"

"I need space." Mila turned away.

"But you're my best friend. I miss you. I nee—" her voice broke. There was a choking sound. "I need you." It was a whisper, barely audible on the cool night breeze. "Okay. No. Sorry. You're right. I'm sorry."

Mila sighed, her shoulders slumping beneath the straps of our carrier. She turned back and watched Becca's defeated silhouette slink into the barn. Tiny whimpering sounds like a wounded puppy drifted out of the darkness.

Mila got into her car and started the engine, but as she was driving past the barn, she turned to look at the quaking figure backlit by the dim glow inside. The car rolled to a stop. Mila dropped her forehead into her hands and let out a long hiss. It was a pretty good one. I would have been intimidated if it had been aimed at me.

"For the love of . . ." She sighed. "Fine."

She turned off her car and padded to the barn. She had uncommonly good night vision and surprisingly quiet feet for a human.

That must be what *magician* meant. Mila was a warrior who practiced her battle skills in play, demonstrating them for others, in order to be ready for any combat to come. Like me with Mousie or the invisible bad guys I defeated regularly.

Her stalking skills were solid. I watched approvingly as she crept up on Becca. Our quarry was slumped against a half-door in the barn. But instead of jiggling her hindquarters and preparing to pounce, Mila made a tiny hairball noise.

My ears flattened. What a wasted opportunity. Becca didn't even jump. And I had been so hoping to discover what a human looked like when it puffed out its hair in shock.

"What are you doing out here?" Mila asked.

"You know the horses calm me down," Becca said. "Ever since I was an angry teenager. Best thing about this job."

Deep in the shadows, movement caught my attention. A horse the silvery gray color of a storm cloud was enclosed in the stall Becca was leaning against. She dropped her head and blew out a warm, hay-scented breath.

She was *massive.* I would have been frightened, except that she smelled like prey. Massive prey, but still essentially harmless.

I trilled at her curiously.

She flicked an ear toward me, turning her head to the side so that one of her huge, dark eyes faced us. "I'm Sage," she said.

Bippity pushed past me. "Pleased to meet you," she told the horse. "I'm Bippity. This is Boppity, and over here is Boop."

"Come closer," Boop purred. "You're so pretty! I'd like to smell your breath!"

"I don't like being near humans who aren't being honest," Sage told them.

"But they're not saying anything," I objected.

"Doesn't matter," Sage gave her tail a swish as if to call me silly. "It doesn't take words to lie to oneself."

I started to protest, but Boop interrupted me. "You're right. Becca's feelings are all garbled. So are Mila's."

But just then, Sage swiveled her ears toward Mila. "This one is about to be brave."

I beamed. Mila was learning courage. Probably because of me.

"Look." Mila drew in a deep breath. "I want to forgive you." She put a hand on Becca's trembling shoulder. "I'm working on it. There's just so much going on. Too much."

Sage bobbed her head and her mouth worked like she was chewing something. "Truth."

"Did you know horses were human lie-detectors?" I asked Bippity.

"Not quite," Sage told me. "We simply don't feel safe around you predators when you're conflicted. If you're hiding something, you're dangerous. When you're honest with yourselves, your tension drops, and we feel safer."

"Huh." For the first time, I could see how having a prey animal around might be useful.

Becca looked up into Mila's face. "All I want is for us to go back to the way we were. I wish none of this had ever happened. I wish Brandon and I had never . . ." Becca's voice broke.

Sage pinned her ears. "Lie." She took a half-step back.

"I know. Me too," Mila agreed. Her chest hitched, jostling our kangaroo pouch. "I miss you." Nodding, Sage stepped forward. "And I'm afraid," Mila continued. "Pete says I'm the only suspect in Brandon's murder. All of the evidence points to me. I'm trying to figure out the truth, but if . . ." Her chest shuddered again. "If I can't, I'm going to end up in jail for something I didn't do. And all these lies . . . All these secrets . . . I don't know what to think. Who to trust."

Sage stepped forward again. "Truth."

"You can trust me," Becca's words tumbled out in a rush. "I know I screwed up. I wanted Brandon so badly, even though I knew deep down that he wasn't mine. I wanted the life he said he could give me. The ease and glamor and comfort. I . . ." She swallowed, squeezing her eyes shut for a moment. "I thought I loved him. But you're my best friend, and that's the love that really matters. I promise I'll never lie to you again. I'll do whatever it takes to earn your trust back. If that means finding out what happened to Brandon, I'm going to help you. You're not alone, Mila."

Mila and Becca crushed us between them in a tight hug. Both of them shook with sobs.

"I'm here for you," Becca kept repeating. "You're not alone."

"Thank you, Becca." Mila whispered. "That means everything. I forgive you. Thank you."

But as they stepped apart, I watched Sage press herself against the back of the stall, gaze darting between the two women. Her tail swished through the night air like a thousand whips.

"Lies," she hissed through flared nostrils. "Terrible lies."

Just as I was about to ask her what she meant, her head jerked up. Her eyes rolled, flashing white around the edges. "Danger!" she screamed, rearing up so that her head nearly hit the beams above her.

The other stalls echoed with shrieks of terror. Hooves clattered against stall doors and shrill cries rose again and again from the throats of the horses and goats. "Fire!"

Becca and Mila flew backward in shock. "What in the . . . ?" Becca started. "Wait. Do . . . Do you smell smoke?"

Mila rushed to the door of the barn. Outside, angry flames roared and leaped as they devoured the second story of Ms. Scarborough's Bed & Breakfast.

Chapter Sixteen
The Fire

Boop.

The air was thick with panic. It came at me from all sides, cloying and dense. Sage and her friends Rosemary and Thyme were screaming, their shrill cries bouncing off the walls and ceiling and hitting us from all sides. Their hooves careened into the heavy oak walls of the barn again and again, louder than thunder. The beams shook, raining dust down from the hayloft. In their smaller stall, the goats, Biscuit and Cookie, huddled together, bleating and shaking.

Mila and Becca were scampering, too. "The house! It's on fire!" Becca cried.

Mila pointed up. "Oh no! Look!"

Outside, fluttering embers rose up from the burning house. They were too terrifying to be beautiful as they flitted through the night air like glowing butterflies and drifted into the window of the hayloft above us.

Smoke began to flow down over us like a waterfall, pouring into the stalls.

Boppity dug fiercely at the zipper to our kangaroo pouch, his eyes locked on the panicking horses. "We've got to save them!" he screeched.

Bippity was forcing herself to stay calm. "We need a plan."

I didn't have a plan. Plans were not my strength. But I could feel how tenuous Bippity's grasp on her calm was, so I stood, feeling my weight travel down through my four paws, into the pouch, and out through Mila into the world. I inhaled deeply, and felt the panic and the smoke and the night all around.

"I am in this moment," I told Bippity. She scowled, but I felt her take a deep breath, too.

"Okay, Mila," she said, letting her voice pierce the chaos with a sharp, determined syllable that demanded action. "You need to call for help."

"Call for help!" Becca echoed. "I'm going to get these guys safe!" She raced to unlock the outer door of each stall so that the horses and goats could escape into their field.

Mila staggered out into the night, coughing. "Oof! Dizzy!" She put a hand to her head. "I don't understand. I haven't inhaled much smoke." She shook herself, wobbling, and dialed 911, informing the human inside the phone about the emergency.

"Ten minutes?" she yelled. "That's not fast enough! There are two people trapped in th—"

As she was shouting, the two second story windows in the face of the house, orange as a murderous tiger's eyes, exploded. Tinkling shards of claw-sharp glass rained down. Below them, the front door burst open, and the black silhouette of a human appeared in its maw, backlit by furious vermillion as though the house had turned into a terrible beast determined to devour everything inside it.

I cowered at the horrifying sight.

"Someone's coming out, but there's still someone inside! Send an ambulance, fire, and rescue! Tell them to hurry!"

Mila zagged toward the house, embracing the smoky, charred Ms. Scarborough as she emerged. "It's okay," Mila murmured. "You're okay." She led Ms. Scarborough to a bench in the garden, as far from the flaming house as possible.

"Mr. Cav—" Ms. Scarborough was interrupted by furious, wet coughing. "Mr. Cavendish. He's still in there. I tried to get to him, but the flames . . . I couldn't . . ."

"It's okay," Mila told her. The shaky, drained feeling of an adrenaline crash was all around us. All four human knees wobbled and gave. They collapsed to a bench, and Ms. Scarborough crumpled into Mila's arms, sobbing.

A car with flashing blue and red lights on its roof growled into the driveway, and Sheriff Pete hurtled out. "Anyone else in there?" he demanded.

"Mr. Cavendish," Mila called. "Pete, wait!"

But he didn't wait. He bolted up the steps and into the raging jaws of the house-monster.

Mila and Ms. Scarborough watched the house, holding their breath. We were all still and silent, staring at the fiery mouth.

Becca emerged from the burning barn and joined us. "Where's Mr. Cavendish?" she asked.

"Still inside," Mila told her.

"And . . ." Becca looked at the empty car with the flashing red and blue lights. "And Pete?"

"Went in after him."

With an anguished groan, the roof of the house collapsed inward. Sparks and smoke gushed out of its eyes and mouth.

"No!" Mila screamed. She leaped up and unbuckled our kangaroo pouch, dropping us in Ms. Scarborough's lap. "Pete!" She stumbled toward the house.

"Mila!" Boppity yowled. "Stop!"

Bippity was frozen, wide-eyed and shaking.

I watched in slow motion, powerless to stop her, as she flung herself up the steps to be swallowed alive.

Becca crashed into her, knocking her flat.

"Let me go!" Mila flailed and fought, but Becca clung to her, teeth bared in a determined grimace.

"Hold her, Becca!" Boppity shouted. "Don't let her go in there!"

Mila thrashed again. Then a heartbroken sob ripped from her chest.

"I know," Becca said, pulling her up and leading her to the bench. "Pete's like our brother. But you can't go after him, Mila."

A misshapen shadow appeared in the crimson doorframe.

"Look!" Ms. Scarborough called out.

Sheriff Pete stumbled down the front steps, a massive lump over his shoulder. He sank to his knees in the garden, spilling his burden on the ground. Sharp coughs wracked his slumped form.

Mila and Becca unrolled what he'd dropped, revealing a fancy rug with a discolored Mr. Cavendish at its center.

He groaned.

"Mr. Cavendish!" Ms. Scarborough gasped. "He's alive!" Her hands flew up and our kangaroo pouch slid from her firm lap. We ploothed to the ground in a kitten-tangle. Shocked astonishment poked out of Ms. Scarborough like porcupine spikes. "It's . . . It's a miracle!"

Sirens wailed in the night, shrill and mournful. They grew so loud that we all cowered together in the corner of the kangaroo pouch. Boots crunched on the ground.

The grim determination of human battle was everywhere. With a series of short, coordinated shouts, there was a roaring hiss, and the smell of water began to battle the smell of smoke in the air. Our mesh windows were mostly against the crush of herbs beneath us, but through the edges of them, everything appeared to be flashing between blue and red, as if the whole world were gripped in a battle to the death between raging fire and calm, insistent water.

"Um . . . hello!" Bippity hollered. She narrowed her huge eyes in annoyance. "We have been forgotten! Rude!"

"Forgotten?" Boppity yowled. "Abandoned! Like when Mother left us! Motherrrrr!"

"Great," Bippity huffed. "Thanks, humans."

"We're fine," I pointed out, starting up a purr. "Mila is fine. She's already tumbling from panicky rage-grief into heavy exhausted relief. Becca is fine, and the horses and goats are fine. Ms. Scarborough is fine. Sheriff Pete is fine. Even Mr. Cavendish is a bit overcooked around the edges, but overall fine. He's a Mr. Cavendish, not an empty Cavendish-body. The humans are fighting the fire-house-monster. Bad things almost happened, but they didn't." I purred louder at the realization, feeling a warm glow in my chest.

"Oh! Kittens!" Mila exclaimed. "I'm so sorry!" She picked up the pouch and buckled it back around herself. "You must have been so scared."

"Terrrrrified! You left us, like Motherrrrr!" Boppity sobbed.

"You're okay, kittens," she told us. "I've got you."

Two people in black jumpsuits guided Mila, Mr. Cavendish, Sheriff Pete, Becca, and Ms. Scarborough to the back of their huge truck-room, aided by a woman in plaid pajamas with a shiny star like Pete's hastily pinned to the front. They investigated the smoke-scented humans with various tools from big black bags.

"Vets." Bippity nodded to herself. "They're vets for humans."

I began to purr. That meant they were making sure everyone really was okay.

One of them looked at Mila's eyes and inside her mouth and listened to her breathing, sliding a hand between us and Mila when she refused to take us off again.

"Pupils are constricted and sluggish. Probably from smoke inhalation. Pulse is low, but within normal. Overall, you look okay. Be sure and get some rest."

Mila wrapped her arms around our pouch. "Okay, loves. Let's go home. Can I go?"

Sheriff Pete pulled off a clear mask that was covering his nose and mouth. "Not yet. I gotta get your statem—" he coughed as if he had the biggest hairball ever, and couldn't seem to dislodge it.

The lady in pajamas put the mask back on his face. "He knows where to find you. You can go." She turned to the sheriff. "You need to rest. You're going to be okay, but you're in no shape to be on duty."

"Thanks, Chantelle." Mila was already heading toward her car as she tossed the words into the air.

* * *

At home, she spent a very long time under the hot rain sprayer from the water room.

I went to check on her when I heard little whimpers echoing inside the tiny, steamy rain-chamber. They were coming from low down, like she was sitting on the floor in there.

"You okay, Mila?" I purred in case she needed to feel warm and safe. Purrs always made me feel that way. I added a trill to my question so she could hear me through the deluge.

"I'm okay, kittens," she called out. Her voice was slurry. Her energy was a muddled tangle of anxious jitters and confused shock, all muffled in a wad of numb exhaustion. "I just need to get this smoke smell out of my hair."

When she came out of the water room wearing her very long black and purple flannel shirt, only the exhaustion was left. Something about the rain room had helped. I couldn't understand how. There was nothing calming about being drenched in a downpour. Mila did it every day, though. Maybe she liked it for some strange reason. I supposed, so long as it made her happy, there was no harm in it.

She played with her new favorite letter-spool toy again before bed. She mumbled and growled as she twisted its letter-rings around and around, blinking groggily. It was becoming a habit, even though she never seemed to have much fun doing it.

Boppity and Boop sat side by side like two identical statue-cats, discussing her puzzle with their ears and whiskers as she grimly played.

* * *

The next morning, after picking up a to-go order from Q's, we headed to Mugsy's. Brutus wag-skittered his way over to greet us.

"Why don't you take 'em out of the bag?" Mugsy asked.

"They could get hurt!" Mila was jagged with anxious shock.

Bippity scoffed. "Ridiculous human. We have more common sense than this addle-pated, flappy-eared slobber-bucket you call a dog." She splayed her whiskers to emphasize her point. She was very impressive, but Mila couldn't see her, so all she heard was a wry little "*yow.*"

"They'll be okay," Mugsy said. "Brutus'll look after 'em. Besides. Cats survive out in the streets just fine. You've got plenty of real problems to worry about, without making trouble out of thin air."

Mila sighed. "Fine." She rustled the bag from Q's, then set us on a table adorned with three little paper dishes the size of meat-feast cans. "Here, kittens. Bacon and wheatgrass goatmilk paw-puddings in cornstarch bowls. Yes, Brutus," she set a larger dish on the floor. "I got you one, too."

I admired his efficiency as he tossed the entire thing in his mouth, bowl and all, and swallowed it after only two chews.

She handed Mugsy a tall paper cup labeled *Q Tea to Go!* "Yerba Maté Latte for you." The second cup, she put on the table in front of herself. "And Mango shortcake tea with tupelo honey for me."

She reached into the bag one last time. "Here's your deviled ham and cress on garlic focaccia and my ube muffin with peanut toffee crumble topping. Want a taste, kittens?" She held out the muffin.

But we were already chops-deep in our puddings. They were creamy and fresh and splooshy, with little crunch-noms of bacon dotted throughout. I couldn't help purr-slurping my treat to show my joy.

Bippity shot me a disgusted look as she lapped away tidily.

Boppity was gobbling with such enthusiasm that he'd somehow managed to splat himself with a big dollop in the middle of his back.

When we finished, we hopped from the table to a chair and from there to the floor, and set off to investigate the scene of the murder.

Bippity and Boppity explored the stage, bickering about physics. I didn't want to bicker, so I trotted around the curtain and backstage. There were wonderful shelves and racks everywhere. Some held clothing or bins of boring human objects like face powder and lightbulbs. Most were empty.

Those were the fun ones. I jumped onto a shelf and tucked myself into a shadow. Above me was another shadow, even darker than mine. I twitched my tail and leaped, tumbling myself into it. Then I spotted another. I jumped again. And again. Soon, I was perched at the very top of the shelf, gazing down at all the beautiful shadows and nooks around me.

Suddenly, I spotted a basket filled with crumples of paper and food wrappers. It looked utterly delightful, so I threw myself at it, savoring the way my belly sank as I dropped through the darkness.

With a satisfying *shoosh*, I sank into a pile of glorious trash. I spun and batted, tossing the magnificent crinkles into the air and pouncing on them with all my grace and might. I spun and pounced with such elegant vigor that the entire trash basket tipped over, spilling its treasure all over the floor.

I hooked one with my claws and threw it across the backstage, watching with wide eyes as it zoomed through the air merrily. I raced to the spot where I knew it would land and very nearly caught it. But it was too clever! It dodged my paws and bonked off of my nose, arcing through the air. When it hit the floor, I thwacked it with my paw. It immediately darted underneath a big chest of drawers with little short feet. Cramming myself into the delightfully low space beneath, I started to retrieve it.

But then I saw a better crinkle. This one was made of crispy white paper, decorated with human words. It had a lacy, jagged edge like it had been ripped. And it was decorated with beautiful dark dots and splotches that had a fascinating smell. Kind of dead and murdery.

"Look at meeeeeeee!" I called to my siblings. "I found the best thing everrrrr!"

They both came galloping up. "This smells like Brandon," Bippity said.

"And blood," Boppity agreed.

"It's a clue!" Bippity did a little victory dance. "We really are detectives! We just found our first clue!"

"Ooo! Me! Mine!" shouted Boppity. He threw out a huge paw and caught the crinkle with his wicked claws. Snatching it up in his jaws, he raced into the depths of backstage.

"Come back! This is not a contest!" Bippity launched herself after him, fury radiating from her in hot waves. "This is serious!"

I wasn't exactly sure why my crinkle merited a game of chase, but if that's what we were playing, I was happy to join in the sleuthing.

Chapter Seventeen
The Curtain

Mila.

Mugsy took a sip of his latte as the kittens and Brutus thundered off to play. "Ms. Scarborough borrowed Q's camper. She wanted a way to stay on her farm and take care of her animals."

"I can understand that," Mila said. "If she was staying in the middle of town, she'd have to get up in the dark to get out there for morning feeding. Besides, the horses need their daily exercise, unless she has guests to take for a trail ride or something. Must be hard, though. Looking at what used to be her home."

She could only imagine how Ms. Scarborough must be feeling after watching her house and barn burn. Mila was still devastated about the whole thing. She'd barely started coming to terms with seeing Brandon's body fall from the catwalk, and now one of her best friends (who also thought she was a murderer, by the way) had nearly died in a fire at the home of her other best friend's mentor and surrogate mom.

They had all come far closer to death than she would have liked. And Scarborough Farms B&B, with its old-world charm and homey accommodations, would never be the same.

Why did terrible things keep happening? And why did she keep finding herself in the middle of them? It was almost like someone was out to get her. Mila shook her head to banish the dark thought.

"What about Mr. Cavendish?" Mila asked. "He can't leave. With Brandon gone, he's got to make sure Luxe stays on track. But where's he going to stay?"

Mugsy had just taken a huge bite of his sandwich. He chewed for a moment, then held his hand in front of his mouth in an awkward nod to polite table manners that perfectly fitted his rumpled fashion mashup of Vaudeville showman and Edwardian dandy. "Oh, actually, Mayor Adams offered to let him stay in his family's ultra-posh RV."

"Really?" Mila popped a morsel of bright purple muffin-top into her mouth. The flavor of ube, like vanilla but richer and more fragrant, blended with the salty-sweet crunch of the candied nut crumble. Tilting her head, she made a questioning noise in the back of her throat, encouraging him to continue.

"Yeah." Mugsy swallowed and gave Mila a crooked grin. "He said it's the most luxurious one on the market, and the only way he can stand to go camping with the wife and kids. I guess he's going to park it at Ms. S's and get his handyman to set up temporary hookups to the utilities there."

"Oh. Huh." Mila frowned. "I'd been thinking he could stay at Brandon's old place. But not for any money. He could just like . . . stay there."

"What, for *free*?" Mugsy reeled back as if he'd been slapped. Horror stretched across his grizzled face, his furry eyebrows nearly touching the brim of his hat. His mouth looked like Munsch's *Scream*.

"I don't know, I just . . ." Mila swallowed. She thought about the way it had felt, standing in Brandon's apartment knowing he was dead. Before heading over, she'd prepared herself for the waves of grief and loneliness that would knock her flat when she opened the door and saw his space without him in it.

And then there'd been . . .

Relief.

It was weird to finally admit that to herself. She'd raged for a bit, trying to stir up the feelings she was supposed to be having, and then she'd shifted her focus to figuring out who'd murdered him.

But the whole thing was confusing. She wanted as little to do with Brandon's loft and the tangled mess of feelings it evoked as possible.

She sighed. Of course she couldn't get away from her responsibilities that easily. Mugsy patted her hand. "It's a kindly thought, but Mr. Cavendish will be fine in that fancy-pants RV. Better to keep Brandon's place open so you can decide what to do with it. Now, what time are we expecting Becca so we can help you unravel this mystery? I'm glad you two made up, by the way.

"Thanks, Mugsy. She should be here any minute." Mila belatedly realized she should have offered to pick something up from Q for her friend. She crammed the remaining hunk of muffin in her mouth and almost choked. Thankfully, she still had a swallow of tea to wash it down. She grabbed her trash and headed backstage to throw it away.

A wild, yowling ruckus arose from Mugsy's office.

"Kittens!" Mila called out, heading for the noise. "What are you doing?" She flipped the switch on Mugsy's office wall, filling the small room with light. It was sparsely decorated in a neoindustrial style, with a scarred oak desk and bulbs caged in black steel. The golden hue of the wood and the plushness of a copper and burgundy area rug gave the space a surprising warmth.

All three kittens were tangled into a fizzing, growling gordian knot in the middle of the rug.

One sharp clap had them leaping apart and staring up at her with three sets of wide blue eyes. On the floor where they'd just been, there was a tattered ball of paper. She bent and picked it up, shaking it at them.

"Fighting over trash? Really? That's no way t—"

Her breath froze in her throat. There was a dot of crimson on the paper.

Evidence.

She should show it to Pete.

But Pete had already told her she was his only suspect. What if this made her look even more guilty? It already had her prints on it, and that brownish red spot looked a lot like blood.

Better to see what it was first. Careful not to touch it any further, she set the crumpled paper on Mugsy's desk. She grabbed two pens from a beer stein full of writing implements and used the capped ends to carefully flatten it.

It was about three-quarters of a sheet of paper titled, *The Companies Law of the Cayman Islands Memorandum and Articles of Association of Commodore Holdings, LDC*. Below the title was an address listed as a post office box in the Caymans, followed by several lines of legalese establishing that the company was founded under limited duration and would be liquidated on or before a date thirty years hence, and per Companies Law, it had a minimum of two members with limited liability. Then it read, *We, the two (2) members named to this Memorandum of Association, wish to be formed into a company pursuant to this Memorandum of Association and the Articles of Association herein attached.*

Brandon's signature appeared above a line that spelled out his name and the words, *Member 1 (Director).*

The rest of the page was torn away.

"Kittens!" Mila exclaimed. "You found evidence! It must have been hidden away someplace where human investigators couldn't find it."

Boppity scaled her leg and hopped up to the desk, grabbing a corner of the page and attempting to drag it away. She shooed him with a little tap on the nose. His ears flicked backward for a moment, and she could almost have sworn he looked irritated. But that couldn't be. He was just a kitten.

"What does it mean, though, Boppity?" she asked. Bippity joined her brother on the desk, sitting opposite Mila and curling her tail around her paws as she gazed down at the paper. She was so serious. She poked at a red spot as though she thought it was a toy, then withdrew her paw and blinked her enormous eyes at Mila.

"Obviously, Brandon was in some sort of partnership with someone," she told Bippity. "And if that partnership was based in the Caymans, it could have been created to shield something shady. That would certainly explain the encoded books. But who was the partner? Mr. Cavendish?"

With a little huff, Boppity stalked onto the page and lay down, his tail twitching.

"Could something have gone wrong, Boppity?" Mila petted him, considering. "This piece of paper being here in the theater, with blood on it, surely means that it was right in the thick of things when Brandon was killed. Maybe he and the killer started to argue out in the alley. It's not very private. Pete sticks his head out the back window whenever he hears a ruckus out there. So maybe they saw that Mugsy's back door was open, and stepped inside for privacy. If so, the whole thing was unplanned. A crime of passion."

Boop clambered up to her lap and settled on her thigh, purring.

"What do you have to say about it, cutie?" she asked, scratching behind their ear. The kitten rolled their head toward her hand, chin already dampening with blissful drool. "If someone shook this in Brandon's face, whatever it is, and it made him mad, I can definitely imagine him snatching at it and ripping this chunk off. Right?" Boop leaned into her hand so hard that they nearly fell off her lap. "It's easy to picture him crumpling it up and tossing it with a sneer."

Bippity leaped to Mila's shoulder, nuzzling her ear. She couldn't help giggling at the tickle of whiskers and snuffling breath.

"But who would have confronted him, Bippity? And why? What were they fighting about? And here's another thing. Should I give this to Sheriff Pete? Or will my prints on something with Brandon's blood be one more piece of evidence against me? It certainly doesn't exonerate me, and that's what we really need."

The club's front door opened. Becca was probably here.

Mila nudged Boppity off of the page, then grabbed two facial tissues and used them to fold up the paper and tuck it into her pocket. She could always give it to Pete later, if it turned out to be important.

Better safe than sorry.

She put Boop and Bippity beside their brother on the desk and headed toward the front, eager to get to work.

But it wasn't Becca who entered.

"Sheriff Pete!" Mugsy rose and extended a broad paw. Pete's palm slapped against Mugsy's as they shook vigorously. "How you feeling?"

"Good," Pete rasped. "Well. Like I've got a chest cold, but fine, considering."

Mugsy gestured to the bar. "Pour you a drink? On the house."

"Um." Pete's eyes darted awkwardly. "It's 10 AM. Plus, I'm here on official business." He looked over to Mila and stiffened.

"Ah." Mugsy looked from Pete to Mila, then back again. His friendly grin vanished. "I see. Well? Out with it."

The sheriff shifted his weight, turning so that Mila was mostly behind him. "Ahem. Glad I caught you alone. I have a few questions . . ." He shot a look at Mila and made an awkward jerking motion with his head, then looked pointedly back to Mugsy.

With a bemused shrug, Mila rose and tiptoed up the proscenium steps and behind the velvet curtain. Mugsy watched her until she vanished.

"Right. No one else is here. That is correct," Mugsy said stiffly.

"Good. Excellent." Pete nodded. He spoke loudly, so his voice carried up the stage to her hiding place. "I have some more questions for you."

Mugsy gave an exaggerated nod. "Okay."

"Great. So the fire chief brought down an arson investigator from the mainland, who found evidence that someone stood between the barn and the house and threw a Molotov cocktail at a second-floor window. The one where Mr. Cavendish was staying. So I need to know where you were last night between the hours of 9 PM and 11 PM?"

Mila's chest tightened. The fire had been set on purpose? Who would do such a thing? She and Becca and Ms. Scarborough and Mr. Cavendish could easily have died. Especially Ms. Scarborough and Mr. Cavendish. It was a miracle they'd survived.

"Am I a suspect?" Mugsy asked.

"Not at this time. I'm just covering all my bases, asking anyone who might be connected to the victim or our main suspect."

Mugsy gestured to the bar. "I was here. Place was nearly empty, though. I assume you're the one who got the scene cleared so quickly. I appreciate that."

The sheriff gave him a nod.

"But that article in the *Corvin's Crossing Courant* entitled 'Mugsy's Latest Show: Murder!' really seems to have put a dent in my business."

"Can you get me a list of who came in and what time?" Pete asked.

"Sure. Not going to be much of a list, but I'll do that."

"I'm sorry to hear business isn't good," Pete pressed his lips together. "We're doing everything we can to catch the killer. Once we have whoever it is behind bars, folks will feel safe again and our little town can get back to business as usual. But let me ask you this. Why wasn't Becca working the bar? Wasn't it part of her regular hours?"

"It was," Mugsy agreed, "but she's been pretty upset. Like I said, business wasn't exactly booming, so I told her she could head out. I'm betting she went to see the horses. They always make her feel better."

Did you speak to Mila? Any idea what she was doing up at Scarborough Farms that late at night?"

"She's no fool, Pete," Mugsy growled. "She doesn't want to go to prison for a murder she didn't commit. I'll bet she went out there to ask Ms. Scarborough or Mr. Cavendish something to help clear her name, but you'll have to ask her directly."

Pete ran his hand through his hair, shifting his weight again. "What with Mila being at the scenes of both crimes and her motive, things are looking pretty bad for her. DNA evidence takes at least a week to get back from the lab, but preliminary print evidence is back on the murder weapon. The handle was wiped clean, but they did find several partial prints at the base of the blade. They could be Mila's." He cleared his throat, pitching his voice so loud he was nearly shouting. "I sure hope she has a lawyer. Things aren't looking too good for her."

Mugsy's eyes narrowed.

"Anyway." He pushed open the door. "Thanks for the drink, Mugsy."

"But I didn't give you a—" The door fell shut.

Shock stiffened Mila's joints as she stepped out from behind the curtain and climbed down the stairs. She felt like she was walking underwater. Every step was a struggle. "I can't believe Pete really thinks that I could have . . ." A wave of emotion rose in her chest and her voice hitched.

"Now listen, kid," Mugsy patted her shoulder awkwardly. "He can't be too convinced that you did something bad, or else he wouldn't have come in here and spilled the beans like that."

Mila drew in a slow breath. "True."

"So." Mugsy squared his shoulders. "What we need to do is, we need to figure out who the real killer is."

The door swung open again and Mila flinched. But this time, it was Becca. Relief flooded through her. "Oh, thank goodness!"

"You okay?" Mugsy asked Becca.

"Yeah. I—oof." Mila crashed into her, and was immediately wrapped up in a huge, warm hug. "I couldn't sleep after the fire last night," Becca told Mugsy over Mila's shoulder, "so I went to check on Ms. Scarborough and the horses."

"How they doing?" Mugsy asked.

"Everyone is fine, and Ms. S already has Q's camper feeling homey. Did you know you can bake cookies in an air fryer? I sure didn't. She had me bring some to Mr. Cavendish with a pot of tea, over in the huge RV monstrosity he's staying in. Makes Q's camper look teeny by comparison, even though it's really nice. But I stayed so late visiting her and the horses, I slept through my alarm. Sorry."

"I don't care." Mila's voice trembled. "I'm just glad you're here."

She'd been through too much, and hearing the doubt in Pete's voice, knowing he was losing faith in her, was just more than she could bear. The weight of everything that had happened crashed through her, and a choked sob ripped from her throat. "Pete thinks I'm the killer! How could he think that?" she wailed.

Becca held her and stroked her hair. "Shhh . . . It's going to be okay," she murmured.

A thought occurred to Mila, jolting her into silence. She pulled back to arms-length from Becca, looking back and forth between her and Mugsy. "Do you agree with Pete? Do you think I'm the killer?" Mila hated the vulnerability she knew was written all over her face.

Their twin expressions of shocked dismay were all the reassurance she needed.

"No!" Mugsy growled.

"Of course not!" Becca agreed. "You could never murder someone. You can't even squish a bug, for crying out loud."

"Well because . . ." Mila's words spilled out in a rush. "Because they have feelings and little families, and some of them may even have a collective consciousness, like bees or ants that react simultaneously when a threat comes for them—"

Becca laughed. "Kinda making my point for me there, Mila." She gave a comforting squeeze. Mila melted into the safety of her friend's embrace. Her hitching breath steadied and slowed. Becca rubbed her back. "There we go. That's it."

Mila reluctantly let go. Becca had come for a reason, and it was more important than ever. They needed to get to work.

As Becca gave her shoulders a final squeeze, Mila thought she saw a slight quiver in her friend's chin. Maybe Brandon's death was hitting her harder than Mila had realized. But before she could say something, Becca put on a bright smile. "We'll figure this out together. It's going to be okay."

"That's right," Mugsy agreed. "We're on your side, kid."

"You're not alone, Mila," Becca put a hand on her shoulder and guided her to a chair. The kittens galloped out of the darkness and swarmed around the legs of her chair, yelling to be lifted into her lap.

Of course, she knew they couldn't understand what was going on. They were just kittens. But it was comforting to think maybe they cared enough to notice that she was upset. Maybe they wanted to help, too.

She looked up at Mugsy and Becca. "Right." She nodded and pulled the scrap of paper from her pocket and the books and codex from her bag. "Let's do it."

Chapter Eighteen
The Suspect

Bippity.

The humans were not very good at solving mysteries. Luckily, they had us.

"Before we go any further," Mila said to Becca. "I owe you an apology. I was so hurt about the affair and the deception that I couldn't help but suspect you might have been capable of anything. So I have to admit that for a little while, I thought you were Brandon's killer, Becca."

Becca's mouth flew open in shock. "What? Why?"

Mila's eyes fell. "I don't know. I was angry. I felt betrayed."

A pained expression flashed across Becca's face so fast that Mila and Mugsy probably didn't notice it. Cats were far more observant than humans.

"I'm sorry, Mila." Her face fell. "I'm so—"

Mila held up a hand. "I know. You're a good person, and you fell for him. I understand that now. He was quite the charmer. I just figured I should apologize for thinking the worst of you and clear the air."

"It's okay." Becca patted Mila's arm. "It's hard to think straight when everything seems to have gone all topsy turvy."

Mila gave her a grateful smile.

"So who do we think did it, then?" Mugsy asked.

Mila opened her sparkly purple notebook. She wrote MR. CAVENDISH in all capital letters on a fresh page. "He seems like the most likely culprit to me. We never had any murders or cataclysmic fires before he came to town."

Becca's eyebrows quirked upward. "You ever read any mystery novels?"

"Not really." Mila tilted her head. "Why, do you?"

"Yeah! Years ago, Ms. Scarborough gave me this book called *The Mysterious Affair at Styles* to read. Agatha Christie, the author, once famously said, 'Give me a decent bottle of poison, and I'll construct the perfect crime.' How awesome is that?" Becca beamed. "Once I read it, I was hooked, and now I can't get enough of them. Anyway, in detective stories, they're always talking about Motive, Means, and Opportunity."

"What are those?" Boppity asked. I had to give him credit. Ever since my lecture, he'd been doing his best to help solve Brandon's murder. He just wasn't quite as clever as I was. I gave him an indulgent look.

"*Motive* means *why*," I said.

"Why don't the humans just say that?" he groused.

"Because sometimes humans think like breaking glass or chasing your tail and falling off the bed, instead of like a ribbon," Boop told him.

Boppity and I looked at one another. What nonsense. "Humans like to feel smart," I told him.

"Can you take a look at Brandon's books?" Mila asked. "You're really good at accounting. Even though we can't decode his secret books, which probably have to do with this Commodore Holdings company, maybe his regular books have clues in them.

"Good idea, Mila," Mugsy nodded. "It's pretty hard to cover up every trace of a financial crime, if you know where to look."

Boppity looked at me.

He was doing his best, so I would be patient with him. "Nobody knows enough yet to have a good *why* for anyone else except Mila, because we can't read Brandon's gibberish books without solving the spool, so we don't know what he was up to. But Mugsy is going to look in some other kind of books to see if they have a why hidden in them." I knew this was all true, but I wasn't completely sure how it made sense.

"Maybe Mr. Cavendish's motive was something to do with the construction being held up and Brandon filing Luxe's bankruptcy paperwork," Mila suggested. "He told me that the day after Brandon died, everything suddenly started moving forward again."

"Really? That sounds like a pretty strong motive to me," Becca said. "Maybe there's more to that. I can ask Ms. S if she saw or heard anything suspicious."

"Great idea!" Mila grinned. "Hey, we're pretty good at this!"

"What about means?" Becca asked.

"The knife does implicate Mila," Mugsy grunted, "but the back door to the club was propped open, so just about anyone could have come in here, grabbed it, and stabbed Brandon."

"*Means* is who had a way to do the murder," I told Boppity. "The real question is who could have gotten Brandon's body up onto the catwalk above the stage."

"The catwalk looks fun," Boop purred.

I had to agree that it was thoughtful of the humans to design a portion of the theater especially for us. I wasn't sure how we would get up there, though. Which brought to mind an interesting question. "How would the killer get the body up there? It would have to be someone very strong, to carry a whole floppy dead human up a ladder, right?"

"Wait." Boppity flicked his tail. "Did you see that box thing Brutus called a 'dumbwaiter'?"

"Rude name," I said.

"Yeah. But I was looking at it, and it had these cables . . ." He raced off, forcing me and Boop to follow.

When we caught up to him, he was darting his gaze back and forth between one of Boop's trash balls and a button on the wall at human chest level. He pushed the trash with his paw and the button pressed inward.

With a whisper-quiet *whir*, a roomy box on a pulley began to climb. When it reached the catwalk, there was a little click and the bit of paper scooted back to its original position. Boppity poked it again, and the dumbwaiter began to descend.

"No Physics!" I hissed.

"The humans didn't see," he insisted, darting his gaze again to disentangle the button from the white crumple.

I wanted to be mad, but Boppity had proved something important. Obviously, anyone who could move a dead human would be able to get it up to the catwalk, climb the ladder, and then unload it there with relative ease.

I sighed. "Good job," I grumbled.

We raced back to Mila, who was now talking about opportunity.

"*Opportunity* means whether or not Mr. Cavendish was busy when Brandon was murdered and stashed," I explained.

"That's a problem," Mugsy growled. "He was in the audience for the whole show. Up on stage right before the body dropped. In the group outside when Pete questioned everyone."

"Right." Mila looked glum.

"But didn't Pete say he'd been dead for three or four hours before he fell?" Becca asked.

"Good point!" Mila brightened. "Mr. Cavendish could have killed him earlier in the evening, and snuck him up onto the catwalk while I was rehearsing."

"Wouldn't you have noticed?" Becca asked.

Mugsy laughed. "When Mila is rehearsing, you could have a brawl in the house and she wouldn't notice until someone hit her with a stray bottle. She's usually pretty quiet, too. Doesn't say her lines aloud, just in her head. So Brandon and the killer might have thought they were alone. And I took a nap with Brutus. Then we went out to get that truckload of supplies for the bar that you inventoried when you came in."

Mila jotted something in her notebook. "So I'll . . ." She bit her lip. "Ah! I'll try to piece together Brandon's day and Mr. Cavendish's. If I can find out where each of them was and when, we can see whether they line up. Ms. Fi offered to make us all dinner tonight, so let's meet up at her place to compare notes."

Mugsy nodded. "Sounds like a plan."

"Listen, guys," Mila looked back and forth between Mugsy and Becca. "Thank you. Truly. I don't know what I'd do without you."

"Always," Becca murmured, her eyes shining.

Mugsy grunted and patted Mila on the shoulder. "You got it, kid."

"Did they solve it?" Boppity asked.

"Not yet," I told him. "But they have a suspect, and that's a good start."

Chapter Nineteen
The Baker

Boppity.

The thing I didn't like about being in the kangaroo pouch was that I couldn't attack anyone. Except Bippity and Boop. But they weren't really enemies, and giving them combat training got old pretty fast.

There were plenty of people I'd have liked to fight. Sheriff Pete was at the top of my list. Everyone seemed pretty sure Mr. Cavendish was Brandon's killer, so I wanted to battle him, too. Mostly because by killing Brandon, he'd made trouble for Mila, and it was my job to protect her. And what about that lie-detector horse, Sage? I'd been convinced by her smell that she was harmless, until the fire. Then she'd hit the barn with hooves like giant hammers and gnashed teeth bigger than my paw. She wasn't an enemy, but she would certainly make a worthy opponent.

Then there was this baker, Q. They sat across from us, cane in hand, telling Mila about how Brandon had met Mr. Cavendish for brunch, but he hadn't ordered anything because he was having an early dinner with the mayor at Rousseau's up on the northern coast. That cane looked like a pretty good pounce target.

But I decided to focus. There were clues to be found. I had already discovered the dumbwaiter in the theater, and snatched the clue with the blood drop, proving once again that I was the most impressive kitten in the family and should surely be in charge.

Preventing me from investigating Q's for evidence was unacceptable. I pawed at the screen and announced my irritation. "Let us out, Mila," I hollered. "Let us oooooouuuuut!"

"Sorry, kittens," Mila said. "It's against health laws to have cats roaming around in places that serve food."

Health laws? Seriously? "Cats are far cleaner than humans!" I told her.

"Even cat cafés have to have two separate establishments," Q agreed. Obviously, it was a conspiracy. "If someone wanted to open the cat-cuddling half of a cat café next door, I'd be thrilled, but I'm not up to the challenge of running both by myself."

"Yeah." I could feel the shake of Mila's nodding head through the kangaroo pouch. "For real. That would be a lot."

"What nonsense," I yowled. "In protest, I will sing you the anger-song of my people."

"Wow." Q's mouth made a flat line. "That little guy is super upset."

"Hush!" Bippity scolded. "You're ruining our investigation! Mila can't ask her questions with you belting out that rage-opera at the top of your lungs. Even if she could, we wouldn't be able to hear the clues she's getting."

I flattened my ears. I didn't want to give Bippity any excuses to claim I wasn't as good a detective as she was.

"I like your rage-opera," Boop said, scooting up against me. "I can feel your voice in my ribs."

At least Boop appreciated me. I gave a final yowl, then subsided.

Boop filled the silence left behind by the cessation of my song with a low, rumbling purr. I decided to lean into their floof and listen. Hopefully, Q would say something interesting.

"What time was Brandon here, exactly?

Q pulled out their phone. "I'm showing the charge for Mr. Cavendish's brunch just shy of eleven, on Friday morning, and I remember that he didn't order until after Brandon arrived."

Mila jotted in her notebook. "And I talked with him in the alley right after he texted me at . . ." she pulled out her own phone. "Ten forty-seven. So he must have come straight here from the alley. How long did they talk?"

"About an hour. Did some paperwork or other. I remember that Mr. Cavendish looked grim."

"Bankruptcy paperwork, I bet," Bippity said.

Mila thought the same thing. "Must have been finalizing that initial bankruptcy filing."

My tail twitched. Bippity thought she was so clever.

Q nodded. "Could be."

"They're not surprised," Boop said. They were comfy, but not the most strategic-minded cat ever. I flicked a fond ear at them. At least they were good at purring.

"So Brandon had an early dinner at Rousseau's. Do you know if he was going somewhere before that?"

Q shrugged. "No idea. Not sure what else Mr. Cavendish was up to, either, aside from going to your show. I recall he mentioned being excited about an afternoon ride with Ms. S to see the southern cliffs, but I'm not sure whether that was scheduled for the same day."

Mila was quiet for a moment. Maybe she was thinking. My mind moved so *fast,* I didn't need time to think. "Ask what he was doing during the show!" I told her.

"Do you know anything else about what Brandon was up to that day or that night?"

Q's eyes shifted. Their beige complexion darkened across their cheeks.

Mila put a gentle hand on Q's wrist across the table. "I don't mean to make you uncomfortable. Hearing all the gossip in here, it must put you in an awkward position sometimes. Never mind. You've been more than helpful already."

Q ran a hand through the thick black hair that stood up in tousled waves atop their head. Then they lifted their eyes to Mila's face.

Huge behind their thick, square-framed rainbow glasses, Q's irises were so close in hue to their pupils that they simply looked deep, like the night sky.

Mila's breath caught and held as Q turned up their palm so they were suddenly holding Mila's wrist.

"Generally, I'm big on privacy," they said, "but in this case . . ." Licking their lips, they looked away for a moment. When their gaze returned to Mila's face, their brows were lifted in the middle, their expression somewhere between sadness and wistful hope. "I . . ."

Mila leaned forward just enough to topple Bippity off-balance. She tumbled into me and Boop. Normally, such an invasion of my space would've been enough to start a wrestle battle, but there was something captivating about the look on Q's face and the way Mila was barely breathing.

I was sure we were about to get a *huge* clue.

Q swallowed. "It might be important, but it's a sensitive subject, and you might not be too keen to discuss it."

"Becca and Brandon, right?" Mila leaned forward. "It's okay. She and I have moved past it." Q released a great blast of air from their lungs. "Oh my gosh, whew. I—wait, you were avoiding Becca at the reception. When did you make up?"

"We talked the next night. But with that, plus the weapon being my trick knife for my show, Pete is getting surer every day that I'm the killer." Mila laughed, but this time it sounded more like sandpaper than joy. "I really hope I can prove him wrong."

Q's expression was stormy now, like a sky about to rain. But the big clue had turned out to be nothing. Investigating was boring. I was starting to get sleepy. This entire visit had been a complete waste of our time.

I buried my nose in Boop's side. At least there was the comfort of napping.

Chapter Twenty
The Chef

Boop.

"What a waste of time," Boppity grumbled. "All we learned was that Brandon got the bankruptcy papers from Mr. Cavendish and then went to meet the mayor at a fancy restaurant. So what? We knew most of that already."

Bippity thwapped his ears. "Pay attention. He was meeting the mayor and then going somewhere *else* during the beginning of the show. Before meeting Becca at the gazebo."

"So? That may be interesting to *you*, but how could it be important?" Boppity had a canny expression on his face. He was trying to get Bippity to admit that she didn't know everything.

"Oh, easy." She flicked an ear casually. "The place Brandon went after the restaurant was probably the last place where he was alive. He never showed up at the gazebo. So when we find out where he went after the restaurant, we'll find out who had the opportunity to murder him." She scoffed at him. "How do you not know that?"

Boppity narrowed his eyes. "But we're not going to the place *after* the restaurant. We don't even know where that is. We're going to the restaurant. Useless."

Bippity's whiskers quirked in condescension. "Again, you're missing the point. The most likely people to know where Brandon was going next would be either the mayor or the people at the restaurant."

Boppity crouched, his ears sleeked back against his streamlined neck. He was ready to pounce. His patience was fraying. "Why not ask the mayor?"

"We were at his office just the other day," Bippity said with a disdainful twitch of her nose. "He didn't say anything about seeing Brandon the day he was killed. Mila wants to get evidence before she talks to him again. Do you get it now?"

Instead of answering, Boppity flung himself into her, knocking her back into me.

"Hey!" I shouted. Then I rolled over and captured her tail.

"I'm going to teach you to respect me if it's the last thing I do!" Boppity hollered at her.

"You're such an easy mark," laughed Bippity. I laughed too. Laughing was fun.

"Kittens! Chill!" Mila scolded. She was already climbing out of the car. "There are no animals allowed in here, so I'm zipping the covers over your windows. You have to stay quiet!"

Mila wanted us to calm down, so I purred, wrapping myself in my best relaxation-feels. The air smelled like secret tidepools and old wood and barnacles. I purred louder. Boppity glowered at me, but I squeezed my eyes shut fondly, and he snuggled down with a reluctant sigh. Bippity scooted over and joined in.

I couldn't see anything even before Mila slipped our pouch off one shoulder, sliding us down into a snuggle-ball in one corner. It was super crowded and comfy.

She pulled open a door, and the space she walked into was full of enticing smells. There was a cool, hushed energy to the room. People murmured all around us. Tiny tinks and scrapes punctuated their conversations. I could feel Mila easing, as if she was in a place of safety and comfort.

Probably because of the smells.

Meat-feast was nothing compared to this. A perfect bouquet of yum drifted through the air-holes in our toasty little cave. My stomach rumbled loudly.

A silky voice drifted to us on the delicious current. "Good evening and welcome to Rousseau's. Do you have a reservation?"

"I don't, but I need to ask you a question. Do you recognize this man?"

"Of course," the host responded. Their voice was a little less warm than it had been a moment ago, I thought.

"He was here recently?"

"Friday afternoon, for our first seating at four o'clock. Is something wrong?"

"You may have seen in the paper that he's been murdered. I need to find out why." I heard Mila swallow. Saying the words aloud had made a tangle of sharp, jittery emotions float around her in a tart cloud.

There was a pause. "Perhaps you should speak with the chef."

"Sure. Thanks. That would be . . . good."

We drifted through gorgeous swirls of fragrant air and into a warmer, steamier room full of bustle and thinly structured chaos. Our pouch slid back and forth across Mila's soft, round hip as she walked, creating a soothing rhythm. Clattering and hissing were everywhere, and voices called out commands or questions.

"*Pouvons*, Chef Michon?" the host called. "This lovely lady has some questions for you about the man who was murdered. Do you have a moment?"

A rich, throaty voice hollered, "*Bien sûr*!"

"The chef's table, *mademoiselle*," the host murmured.

"In the kitchen?" Mila asked.

"It's a great honor, usually reserved for the Chef's close personal friends."

"Oh! Well . . . thank you." She sat and put our pouch in her lap. I could have happily stayed forever in the warm darkness, at the bottom of this furry sibling-pile on Mila's cushy lap, breathing in this beautiful-smelling place.

The chair opposite Mila slid out and someone sat. "Hello, *mademoiselle*. I'm Chef Michon Rousseau."

"Mila MacAllister."

"*Enchanté*. He was your boyfriend, the victim, if I remember the article in the *Courant* correctly?"

"Yes. And business manager."

"I'm sorry for your loss. How may I help?"

"I believe Brandon met Mayor Adams for dinner on Friday night, right?"

"He did, yes. It was an early reservation, four-thirty in the afternoon. Our first dinner seating."

Mila's pen scratched in her notebook. "To file bankruptcy paperwork for the Luxe Resort?" she asked.

The chef made an elegant furball noise. "It was rather more than that, *m'selle*."

Mila froze. Her body stiffened, and cold, staticky shock erupted in her chest. "What does that mean, more?"

"They were making some sort of plans." Chef Rousseau gave off waves of even, gentle calm. "I am sure we were not supposed to overhear them, but these are the sort of men who do not even notice service and hospitality professionals. To them, we are nothing. Therefore, we are invisible."

Boppity had fallen asleep, but Bippity's ears stood up. I supposed that meant the humans were talking about something interesting.

"I'm sorry," Mila murmured. "That must not feel very good."

"Eh, we are unbothered. There is no use being vulnerable to the opinions of men such as this," the chef told her. "Crooked, self-important bombasts with no finesse and absolutely horrible taste in wine."

Mila giggled, a sound that seemed to startle her as much as it did me.

"Ahhhh . . ." Chef Rousseau sighed. "You retain your capacity for joy, even in such trying times. What a lucky man this Brandon was."

"He didn't think so," Mila's voice hitched. A jolt of pain, weak but unexpected, vibrated in her chest and echoed through mine. I redoubled my purrs to quell it.

"Then he was a fool. *Quelle andouille.*"

"Do you know what kind of plans they were making?" Maybe my purrs were helping. Her voice did sound steadier. She was a good human. *I'm proud of you,* I thought. "You said something about crooked?"

"I'm afraid I didn't pay particularly close attention," the chef murmured. "All I know is that it had something to do with the fate of the Luxe Resort after Mr. Cavendish was no longer involved, and as he was leaving, the slick one, Brandon, asked to meet with me about a future business opportunity. As if I would ever go into business with a man such as this."

Mila wrote in her notebook, her emotions suddenly in a furious swirl. "After Mr. Cavendish was no longer involved? What kind of *after* would there even be? I mean . . . What could Brandon have . . ." Under her breath, I heard her whisper, *Who was he, really?* Her breathing quickened. My purrs faltered as my own breath raced in empathy. I blinked and breathed out slowly through my nose, then drew in a lungful of delicious aromas.

My stomach rumbled again and I restarted my purr. Mmmm. It smelled so good in here.

Mila drew in a deep breath. "Do you have any idea where he was going next?"

"I believe both men planned to meet back at the mayor's office. Something to do with additional paperwork. 'Now that we have amended our agreement,' I believe Brandon said. After that, he said he was going to meet someone else. I am not sure who. He said something about a loose end, or maybe a loose cannon." The chef made a little grunt. "Some such colloquialism."

"Huh. And what time did he and the mayor leave?"

"Just after five."

"Okay. Thank you, Chef Rousseau. You've been a big help." She stood, sliding us onto her shoulder again. "Truly."

"It's my pleasure. I'm very sorry for everything he's put you through."

"It's okay," Mila nodded. "He just wasn't who I thought he was. I guess I never knew him. All the feelings I thought I had for Brandon were just a fantasy."

"Oh, one more thing, *m'selle*." There was a slight pause. "This may be indelicate of me to say, but the mayor did not seem particularly satisfied with the outcome of their discussion. Perhaps Brandon wasn't who *he* thought, either."

Chapter Twenty-One
The Discovery

Mila.

When Mila stepped into Ms. Fi's home, the smell that washed over her had her stomach rumbling eagerly. It smelled warm and comforting, meaty and spicy—like the kind of home she'd never had but always wished for.

"Mila, dearest! It's so good to see you." Ms. Fi gave her a warm hug. "Let's turn those kittens loose and get you settled." She pressed her lips together, appraising Mila from the scuffed tips of her purple canvas sneakers to the top of her wind-scrambled mane. "Hmm. You do look a bit of a mess." The barest hint of a fond smile turned up one corner of her mouth. "But we'll set you right. Come on in, dearest. Let's get you fed."

Mila toed out of her shoes and padded across the plush burgundy Persian rug and past the sitting room with its merlot leather sofas.

At the scarred oak kitchen table, Mugsy and Becca sat behind heaping plates of food. Mila sank gratefully into a velvet and hobnail dining chair. Faster than should have been humanly possible, Ms. Fi made up a plate and set it before Mila.

A thigh and wing of fried chicken nestled in beside a heaping scoop of mashed potatoes with a lake of gravy, golden okra pinwheels rolled in cornmeal and fried in bacon grease, a fluffy buttermilk biscuit, a beautiful mess of mustard greens, and a mound of black-eyed peas.

In the center of the table, towering above the massive platters of food, stood a cut crystal cake stand with a triple-layer hummingbird cake iced in cream cheese frosting and decorated with toasted pecans.

"Thank you, Ms. Fi, this looks incredible!"

"It does," Becca agreed, gazing longingly at her biscuit. "And there's so much of it."

Mila nodded. "You're too good to us, Ms. Fi." In truth, it was a ridiculous amount of food for four people. Still, the massive spread just added to the welcoming energy filling the house.

"Well, dig in." Ms. Fi waved her hand, then made herself a plate and sat.

Sinking his teeth deep into a drumstick, Mugsy grunted with pleasure. When he'd chewed a few times, he scooped a forkful of greens and mashed potato into his still-full mouth. "So good, Ms. Fi."

Turning to Mila, he swallowed. "There was something interesting in Brandon's books."

"None of that talk at the dinner table." Ms. Fi's voice was light, but her eyes were steel. "This has all been a lot. Let's give Mila a moment to breathe and just enjoy a meal with people who love her and have her back."

A lump rose in Mila's throat. She took a long chug of sweet tea to hide her watery smile. Dinner passed in pleasant conversation, though Mila was itching to compare notes and learn what the others had discovered. When everyone was stuffed, Ms. Fi herded them into the sitting room for dessert.

Becca excused herself. "I just need to make a quick call to check in on Ms. S," she said. "I'm too full for cake right now, anyway. I'll be back in a sec."

Ms. Fi nodded. "Give her our best."

The hummingbird cake was as light and sweet as hope, the coffee strong but not bitter. When they'd finished, Mugsy took a last swallow of coffee. "Okay. Down to business."

He exchanged looks with Ms. Fi. Mila stiffened at the worry lines that furrowed his forehead. "I have some hard news."

"Okay, I'm ready." Mila wasn't sure she was, but regardless, she wanted to know.

Mugsy grunted, eyes misty for some reason. He sniffed. "Okay, kid. Here it is. Brandon was stealing from you."

"What?" Mila's brow furrowed. "I don't understand. I didn't have anything to steal."

"That's because of Brandon," Mugsy said. His face was like a sheet of paper crushed in an angry fist. "He wasn't just taking his fifteen percent commission from your profits to manage your career. He was taking more. Lots more."

Mila blinked. "How can that be? I've barely been hitting the booking rates and scheduling goals he mapped out for my career plan."

"What career plan?" Ms. Fi asked, her tone sharp.

"Brandon was always honest with me." Mila heard a tinny ring of defensiveness in her voice. "I know I'm not good enough for real fame or success. My shows sold pretty well, even off-island, but only because ticket prices were low and they were never at top-tier venues."

Mugsy bristled. "What are you saying about my club?"

"Except yours, of course!" Mila held up her hands.

"What?" Becca screeched from behind her. She crossed the room and sat beside Mila. "You have enormous talent! You're a star! You've always been a star!"

"I'm just being realistic." The words tumbled out of her in a rush. "I'm a B-list magician. A second-rate performer."

"It's hard for me to hear you undercut yourself, dearest." Ms. Fi put a hand on her forearm. "Becca's right. You're a star. You deserve better than that swine."

Becca was rigid beside her.

Mugsy grunted. "Whatever Brandon was telling you about your bookings, it wasn't the truth. He wasn't giving you anywhere near your share. A huge chunk was getting siphoned off."

Mila's head spun. "How much are we talking about?"

"I'm not a forensic accountant." Mugsy frowned. "And without those coded books, I can't give you any specifics. But if I'm piecing this together correctly, he was taking maybe three-quarters of your profits, Mila. It was a lot. And there were definitely other victims, too."

"Other victims?" Becca asked. "Do you know who?"

Mugsy shook his head. "He did a pretty good job covering it all up, but my guess is he was stealing from most of his clients, which means our suspect list just went from short to enormous."

Mila squeezed her eyes shut. Her heart hammered in her chest. It was all too much. "I need to . . ." She looked around. "Where are the kittens? I have to go home. I need to think."

Ms. Fi stood and put a hand on Mila's shoulder. "I'll get them."

Mila looked from Becca to Mugsy. "I'm sorry, I just don't know how to deal with this. I mean who even *was* Brandon? What was he doing? Did he ever actually love me?"

"He was a dirty, worthless thief," Mugsy told her. Becca shook her head helplessly, eyes wide and mouth tight.

Shame and remorse surged in Mila's gut. She imagined Becca was feeling a lot of the same things she was, but unable to say them because of her affair with Brandon. She reached out and wrapped Becca in a hug. "I'm sorry," Mila said. "It seems like he fooled us both. This must feel really bad, learning all of this about him."

Becca went stiff in her arms, then shuddered and melted. A sob choked out of her, and she pulled away and clapped a hand over her mouth. "It's not my place to . . ." She shook her head. "I mean, it's your feelings that matter here. I never had the right . . ." A tear rolled down her cheek.

The tangle of emotions in the pit of Mila's belly churned and roiled. She was trying to figure out what to say when Ms. Fi reappeared, still cradling her kangaroo pouch.

"Little dears were smooshed into Hylia's belly-fluff. Never seen her looking so protective or so irritated. I think I got them resettled in here without waking them."

Mila took the pouch carefully and shoved her feet into her shoes by the front door. She just wanted a hot shower and bed. But when she climbed her own porch and stepped inside, a scream ripped from her throat. Mugsy, Ms. Fi, and Becca raced out of Ms. Fi's half of the duplex and up onto Mila's, coming to a halt beside her. In her kangaroo pouch, the kittens woke with a start and began to yowl.

Her apartment had been absolutely trashed. The cushions of her sofa were slashed, stuffing pulled out and thrown everywhere like the fake snow at a shopping mall North Pole. The books had been hauled off her shelves and dumped all over the floor. Their pages fluttered in the evening breeze like injured butterflies. Lamps were knocked over, the shades ripped off.

Mila rushed through the mess to the room where she worked on her tricks, with the others following close behind. A strangled cry wrenched itself from her throat. Her props and equipment had been pulled down and broken open. Tattered scraps of fabric and shards of broken mirror dotted the rubble. On the back wall, in crimson spray-paint that dripped like blood, was the warning:

Keep your nose out of other people's business.

"I'm calling Sheriff Pete," Ms. Fi said.

"No, wait!" Becca held up a hand. "Do we really want the law involved? As it is, Pete seems convinced Mila is responsible for Brandon's death."

"How could anyone think a break-in would make Mila look guiltier?" Ms. Fi asked. "Whoever did this probably left behind some sort of evidence. We should give Sheriff Pete a chance to find it."

Mugsy shook his head grimly. "Becca may be right. You didn't see the sheriff, Ms. Fi. He was really convinced Mila's the killer. I wouldn't put it past him to think she did this to her own place."

"That's ridiculous." Ms. Fi scowled.

All three of them turned to Mila.

"I trust the sheriff. And there could be trace evidence."

Mila put in the 911 call, then turned to Ms. Fi. "Can I crash at your place? I suppose I could go to Brandon's loft, but I really don't want to be alone tonight."

Ms. Fi's face softened. She herded everyone outside and shut the door. "Of course you can. Let's just lock this up for now."

Wrapping an arm around Mila's shoulder, she guided her gently to her own porch. "I'll make up my guest bed, and you'll stay as long as you need to."

She gave Mugsy and Becca a disapproving shake of her head as she led Mila away.

Chapter Twenty-Two
The Shoe

Bippity.

We were back in Hylia's Queendom. It was difficult to be disappointed with this outcome because Hylia was so lovely and soft. Perhaps she would allow us to snuggle-pile her again.

"Come on, siblings," I said. I trotted toward Ms. Fi's room, where we had found Hylia before.

A wide bed clothed in deep purple velvet dominated the space. In the corner, an elegant armchair with a winged back bore stripes of cream and lavender. Colorful little burlap fish stuffed with some sort of fragrant herb were sprinkled around like confetti.

Hylia's queendom really was magnificent. But where was she?

A trill drew my attention upward. On the wall, four shelves wrapped in jute described a pattern like ascending stairs, and high above the head of the bed, where a fifth step should have been, there was a hexagonal box. Hylia gazed down at us from inside it.

The leap from the chair to the first wall-step was far. Too far for little kittens like us. There was no way we could—

"Hiiiiiiiiii Queeeeeeeen!" Boop trilled, flinging themself fearlessly through the air between the top step and Hylia's throne-nook. They landed atop her hindquarters and slid down her rump.

"How dare you . . ." she started, but as Boop opened their mouth and began a deep, moist purr, Hylia tilted her head. "Huh. You're a funny one, aren't you."

They burrowed into her underfluff.

How had they gotten up there? It was impossible!

"If Boop can, I can!" shouted Boppity, leaping from the chair-back to the first step and barely making it. Jump after claw-hooked, death-defying jump, he continued upward until he, too, threw himself boldly into the air.

He hit her square in the face, wrapping his forepaws around her head and scrabble-kicking with his back feet until he found purchase on the lip of the throne room. Before she could protest, he buried himself in the chest-floof between her front legs.

It should have been impossible. He'd barely made it. The jumps were too high. Too wide. I yearned to be in that queenly snuggle pile, warmer and more comforting than anything we'd known since Mother.

But as I scaled the back of the chair, I began to shake. In my mind, I was falling from Mila's shoulder again and again, twisting and swimming through the air and knowing that even if I organized my paws perfectly, I wouldn't survive that terrible impact.

I didn't want to die.

I decided to demand that everyone come down and share their cuddles on the bed, like any sensible cat would do.

But the sound that came out of my throat was a terrified, mournful yowl.

Some leader I was. Shame flooded me.

Ms. Fi came running into the room, cell phone still in her hand. "Yes, Pete, thank you for letting me know you're on your way. She's over at my place. Yes, I locked it up right away. Okay. Thanks." She hung up her phone. "What's happening here, kitten?"

"I am ordering my siblings to come down, and politely requesting the Queen join us as well," I tried to tell her. But instead, I yowled again, staring up at the cuddle pile so near and yet so far beyond my reach.

"Aw. Poor little thing," Ms. Fi lifted me in cupped hands. "You must be Boop. Cute and cuddly but sometimes a bit confused. That's how Mila described you."

I bristled, my tail poofing into a bottlebrush. "How *dare* you?" I lifted my paw to swipe at her, but she was depositing me gently in front of Hylia's warm belly. Boop turned up their purring until it was so deep and rumbly that they vibrated the entire throne room.

I wanted to be furious, but instead, I pushed myself under Hylia's glorious fluff, ignoring the snickers coming from Boppity. I didn't want to think about my failure. I closed my eyes and settled into the comfort of the purr pile.

I woke up to voices in the sitting room. Mila, Ms. Fi, and a third voice that I recognized as Sheriff Pete.

Boppity was gone and Hylia was sound asleep, her breath deep and slow. Boop purred beside me, gazing at my face.

"Boppity went to guard Mila, and I stayed to show you the way down," they said. "In case you didn't want to figure it out all by yourself. Alone isn't nearly as much fun."

Then they flung themself from the edge of the hexagonal throne room, falling through the air for what seemed like an eternity, before landing on the bed with a little *mmph* sound, bouncing once, and giggling about the fun ride.

I looked down and felt my stomach clench. This couldn't possibly be the way down, could it?

"You can do it," Boop told me. "You're so courageous. Facing scary things is the bravest. I believe in you."

But even though they believed in me, I knew I couldn't do it.

"It's okay," they told me. "Don't worry. I'll help you." They raced up the chair back and leaped boldly up each of the steps until they were once again beside me.

"Ready?"

"Ready for wh—?"

Before I could finish asking, they'd wrapped their forearms around my neck and leaped, yanking me into the abyss with them.

I was going to die.

But I didn't. Instead, I hit the bed with a *bong* and bounced, fizzing with rage.

"See?" they trilled. "Fun!" When they saw the wrath in my eyes, they bolted. I followed, my fury morphing into curiosity as I overheard the humans ahead.

What time did you return to your house and find it ransacked?" Sheriff Pete asked.

"Around eight. Right before I called 911." Mila sat on the edge of a burgundy sofa cushion, hands curled into fists and tucked under her chin. She was staring at the ground, her shoulders rigid. I knew what she was feeling. She was trying desperately to be brave.

"And did you ever step outside?"

"Mila spent the evening here with Mugsy, Becca, and myself." Ms. Fi's voice was angry. "What do you intend to do to find out who could have done this?" She made a *hmph* sound deep in her throat, eloquent with scorn.

I raced over to Mila, who was staring at Pete's face, her eyes hollow. Climbing delicately up the leg of her fleece pajama bottoms and up the front of her top, I tucked myself beneath her left ear. "I'm here," I whispered comfortingly.

Her hand uncurled and reached up to pet me. Below, Boop settled across one of her bare feet, purring.

"Did anyone leave the dinner party?" Pete asked.

"I don't think so." Mila tilted her head. "Wait, no. Becca made a phone call. But she didn't leave, I don't think?" Poor Mila. Something about Pete's icy blue stare seemed to be draining her strength. I rubbed my cheek against her neck to remind her that she and I had one another no matter what.

I was sure that Boop's purring was helpful, too. And Boppity . . . wait, where *was* Boppity? I searched the room, but he was nowhere to be seen.

"Deputy Chantelle is canvassing the neighborhood. Hopefully, someone saw something. But so far, we're coming up empty." A muscle twitched in Pete's jaw. "I'm trying to find an explanation for everything that's been happening. I'll be honest, though. The evidence against you is piling up, Mila."

Her chest hitched, and her hands curled back into fists.

"I need you to leave, Sheriff." Mila's voice was sharp. "I don't feel comfortable answering any more questions without legal representation present."

"Boop?" I looked down at my sibling, who gazed up at me through half-closed eyes. "Have you seen Boppity?"

"Nope," they purred.

"Let us know what you find out, Pete." Ms. Fi opened the door, and the sheriff stood to leave.

Just then, Boppity appeared at the doorway to the Queen's bedroom, carrying . . . oh no. He was carrying a pink stuffed fish, and everything about his body language was eloquent with the fury of a warrior about to strike.

He dropped the fish, darting his gaze between it and the sheriff.

"Boppity!" I shouted. "No! It's forbidden!" But even though I used my voice to be sure he heard me, his focus didn't waver. With a malicious grimace that was part rage and part glee, he smacked the fish, shooting it across the room. Pete's left foot shot out from beneath him and he hurtled toward the door, barely catching himself on the doorframe.

"What the . . . ?" he shouted, his eyes shooting around the room.

He would spot Boppity, and that would be the end of everything. I didn't want to be captured and have the humans showing one another our guts. Thinking fast, I shooed all the photons away from the sheriff's eyes. He released the door, arms waving in the air.

"I can't see! I can't—"

He stumbled backward through the door, and just as his weight was resting on his left foot, Boppity hit his fish again. Pete flew backwards down the front porch stairs.

I hurriedly redirected the photons around the fish, rendering it invisible, so the humans wouldn't see it careening and whirling across the room in mimicry.

Mila leaped up. "Pete!" she shouted. I fell from her shoulder and hit the sofa with a bounce not unlike the one I'd experienced when disembarking from the Queen's throne room. The impact broke my grip on the photons, and they all flew back to their normal paths of travel. The fish reappeared, and Boppity hastily disentangled it from the sheriff's shoe hanging in the air over Ms. Fi's front yard.

The shoe fell to the ground with a thud as Pete flung himself back to his feet, rubbing his eyes.

"Everyone always says you have some mystical ability," he said, pointing an accusing finger at Ms. Fi. "But I never believed it . . . until now."

Hylia stalked across the sitting room, pinning each of us with a stare as sharp and cold as death. She settled herself neatly by her human's ankles, sitting with regal grace and curling her tail around her paws.

Ms. Fi's shocked expression relaxed and her eyes narrowed in contempt. "Come now, Sheriff," she tutted. "You merely had a bit of a dizzy spell. Forget to eat dinner tonight, did you?"

He opened his mouth, then closed it again.

"That's what I thought." Her eyebrow gave a wry twitch. Her lips quirked, and I couldn't help thinking that if she'd had whiskers, she would have been scoffing. "Don't worry, Sheriff. I'll forget all about your foolish talk of hocus pocus. I know you'll feel silly about all of this once you've had a good meal and a little rest."

Pete blinked. He rose, dusting himself off, and grabbed his wayward shoe. He was still mumbling to himself, shaking his head in bemusement, as he drove away.

Chapter Twenty-Three
The Code

Boppity.

We were living in the super-slick loft now. Best news *ever!* Mila's place was a crime scene, so we needed somewhere to live since Sheriff Pete was collecting evidence.

I was so proud of myself for setting that guy straight, I almost didn't mind the lecture from Hylia that came afterward, about the consequences if we ever risked discovery by the humans again. "Remember. The relationship between cats and Physics must be kept secret," she'd said as Boop climbed onto her tail and began to purr. "They must never know. As I have told you before, it is the oldest and most important Law of Cats." She'd used that scary command voice that made me freeze and vibrated my bones.

Obviously, she meant business.

Even now, I was still confused about what she'd said next.

"The rules are a little different when you're protecting the human you've bonded with." What could that mean? "Have you decided about Mila yet?"

"Bonded?" Bippity asked. "Are you asking if we like her?"

Hylia sighed. "It's so much more than that. There is no more important decision for a cat than which human to bond with."

"What if we're with the wrong one?" I'd asked her. I was trying my best to be brave. But I could *feel* the uncertainty echoing through my question.

"Are you?" Her deep golden eyes, the color of rising harvest moons, bored into me.

"I don't know." I looked at Bippity. For once, I saw the same doubt and confusion in her eyes. It was comforting. I scooted close to her, letting myself lean against her, shoulder to shoulder and ribcage to ribcage.

"How can we tell?" Bippity asked.

"Look, kittens." She tilted her head indulgently, then pulled Bippity forward and gently knocked her down to groom her. "I can tell you about my bond with my human, but in the end, you have to decide for yourself how you want to live this life. Do you love Mila?"

Uncertainty coursed through me. I *wanted* to love Mila. But what if she got sent to the human pound, and we were alone. What if she abandoned us, just like Mother had. What would that mean for me and my siblings? What would happen to us? "I . . . how do I tell?"

Tugging her tail out from beneath Boop, Hylia gave it a wry swish. "If you have to ask, then the answer is no. Maybe someday, but not yet."

Bippity pulled her face out from under Hylia's huge paw. I struggled not to laugh. Her fur was combed into damp peaks, all swirling to the left. She looked like she'd been hit with a tiny tsunami.

"We're her protectors, just like we've been told to be. We're good, loyal cats, and Mother would be proud of us." She glared at me. "Obviously, we love her. Of course we do."

"Ease up, little Queenlet." Hylia had glanced at her flank, which Boop was creeping toward, making their best effort at stealth. She pretended not to see them. "You don't always have to have an answer to every question. You don't have to know how you feel about her yet. It's clear she needs to be fostered, at least. You can protect her for now. It doesn't mean you have to keep her."

Listening to Mila cry herself to sleep as I lay awake beside her, pondering Hylia's words, had left me tired and confused.

But now, in our shiny new home, she must have been inspired by my fighting spirit when I faced that bully sheriff, because she wore a determined expression as she tucked us into our kangaroo pouch.

"I suppose I could leave you guys here," she was saying. "But having you along is so comforting. Maybe I should start leash-training you."

"Good idea, human!" I said. I wasn't sure what that was, but anything that meant us getting to go along on adventures, I was up for.

When we arrived at our destination, I was pleased to see that we were at the burned farm where we'd met the lie detector horses. They seemed really useful. I figured Mila was going to interrogate them, but instead, she headed for a massive, shiny vehicle parked out in the horse field. It was red and swoopy and bigger than a bus, with at least as many wheels. It had a wide, pointy face and a bubble-shaped see-through forehead. A black staircase with burgundy carpeting led up to a wide door on its side.

It was parked like the long part of an L beside a much smaller boxy white thing with two sets of wheels and no face at all. Its metal neck rested on a cement block.

Mila climbed the stairs of the grander vehicle and knocked on the door, but nobody answered. When we walked around to the inside of the L, there sat Ms. Scarborough and Mr. Cavendish in two comfortable-looking chairs with a square folding table, sipping tea and eating cookies as they watched the goats and horses graze in the distance.

"Mila, honey!" Ms. Scarborough's face lit in a smile. "Join us! You can take my seat. I'll go grab another chair and a teacup. Won't be a second!" She leaped up and scurried off before Mila had a chance to respond.

"Your Ms. Scarborough is quite a charmer," Mr. Cavendish chuckled, gesturing to the seat she'd left empty. "She's full of stories, too. Did you know she got married in the seventies, right around when I was born? Back then, women weren't legally allowed to get a mortgage or a credit card without a husband's approval. Can you imagine? She has this amazing story about her husband getting angry at her for attending a protest for women's rights, because when he came home from work, she didn't have dinner on the table. Have you heard this one?"

"No." Mila leaned forward. "Tell me!"

"Apparently, she spent all day making his favorite meal of slow-roasted beef tenderloin, watermelon pickles, homemade dinner rolls, mushroom cream gravy with black pepper, caramelized carrots and pearl onions, and apple pie for dessert. Then she served it all up on the best bone china they had and set it out for him . . . right inside the front door. When he came home that night, he literally put his foot in it."

Mila and Mr. Cavendish burst out laughing, her high tinkling giggles floating above his deep booming guffaws. Personally, I couldn't see what was funny. Putting your foot into your food was a great way to make sure your face was lowered to the perfect height for eating, and plus it made your toes extra nice to groom afterward.

"I thought Mr. Cavendish was our murderer," I said sourly. "Why is Mila being nice to him?"

Bippity flicked an ear. She was so condescending. "Oh, silly brother," she said. "Being nice disarms him. He's more likely to slip up and give something away if he thinks we're his friends."

She was talking like she thought she and Mila were doing this together. I was about to swat her rude face, but Boop sidled up to me.

"Let's listen. Maybe they'll say something interesting," they suggested.

It wasn't the worst idea ever. I kind of wished they'd start purring, but they seemed intent on the humans.

"What are you two laughing about?" Ms. Scarborough asked, setting a clean teacup on the table and opening the folding chair she'd brought.

"I was just telling Mila about that special dinner you made for Mr. Scarborough."

Ms. Scarborough joined in the merriment. "Oh, yes. Right about then, I'd catch him looking down at his wedding ring, and I swear I could hear him thinking, *what have I gotten myself into*?"

Everyone continued to laugh as Ms. Scarborough poured Mila a cup of tea.

"So what brings you out our way, Mila?" Ms. Scarborough asked. "Not that we don't love the company, but you youngsters are always zipping from place to place, busy as bees. Seems pretty rare you'd come just for tea and conversation."

Mila spread her palms open before her. "You got me, Ms. S. I came by because my place got broken into, and I was wondering if either of you happened to be in town last night? Maybe you saw something?"

"Oh, Mila, honey! That's terrible," Ms. Scarborough's brow crumpled with worry. "Are you okay? Was anything taken?"

"I'm fine. I'm not sure if anything is missing. Pete's still sifting through the mess."

"We were here all night," Mr. Cavendish said. "I went to bed early, and even though I do seem to sleep uncommonly well out in all this peace and quiet, I'm a light sleeper. I'm sure I would have heard Ms. Scarborough if she'd left."

She nodded vigorously. "I'm an early to bed, early to rise sort anyway," she agreed. "But it's true. The gravel sound of cars coming and going always wakes me. Neither of us left last night."

Mila's shoulders slumped. "Okay, well. Thank you both anyway."

"Where are you staying, honey?" Ms. Scarborough asked.

"At Brandon's place."

"Okay, dear, well you be careful."

"Take care," Mr. Cavendish agreed. "And don't forget to work on that magic act."

Mila showed her empty hands, and then produced a cookie with a flourish. A slight rattle in her sleeve, too faint for humans, had my ears standing up.

"You hear that?" I asked.

"What?" asked Bippity.

"Laughter," said Boop.

Heh. Bippity wasn't so impressive after all. Good thing I was here to keep an eye on things.

* * *

Back at our new sky-cat home, Mila pulled the spool from her sleeve, fidgeting with it like she had so many times before. She paced around the loft as she twisted it, muttering. Then, all of a sudden, she came to a stop before a huge portrait of a man with squinty eyes, a long nose, and a shiny head. Evidently, he'd removed all the hair from up there and put it onto his cheeks, because each of them had a huge, billowy poof on it.

Below it was a brass plaque that read, *The Commodore.*

She froze. "Of course!" she shouted. I jumped, casting my gaze about to make sure there wasn't an enemy approaching. "Ha! That *has* to be it. I mean his license plate and . . ."

She began twisting the codex, muttering. "T . . . H . . . E . . . C . . . O . . . M . . ." she continued saying letters until she reached E. Then there was a click, and the letters sunk into the spool a little way.

"Ha!" she shouted. "I did it!" She pulled out her phone. "Mugsy? Come quick! I solved the spool! We can decode Brandon's books!"

Finally! I wasn't sure *exactly* what this meant, but I was confident it meant we were getting closer to catching the murderer. I raced around the loft, shouting terrifying threats at invisible bad guys and warning the real one, whoever they were, that we were coming for them.

Chapter Twenty-Four
The Turnover

Boop.

Ms. Fi came through the door carrying a big roll under her arm. Her pockets were bulging. "Happy housewarming," she said, unfurling the roll into a huge soft rug with swirls and dots of purple and black that suddenly made the slick white floor look welcoming. Reaching into her pockets, she tossed fistfuls of crinkly poms, little fish, and feather-tailed bounce balls into the air.

Boppity trilled in delight, his pupils huge as his eyes zipped from pounce-target to pounce-target. He leaped and batted and tumbled, exploding with noisy glee. Bippity raced toward the rug, landing on it and sliding it across the floor as it accordioned beneath her.

"Oooooo!" shouted Boppity. "My turn! My turn!"

Becca came in next. "Happy housewarming!" She threw four fat pillows covered in long, thick plum-colored beastie fur onto Brandon's slippery sofa, and then handed Mila a squishy stuffed pink pineapple as big as her whole body.

Brutus trotted in, two large bags hanging down his sides, tied together over his back by the handles. "Look at me," he announced proudly. "I'm so helpful!"

"Wha . . . ?" Mila's mouth hung open.

"Erm, happy housewarming." Mugsy set a bag from Q's on the kitchen counter and handed Mila a purple box that said *Lava Lamp*. Then he zipped open a thick package tucked under his arm and threw a lavender and fuchsia blanket over the slick gray bed half-obscured by its frosted glass wall.

"Becca said Brandon's place was ultra-modern and kind of lifeless." Ms. Fi led Mila to the sofa.

"Yeah," Mugsy agreed. "So we figured we'd bring you a few things to Mila the place up a bit. Make it a little less . . ."

"Depressing," Becca finished. She grabbed the lamp box and began unpacking it.

Ms. Fi pulled a rainbow cat night-light from her pocket and plugged it into the bathroom outlet. Then she took suction cups, curtain rods, and velvety-looking pink and purple curtains from one of Brutus's bags and hung them from the huge windows, giving the bright afternoon sun plenty of lovely nooks of fabric to hide in and throwing fascinating shadows across the big room.

Mugsy pulled slippers and a fluffy pink robe from the other bag. In minutes, our loft was a place of pink and purple glory and Mila looked like the queen of cozy.

She sank to the sofa, her shock dissolving into tears.

Boppity spat out a bouncy ball, feather-floof clinging to his tongue-combs. "Who should I kill first?" he demanded. "Who hurt Mila?"

Bippity raced to Mila's shoulder, shoving her face into Mila's ear and whispering reassurances.

"Don't worry," I said. "She's not upset."

Boppity tilted his head, confused. "But she's making that salty human face-rain."

I couldn't help purring. "Looks like they can do it from joy, too," I told him. These humans were magical. They had filled the huge, empty space with joy. It was everywhere, sweet and warm and vibrant.

"I'll put the kettle on," Becca said. A purple glow emanated from the odd, watery lamp she had set up atop the bookcase. It gave the silver teakettle a lavender hue as it sizzled on the stove.

When everyone was settled amidst the color and fluff with matte black mugs of Mila's favorite ginger peach rooibos and plates of flaky strawberry and coconut cream turnovers, Mugsy pulled out Brandon's secret books.

"Everyone ready?" he asked.

They all nodded.

"Mr. Cavendish absolutely had motive," Mugsy said. "I'm still working on decoding the books and making sense of them, but I uncovered a plot."

"A plot!" Boppity settled in. "This is going to be good!"

"Shush." Bippity's tail twitched. "Don't interrupt."

"Look here." Mugsy pointed at one of the books. "This is the accounting for the Luxe Hotel and Resort holding company Brandon created to shield Mr. Cavendish from personal liability." Now he pointed at the other book. "This is the accounting for that company registered in the Caymans you found on that scrap of paper, Mila. The one called Commodore Holdings. You see these amounts here?" He pointed to the margin of the Luxe ledger.

"They match those amounts over there," Mila said. "So Brandon was embezzling directly from Luxe?"

Mugsy gave Mila a fond nod. "Clever of you to spot that. He sure was."

"What's embezzling?" Boppity asked.

Bippity's ear twitched. "It's like guzzling. Drinking very fast."

"You don't even know, do you?" Boppity's whiskers were smug.

Bippity flattened her ears. "Hush! Listen."

I crept toward the purple pillow next to Mila. It looked super soft. But halfway there, I sniffed the air drifting toward me from her partially eaten turnover. The cream smelled magnificent. I decided to lie down and slowly, slowly stretch my paws toward it. I was the most casual kitten in the world.

"These numbers are huge, though," Ms. Fi protested.

Mugsy nodded. "Big enough to sink the project, for sure. Especially with all the permitting delays and such."

My paws were fully extended, so I slowly moved my body forward, tucking my elbows under myself and purring.

"Why would he want to ruin Luxe, though?" Becca asked. "Isn't that short-sighted? I mean, wouldn't it be better to embezzle a little at a time over years? He was managing the Luxe LLC, right? So wouldn't he make more if he just kept taking a little bit every month indefinitely?"

"That's what I was thinking." Bippity tucked her chin primly.

"Is not," Boppity chided. "Don't lie. Your whiskers give you away every time."

"Hmph." Her tail fluttered in chagrin.

I was in full meatloaf configuration now, paws tucked under my chest. The turnover was nearly within reach. I yawned and stretched my paws out, only a claw's breadth away from touching the plate. Nobody noticed. My stealth was maybe not quite as good as Boppity's stealth, but it was pretty good. Even my siblings didn't seem to notice.

Mugsy scratched his chin. "He would. But one thing is for sure. He was aiming to sink Luxe. I'm just not clear on why."

"It's becoming more and more obvious that he was a bad person," Mila said. "Only someone really unscrupulous does stuff like this." Mila and Becca exchanged a long, serious look. Waves of misery flowed from Becca for some reason, along with something sharp that felt like anger. Mila was a tangle of heavy, difficult emotions.

If they had any common sense, they'd lie in a big cuddle pile. Instead, they just continued to stare at one another wordlessly. Humans were strange. Sometimes, I didn't know what to make of them.

At least I was back in meatloaf shape. One more stretch, and I'd have the taste of coconut cream I was yearning for. I yawned and extended my right paw, hooking my claws into the tender, crispy pastry.

"Hey!" Mila shouted.

I jerked at the sharp burst of sound, yanking back my paw by instinct. The turnover shot into the air, arcing high overhead. We all watched it soar above us like a bird in flight. In slow motion, it reached its apex and began its languid downward trajectory. Down and down it fell.

Right into Brutus's waiting jaws.

Before anyone could react, it was gone. His long tongue darted out to tidy his stubby whiskers. "Nice one little bud," he told me.

"Hey! Bad!" Mila scolded. "Naughty thief!"

She was looking at me, but I was sure she meant Brutus. After all, he was the one who had swallowed her dessert. I'd only wanted a tiny little taste. And Brutus didn't seem to feel ashamed at all. In fact, he was wagging, a crooked grin on his face.

"Boop!" Bippity was shocked. "I would never have thought you would do such a thing! Boppity, maybe! But not you!"

"I would have succeeded," Boppity snickered. "Instead of just feeding the *dog*."

Had I actually done something bad? I hated that thought. My ear-tips drooped. But maybe it was all a big misunderstanding. What should I do?

I decided to purr, tilting my head to the side. "Did I do something wrong, Mila? Did I make you sad?" I asked, padding across the empty plate and reaching up toward her face. "I'm sorry if I did. I can pet you. Pets always help." I gave her a questioning trill to clarify my intentions.

Mila's shocked expression of disapproval dissolved into giggles. Soon everyone was laughing. Even Brutus.

I wasn't sure why.

But my own joy was eclipsed by a sinking feeling I couldn't shake. If we didn't help Mila figure out who Brandon's killer was, these moments of happiness might be numbered.

Chapter Twenty-Five
The Foundation

Mila.

When Mugsy and Becca left to open the club and Ms. Fi headed home, Mila found herself alone again. She loved the irreverent, homey touches her friends had left all over the loft. But without their voices, the space felt hollow. The kittens were piled in a heap on the furry comforter Mugsy had put on her bed, and she desperately wanted to hug them, but she couldn't bring herself to wake them up.

So instead, she shook off her fluffy pink robe and slippers and paced. She'd been carrying this restless feeling behind her breastbone all her life. She remembered the first time she'd felt it, at the tender age of five.

Camille Louise MacAllister, you should be ashamed of yourself. Her mother's voice, calm and yet colder than ice, had cut right through her. Only the barest hint of her rage and disgust showed on her perfectly smooth face. *I'm ashamed just looking at you. You're a stain on the MacAllister name. Get out of my sight.*

The memory overtook Mila as if it were happening all over again. The mud staining her palms and her patent leather shoes and the hem of her silk organza tea dress. The slam of her bedroom door. The click of the lock. The laughter and merriment far below her window. Laughter that she was learning was for other children. Not for her. Never for her.

It was the moment she'd first understood that *family* was not what the storybooks said. Family was about reputation and appearances, about living up to the MacAllister name and all of the culture and elegance and good taste that went with it, and most of all, about duty to the legacy of her noble forebears and bending her knee to the responsibility of the Great Families to shape the future of America and the world.

It was the moment she'd begun searching for a way out.

Eventually, she'd managed to make a clean break. She'd come to Corvin's Crossing to start over, to build a life and eventually a family based on love and trust and kindness. That was one of the things she'd cherished most about Brandon. He never cared where she came from. He never even knew. She'd tried to tell him a couple of times, but he'd always stopped her and told her that where she came from didn't matter. Only where they were going together.

Now it seemed like he'd been lying to her about who he was. Cheating. Embezzling. Maybe worse.

Obviously, family and home just weren't for her. She was destined to be alone. Something about her attracted bad people.

She sighed. It was what it was. No sense throwing herself a pity party.

Instead, she texted Mugsy. *How's it going with decoding the books?*

I found something strange, Mugsy replied. *I'm not sure yet, but it looks like Brandon was paying Mayor Adams.*

What do you mean?

There are regular payments to Mayor Adams from Brandon's holding company in the Caymans. $10K each month.

Mila's brow furrowed. Why would Brandon be paying Mayor Adams? Maybe it had something to do with the meeting in the restaurant.

Maybe it had something to do with Luxe's permitting issues.

For sure, the mayor was hiding something.

I'll look into it, she texted. *Thanks, Mugsy!*

Mila plated three cans of cat food and set the dishes beside the water and crunchies, then let herself silently out of the loft.

It was the first time she'd been apart from the kittens since rescuing them. She was surprised to discover how much she missed them. Even when they were sleeping, their comforting weight against her belly made her feel less alone.

When she parked in the municipal lot, it was mostly empty. She glanced at her phone: 4:48 PM. She'd barely made it before the mayor's office closed. She hurried through the door and past the receptionist, who was tidying up her desk for the night.

"Mila? You don't have an app—"

Mila held up a hand and kept walking. "It's okay, Larissa. Mayor Adams won't mind." She was shocked at her own audacity, but she was running out of reasons to be well-behaved. She didn't give Larissa a chance to say more. Instead, she pulled open the mayor's office door and stepped in, closing it behind her.

". . . from the holding company and revert to the land trust. Yes. Immediately." Mayor Adams looked at her with startled hazel eyes. He held up a finger, then spoke into his phone. "Right. No, something just came up. I'm going to have to call you back. Sure. Okay, sounds good. Yep." He hung up.

"Mila." He leaned back in his tan leather chair, running a hand through sandy salt-and-pepper hair. "Hello. What can I do for you?"

"I'm sorry to bother you so late in the day, I just . . ." Why was she apologizing?

Her pause was all the opening he needed. "I'm actually heading home. You can make an appointment with my receptionist for whatever it is you'd like to discuss." He rose, holding out an arm like a hook and walking toward the door. It was just the sort of thing Brandon would have done. She could feel the social force of his expectation that she would allow him to guide her out of the office.

How many little ways had she been trained to unconsciously undermine herself? To allow others to undermine her? She was sick of being guided. Of being controlled.

She sidestepped his arm and pulled out a chair at the little table in his office. Before she could freeze in shock at her own boldness, she sat.

For a long moment, the mayor stood, arm still cupping the space where she'd been, staring at her. Then he cleared his throat awkwardly. "Right. What do you need? I only have a minute."

A heady surge of victory shot through Mila. "I just have a few questions about Brandon," she said.

Mayor Adams flushed beneath his expensive-looking tan. "I can't comment on the investigation. You're going to need to direct your questions to the sheriff's office."

"I know," Mila said. "I wanted to ask you about the money Brandon was paying you. You know, the Luxe money?"

He blanched. "I don't know what you . . . That is . . . He wasn't . . ." Clearing his throat again, the mayor strode behind his desk and sat. "You must be referring to the permitting costs and fees he was paying the town via my office, on behalf of the Luxe project." He tapped at his keyboard for a moment. "Yes. I have those records here. But I'm not at liberty to discuss the financial details of a project you are not a part of."

"Can you tell me why the permitting kept presenting such a problem?" Mila asked. "Mr. Cavendish told me that as soon as Brandon was out of the picture, those permits all sailed through. The very next day, in fact."

"Exactly what are you implying?" he spluttered.

"Nothing," Mila blinked innocently. "I'm not implying anything. I'm just asking about how it's possible that Brandon was paying you all this money and the permits were all getting held up, and then the day after he died, they all went through without a hitch."

"Well." Mayor Adams's face reddened and his brows lowered ominously. "I'm not sure what you're getting at, but whatever it is, it's baseless. Also, Mr. Cavendish's project is on hold again. The foundation had an insufficient density of rebar for the size and mass of the structure. It wasn't up to code and failed inspection. It needs to be ripped out and redone from scratch."

Mila's jaw dropped. So Luxe was on hold again? "What does this mean for the future of Luxe?" Mila asked. "I know that it was on the verge of bankruptcy before. It seems as though something like this could tip it over the brink."

Mayor Adams harumphed. "Again, I am not in any position to give you confidential information about business dealings in which you have no role."

"Of course." Mila nodded. "Does Mr. Cavendish know construction of his resort is on hold?"

"Yes. I told him last night over a nice snack of Ms. Scarborough's famous bedtime tea and cookies. I don't mind admitting, I slept like a baby." He gave her a fake grin, like a happy customer in a pharmaceutical commercial.

"You had dinner with Brandon the evening he died. Chef Rousseau tells me you were discussing business and agreed to meet back here after the meeting for some additional paperwork." Mila flipped through her notebook. "Brandon mentioned you had amended your agreement. What agreement was that?"

Mayor Adams's face darkened. "Again, I am not at liberty to discuss private business dealings in which you have no part, nor can I talk about the ongoing investigation."

Mila ground her teeth. "Can you at least tell me what time he left from the meeting at your office that evening?"

"He never arrived." The mayor stood, extending his arm into a hook again and actively shooing it toward Mila. "Now unfortunately, I'm out of time for this evening." He made another swooshing motion with his arm.

Mila stood, nodding, and headed to the door. "Thank you for your help, Mayor Adams."

Mila's steps were light as she walked back to her car. She wasn't sure what it meant that construction on the Luxe resort was on hold again, but she hoped it wouldn't go bankrupt. Her big shot at a real stage career would go up in flames if it did.

Regardless of what it meant, she'd made herself seen and heard. That had felt good. But as she drove home, she missed having the kittens to talk to about it. She knew it was silly to feel that way. They were just cuddly animals, more concerned with toys and canned food than with the nuances of nonverbal power dynamics and socialized compliance. Still, she hoped they'd be awake when she got home.

As soon as she opened the door, she heard their high, sonorous voices racing toward her. She yanked off her shoes and dropped her purse just in time. The trio arrived in a thundering tumult of little paws, hollering wildly.

Bippity sat before her and began to trill and yowl, huge eyes wide and one ear flicking occasionally. She almost looked like a tiny professor. Boppity pounced on her left shoe, wrapping his huge paws around it and biting it furiously as he rolled into a somersault. Midtumble, he rabbit-kicked so hard her shoe flew across the room, landing on the sofa with a *thwap*. Boop settled across her bare foot, nestling their round face between dainty paws and punctuating their purring with bird-like chirps and the occasional wet gulp.

"Oh my gosh, kittens, what happened?" She scooped them up, and they smashed themselves onto her chest, Boop at the bottom of the pile rumbling and slobbering blissfully. They still had wet and dry food, plenty of water, and a relatively clean cat box. The only explanation for their behavior was that they must have missed her.

Her chest felt warm inside and out.

"I missed you too, loves," she whispered into their soft fur.

Chapter Twenty-Six
The Motive

Bippity.

"Then don't leave without us ever again. *Ever!*" I told her. It was the best scolding I had ever given, and that was saying something, because I was a master scolder. I was confident I'd made my point. Even with her limited language skills, she certainly understood. After all, I'd used all of my best vocal scolds to punctuate key elements of my lecture. I sighed, relaxing into her fingers as they swirled in the fur behind my ear. "Okay. We forgive you."

"We do?" Boppity shot me a glare. "Speak for yourself!"

"What, you don't forgive her?" Boop opened their eyes halfway, startled by what Boppity was implying.

"No, of course I forgive her. Obviously." Boppity huffed. "Just don't *assume* you know how I feel."

I rolled my eyes. "Whatever."

He smacked me in the face. I pinned my ears, ready to launch myself into him, but Mila dropped us all on the furry bed.

"Now look what you did!" I shouted as she headed to the shower. "You made her leave again, after we just got her back!"

"Nooooooo!" he shrieked. "Abandoned! Just like Moth-errrrrr!" He began to yowl. Great. I'd let myself get mad, and I hadn't thought things through. He'd been inconsolable the entire time Mila was gone.

"She's not *gone* gone," I told him. "Hush, now. She's still here. She's just taking a shower."

"Shower," Boop cooed. "You know, weird hot human indoor rain?"

But it was no use. He was lost to his misery. There was no way to help him once he got like this.

"I know," Boop said, their little ears perking up atop their big round face. They darted into the bathroom and vanished into Mila's clothing, then reappeared rolling her codex-spool. When they whacked it hard enough to send it crashing into Boppity, he pinned his ears and pounced on it, his fierce warrior instincts taking over. He chomped at its edge, put it in a choke-hold, and then rolled it over and smacked it with a powerful left hook.

It soared through the air and smashed into the thick plate glass window between us and the world with a deep, resonant *thunk*.

When it hit the floor, it was in three pieces.

There was the spool we were all used to seeing Mila play with, except it was open at one end. Beside it was a smaller spool, plain and black and hollow. Spilling out of that, there was a little silver key.

"You broke it!" I shouted.

"Oooooo!" Boop said. "Discovery!"

"Oh noooooo!" Boppity cried.

"What are you kittens up to?" Mila called. Her bare feet splatted toward us. Before I could block her view of the ruined spool with my body, she bent down. "What's this?"

We all watched her, eyes wide. Boppity poked the key once, as if urging it to vanish.

"Oh my gosh, Boppity! What did you discover? What a clever kitten!" she exclaimed.

Huh. Apparently, Boop had been right.

"It's a key. It says, *KeepSafe.*" She squinted. "Huh. That's a wall-safe company, isn't it? So—" She took off at a run, her flat human feet making more splat sounds on the floor. We followed silently. Her gaze darted around the room and landed on the huge portrait of the man with the bushy sheep-cheeks.

"Sorry, Commodore," she said, lifting the painting off the wall. Behind it was a little silver door with a keyhole in it.

When she stuck in the key and turned it, she gasped. Inside were several wads of stinky human paper money. Once she lifted them out, she found a small blue booklet with an extremely fancy golden picture of a lion and a unicorn playing with a shield. "What?" Mila asked it.

"Why are you asking it?" I trilled. "It can't talk."

"It's a passport for the Cayman Islands," Mila said. "It lists Brandon as a citizen. Here's his US passport. And look, here's a third one, for a country called Montenegro."

Mila grabbed her phone from the counter. "Hello, Mugsy?" she asked it. "Can I come over? I know it's late, but I . . ." She shook her head. "No, I just found something really weird. The kittens discovered there was a key in the center of the codex-spool thing. I found a safe in the apartment, and inside there's money, passports, and a stack of files." She shook her head again. "Just a second."

She reached back into the safe and pulled out a big stack of beige files. "There's one that says Luxe and one that says Commodore Holdings, and then below that are so many more. This one has my name. The next one has yours. There's Becca, Mayor Adams, Ms. Scarborough, Reverend Bak, Q . . ." Mila's voice tapered off.

She nodded. "Okay." Grabbing the kangaroo pouch, she tucked the money, the little booklets and the files inside, then looked down at herself. "I'll be there in fifteen minutes. Can you call Ms. Fi and Becca? Yeah. I think we need everyone for this."

* * *

At the club, Boop ran off to play with Brutus. I tried to convince Boppity to stay and focus, but he couldn't resist the sounds of their mischief. I sat in the center of the table, listening as best I could.

I was missing an epic game of shadow tag, which I was the best at because of my ability to bend and redirect light. But this was more important.

"How come the spool wasn't in your apartment when it got burglarized?" Becca asked.

"I've been keeping it up my sleeve." Mila said. "Fidgeting with it got to be a habit before I solved it. Afterward, I guess it was just weirdly comforting."

Becca shook her head, bemused. Something tantalizing and golden was in her hair. My whiskers spread wide as I crept across the table toward her. Perhaps I could be a good leader and have some fun at the same time. Mother had always said only the wisest of cats could catch two birds with one paw.

"Lucky," Mugsy grunted. "Otherwise, you never would've found all this."

"Okay," Ms. Fi said. "We need a strategy. How about if Mugsy and I look at the Luxe and Commodore files, and Mila and Becca look at the others. It's probably just records and receipts from siphoning your money, but let's be sure."

Mila and Becca stared at their papers, muttering to themselves.

"Mayor Adams! Naughty, naughty! So that's why you go out to the mainland on Friday nights. What would your wife think?"

"Is embezzling from a church a special kind of extra-bad crime? Because it should be. That's low, even for Brandon."

"Did you know Mr. Scarborough died after a long illness? Look at all these medical records. Tetanus? And he was trying to sell the farm, probably to cover medical expenses."

"Mugsy! Brandon was stealing *so much* from you!"

"Mila! You're one of *those* MacAllisters? Your family is richer than Midas!"

Mila scowled at that. "I guess he *did* know. So even that was a lie."

Occasionally, Becca shook her head, making the tantalizing toy in her hair shine in the dim light. I crept toward her. It was nearly within my reach.

"Looks like Brandon is registered as the . . . Huh?" Mugsy said. Everyone looked up at him. Becca's hair swung back over her shoulder and out of reach. Never mind. I wouldn't give up.

Mugsy pushed his file toward Ms. Fi. "If I'm understanding this right," he pointed to a paper, "It says that if the Luxe holding company goes bankrupt, the property goes to the Corvin's Crossing Land Trust for disposition."

"Yep," Ms. Fi agreed. "That's what I see too. Wonder if Mr. Cavendish knew Brandon wrote that clause in."

"Right," Mugsy was still staring at the papers. "But then this here shows who runs the Corvin's Crossing Land Trust. Brandon is listed as the director."

"Explains those huge payments Brandon was making to the mayor," Ms. Fi said. "The Mayor's been letting Brandon manage the Land Trust for a long time. Years, now. Who knows how many crooked deals he's made? How much he's skimmed?" She scowled and sucked her teeth.

"Does that mean if Luxe went under, Brandon would have gotten to decide what happened to it?" asked Mila.

"Right," Mugsy nodded. "Then here, I have what seems to be preliminary paperwork from the Land Trust, preparing to sell the Luxe property to Commodore Holdings, which is Brandon's company in the Caymans. And look at this selling price."

Ms. Fi gasped. "That's practically nothing!"

"What?" Mila asked, looking back and forth between Mugsy and Ms. Fi. "What does it mean?"

Mila and Becca both leaned forward. Becca's hair swept in front of her shoulder. My prey was once again within reach. I crept forward. Just two more steps.

"Well," Mugsy cleared his throat. "If Brandon made Luxe go bankrupt, the entire Luxe property would be deeded over to the Land Trust. Brandon was planning to sell it to his own management company in the Caymans for pennies on the dollar. He'd have been rich."

One more step now. I crouched, quivering my haunches and gauging the distance.

"If Mr. Cavendish knew . . ." Mila's eyes were wide.

"That would be more than enough motive for—Ouch!" Becca shouted. I caught my gleaming prize and locked my jaws around it, wrapping myself up in Becca's hair to keep from falling.

It was even more crispy and twiggy and glorious than I'd imagined. I shook my head, crunching it gleefully.

Mila wrapped her hands around me and pulled me from Becca's long black tresses.

"Ow!" Becca shouted again. "Kitten! Why?"

"Treasure!" I grrred around the magnificent prize I'd won. It was hollow, and crushed and splintered as I chomped. I shook my head, assuring it was well and truly slain.

"Sorry!" Mila didn't sound sorry. She was giggling. "Did you come from the barn? You had a piece of hay in your hair. Now Bippity looks like a little farmer."

Everyone started to laugh. Even Becca.

But Ms. Fi put up a hand. "It hasn't hit you yet, has it?" She asked Mila.

"What?"

Mugsy looked down at the papers. "This is more than just information. This is cold, hard—"

"Proof!" Mila shouted. "It's proof that someone else had a better reason to kill Brandon than I did. We have to get this to Pete right away."

"Let me spend a few more hours going through this and the books," Mugsy said. "Make sure I find everything there is. I want to make the strongest case we can when we talk to the

Sheriff. Meet me here tomorrow morning at eight, and we'll go over everything together and show him what we've learned."

Mila's eyes were full of tears. I scaled her shoulder, still chomping on my prize. "Don't worry," I told her. "It'll all be okay. I'll share my crunchy with you." I pushed it toward her.

"Oh my gosh, *thank you*," she said, tears spilling down her face. But she was smiling now, the biggest, brightest smile I'd seen on her face since the day she found us.

"You're welcome," I told her.

"Thank you all!" she said.

Ms. Fi gave Mila and me a hug. "It's late for these old bones," she told us. "Call if you need me."

Becca hugged us, too. "I've got to go finish up at the barn, so I'll be up if you need to talk," she said.

Mugsy stood and Mila threw herself into his arms. "Thank you so much, Mugsy," she murmured into his shoulder.

"Mmrph," I said. "Rude."

But as Mila tucked my siblings and me back into the pouch, I remembered what Mugsy had said. Proof that Mr. Cavendish had been the one with motive to kill Brandon. Tomorrow, we would be getting Mila's name cleared. I couldn't wait to tell my siblings about the important things I'd achieved.

Chapter Twenty-Seven
The Attack

Boppity.

Mila woke us up *early*. It was so early that we were all squinty. We tried to tell her that it was still time for sleeping, but she insisted. She even managed to resist Boop's cuddly goodness, which was impressive.

"She's in a hurry because she's excited about my proof!" Bippity chirped.

"It's *my* proof!" I told her. "I'm the one who opened the spool and found the key!"

Boop was asleep again, but I was sure they'd agree with me if they were awake. They'd be proud of me.

Bippity pinned her ears, but she couldn't argue with me because I was *right.*

Mila was so excited, she practically trotted through the open door and into Mugsy's. The second we got inside, I knew something was wrong. My fiercest warrior instincts roared through me and my fur stood up. I poofed my tail, ready to terrify whatever evil was here.

"Danger," I signaled to my siblings.

"Mugsy?" Mila called. "You ready to go?"

My pupils opened wide, letting in every bit of light as I scanned the room again and again. Where was the danger? I knew something was wrong.

"Mugsy?"

Mila stiffened. She was beginning to feel it too. Maybe the combat lessons I was giving her were finally starting to pay off.

"Brutus?"

Mila was right. That goofy dog should have raced up to us immediately.

"Coming, kid. Coming." Mugsy's voice rumbled up from backstage. When he emerged from the shadows, he was wearing a big white bandage around his head. He smelled injured.

Mila gasped. "Mugsy! What happened?"

"I was attacked last night. Just before dawn, I think. I was working on the books and I hadn't locked up and gone upstairs to my apartment yet. Someone snuck in and conked me on the head with something metal. Crowbar maybe."

He winced, touching his bandaged head gingerly. "I was dazed, but I felt something going around my neck. Something rough, like rope. Last thing I heard was Brutus snarling. When I came to, everything was gone. Money. Passports. Files. And Brutus was lying there . . . he . . ." Mugsy's legs went wobbly. He sat in a velvet chair, blinking.

"Brutus?" Mila's voice was tremulous. "Is he . . ."

"He's gonna be okay, kid. He's a hero. Saved my life." Mugsy's gravelly voice hitched and went mushy. "Fought the guy off.

I came to and found a pool of blood where he'd bit him. Did some real damage. But the guy must have had to hit him to get him to let go. That's what Doc said. He's g—"

Mugsy made a strange croaking sound and then coughed. Mila sat beside him, putting a hand on his arm.

"He's got a concussion, like me, plus a bunch of cuts and bruises. Dog deserves a damn purple heart."

"Oh, Mugsy!" Mila crushed him in a hug. "How horrible! I'm so sorry! This is all my fault."

"Pah!" Mugsy pushed her out to arm's distance, holding onto her. "It's my own fault. I should've locked up. Should've known better, what with the murder and the fire and the break-in at your place. Corvin's Crossing's not safe anymore. Not until we catch this killer."

Mugsy made another croak-cough, this time ending with a *rrrumph.*

"Thing I can't bear is, I really let you down, and it breaks my heart. All the evidence is gone. We've got nothing to give the sheriff." He leaned forward, staring into Mila's face. "I'd do anything for you, kid. Anything."

There was a long silence before Mila nodded. "I know, Mugsy. It's okay. We know who to go after now, and we know why. There must be other ways to get those records. I'm just worried about you." She reached out toward his head. "You and Brutus. You want me to take you to the hospital?"

Mugsy swatted her hand away. "Nah. I'm fine. When I carried Brutus into Doc's, she called the EMT and they checked me out. Just a concussion is all."

"They didn't tell you to go to the hospital?"

Mugsy grunted. "It's nothing. Just a headache." He stood, heading for the bar. "Can I get you . . ." His knees wavered. Mila leaped up and grabbed his elbow, steadying him.

"That's it." Mila's voice was stern. "You're going to the hospital." She hauled him toward the door.

But he set his feet and refused to move. "You know I hate that place," he said. "I'm fine."

"Well at the very least, I'm taking you to stay with Ms. Fi."

Mugsy's eyes widened. "No way. She'll scold me 'til my ears fall off."

Mila leaned into him, propelling him outside. "It's Ms. Fi or the hospital, Mugsy. I'll call 911 if I have to."

He let out a disgusted sigh. "Fine. Let me just lock up. But she'd better not be screeching at me about common sense and thick-headedness."

"When did Ms. Fi ever screech at anyone?" Mila asked drily.

Mugsy chuckled. "Good point."

Once Mugsy was settled in at Ms. Fi's, Mila dragged us to talk to the bank about the accounts she'd inherited, then to town hall to request public records, then up to Rousseau's to ask about the business opportunity Brandon had mentioned, and finally down to the Luxe construction site, which was quiet and spooky like huge bones sticking out of the ground. Eventually we ended up at Ms. Scarborough's to try and find out what Mr. Cavendish knew without making him suspicious.

All we managed to get was a copy of the certificate of registration for Brandon's company in the Cayman Islands. But the only names on it were the assistant registrar of companies for the Cayman Islands, John Coe, and the company, Commodore Holdings, LDC. Nobody had anything new to say, nobody had seen Brandon the evening of his murder after he left the restaurant, and nobody had any proof of anything at all.

By the time we got home, we were hungry and tired and cranky. I nearly faceplanted into my meat-feast when Mila set it down, I was so ravenous. I growled as I ate, just in case anyone got any ideas about me sharing.

When Mila got out of the shower, she looked like she'd been scrubbing her face a lot. Boop trotted over.

"Poor Mila. Scared. Sad." They clambered up onto her lap. "It's okay, Mila. You're not alone." They purred, rubbing their open mouth on her nose.

"Oh! Ew! Boop! Urgh!" She wiped her face with the back of her sleeve.

Boop's purrs sputtered and nearly died out.

"Hey!" I told her. I stuck my tail up tall like a flag. "There's no call to be mean to poor little Boop like that!" I sniffed their wet nose and butted my forehead against their juicy chin encouragingly. Their purr rumbled back to life.

"What are you two doing?" Bippity asked. "We should be making a plan. We need to get more evidence."

"Mila's sad," Boop said. "We should help her. Purr pile."

But our snuggles and Boop's purrs didn't seem to help.

"Everything is falling apart, kittens." She stared into the distance. "A week ago, I was about to get my big break in my nice safe little town, laughing with my friends, enjoying life. But the man I thought I'd found and the life I thought I was building were all just illusions and lies." Mila's face crumpled, and she squeezed her eyes shut. But her shoulders didn't shake. No wails came from her throat. Her eyes didn't rain.

"What's happening?" I asked.

"I . . . don't feel anything," Mila said. "I'm sad when I think about the dream that's gone, but when I think about Brandon, the actual man, being gone . . ."

Her eyes darted from side to side as if she was searching.

"Nope. I don't miss him. Nothing. What's *wrong* with me?"

Boop stalked up her front, purring through their open mouth. "Nothing. It's okay. You get to be you," they said. "You get to feel what you feel." They tucked themself under her chin. "It's all okay."

Mila drew in a deep breath and let it out through pursed lips, like she was trying to make a zephyr in the loft.

"Nice breeze," I told her, wanting to help too.

"Okay." She nodded. Obviously, my compliment had given her strength. "I'm okay. I don't have time to feel bad about not feeling bad. I'm just not sure where to take this investigation next. I've exhausted every lead. Mugsy's all banged up. Even I can see Sheriff Pete's point. The only hard evidence we have all seems to point to me. What do you think, Boppity? What should I do?"

Was she asking for my advice? I decided to say something *super* wise. "The best warriors prepare for war, but hope for peace." Yes. Perfect. I punctuated my important message with a crisp *myeah.*

"What nonsense." Bippity pinned her ears at me. I was reaching back to thwap her, but Mila's phone rang.

She lifted it. "Hey, Becca! I was actually just thinking of calling you. I—"

Mila shot to her feet. "What? You found something? What is it?"

She began to pace. "Becca? You're breaking up! Mugsy's? Meet at Mugsy's? Okay! I'll be there!"

Mila rolled her shoulders. "Okay, kittens. Good news. Becca says she found something. A game-changer, she says. Maybe we can figure out who killed Brandon, and I won't have to go to jail after all!" She unzipped the kangaroo pouch and set it on the floor. "Let's go!"

I was the first one in.

Chapter Twenty-Eight
The Gazebo

Boop.

It was a clear, lovely night. Mila had kept her promise not to leave us alone again, but not her promise to get us leashes. Brutus had said that leashes were for walks and poopsies on the grass, which sounded sort of fun. Poor Brutus. Brave dog. A sympathy purr rumbled to life in my chest.

Mila stepped out from under the lamp where she'd parked our car beside Becca's, plunging us into the river of darkness we had to cross to get to the next circle of coppery light. She was still worried, but excitement rounded her edges and made her buoyant, so floating along on her bouncy steps was easy. Becca had a clue, so Mila was full of hope.

Hope was the best.

The trellised gazebo in the center of the green glowed like gold up ahead. Beyond it, Mugsy's club stood in the distance, its marquee lights barely visible in the night. I should have been happy, like Mila. But instead, an unpleasant, itchy feeling started itself up in my whiskers and began to fill my chest. My fur stood on end.

My purr faltered.

"Something is wrong," I said. "Boppity. Something is wrong."

He stood, pressing his nose against the screen of our pouch. His muscles rippled beneath his fur. Bippity scanned the darkness with her piercing gaze.

Mila stopped, hunching her shoulders and leaning forward. A strange moaning sound drifted to us on the cool night breeze.

"Hello?" Her voice was high and tense. She crept forward, one step at a time, her body rigid. Her bounce was gone, replaced by something stabby and tight.

Fear.

But there was something else.

Something worse.

A terrifying feeling came in vicious waves from the darkness inside the gazebo.

We all held our breath.

Another groan, this one louder, rose up into the night.

Mila jerked to a halt.

"I smell violence," Boppity hissed.

There was a human form lying on the gazebo floor. A deeper shade of black at the heart of the gold-tinged shadows. "Merciful Goddess," Mila whispered. She pelted toward the gazebo and leaped inside.

There, splayed across the cobblestone floor, lay Becca in a broad pool of crimson. She was moving her arms feebly. The air smelled coppery. Terror ripped claw-sharp gaps in the air all around us, but behind it was something bleak and heavy and still. Something that pulled at Becca with cold, patient insistence.

I felt a desperate stab of dread.

"Help!" Mila screamed. She hurled herself forward, lifting Becca into her arms. A big black and silver handle protruded from her chest. *Oh, Becca.* The words were barely audible on Mila's shaky, exhaled breath. *How did this happen?*

Becca grabbed Mila's shirt, clinging to her like a lifeline.

"It's okay, Becca. I'm here," Mila murmured in a tone that was probably meant to be soothing, but sounded hollow with panic. "You're going to be okay. I've got you."

She whipped out her phone and dialed 911, demanding an ambulance at the gazebo immediately. Then she carefully lay Becca flat, steadied the knife, and pressed her hands down on either side of it, her arms stiff.

Becca groaned weakly.

"I'm sorry, love. I'm so sorry. I need to put pressure on the wound." Mila's eyes were rolling like the horse in the fire-barn, but she forced her voice to stay low. "This is all my fault."

Becca opened her mouth, but no sound came out. Tears spilled from the corners of her eyes. She was a dizzying storm of anxious urgency. Beneath her fear and pain, that deep, patient darkness loomed larger and larger.

She struggled to inhale, but couldn't seem to manage it. When she opened her mouth again, only a hiss came out. She reached down to pull the knife from her chest.

Mila pushed her hand away, grabbing the handle of the blade to steady it in place. "No, love, you have to leave it. You're going to be okay. Help is coming. Just hang on."

Becca opened her mouth again. Her arm wavered in the air, shaking. She fumbled at her waist, slipping her fingers into her pocket and pulling out a crumpled ball of paper.

She shoved it at Mila with a trembling hand, a desperate look in her eyes. Her urgent stare darted from the paper to Mila's face. Their fingers met as Mila took the ball of paper and crammed it into her own pocket. The corner of Becca's mouth shuddered upward. She reached up to set her fingertips gently against Mila's cheek. Terrible sadness and weak, perfect love drifted up from her and washed over Mila like warm, delicate rain.

Then her arm dropped. Her body went limp.

"Becca!" Mila screamed.

We sat in our pouch, watching Mila press on Becca's chest, whispering *I'm sorry, Becca. So sorry,* over and over like a prayer. We all heard Becca's heart grow slower and weaker with each beat. But there was nothing we could do.

Time went all wiry and strange.

Eventually, red and blue lights splashed across the scene. I couldn't seem to move. The jumpsuited helpers had to pull Mila off of Becca before they could lift her onto their rolling bed.

"We've got her, Mila. You did good," one of them said.

"Stay right there on the grass," said the other.

They loaded the bed into their human vet vehicle, and with an ear-splitting wail, the flashes of color vanished into the light.

Mila spread her open hands against her lap, shadowy in the darkness. She stared at them as the night pressed in on us from all around.

Another wail broke the silence. More blue and red lights, first dim, but soon growing brighter, flickered over us like fire and ice.

Mila jerked as if something had shocked her back to life. She reached into her pocket and pulled out the ball of paper, now dark with blood.

Mila twisted her wrists and flicked her fingers, and when she turned her palms upward again, the paper was gone.

The thunk of a car door was accompanied by the sound of Sheriff Pete's voice. "Mila . . . Are you okay?" he asked. Mila barely nodded.

The shrill ring of his phone pierced the night. "Deputy? What is it?" His whole body stiffened. "Okay. Thanks."

He turned to Mila. "Becca is at the hospital. They're working to get her stabilized. Deputy Chantelle says she has a fighting chance because of you."

Mila let out a rush of air. "Oh, thank goodness!"

"But the ER doctor told Chantelle that the knife in Becca's chest was a trick knife, just like the one that killed Brandon."

"What?" Mila went from still to frantic. "No! Pete, someone is setting me up! You have to believe me! The killer must have stolen my backup knife when he broke into my apartment!"

Pete's tone was grim. "If that's true, I'm sure we'll figure it out. But for now, I have to do everything I can to protect the people of Corvin's Crossing. I'm sorry, Mila, but you're under arrest."

Mila's arms wrapped protectively around our pouch. "What about my kittens?"

The sheriff slid the straps of the pouch off her shoulders. "I'll get them to Ms. Fi. I'm sure she'll take good care of them for you."

He set us in the passenger front seat of his car. The world flashed crimson and cobalt around us.

It was a short, silent ride to the sheriff's station. When we arrived, I watched helplessly as Sheriff Pete helped Mila out of the car and led her, hands now tethered behind her back, toward the big building.

"Mila!" I cried. "No!" My wail unspooled like a ribbon of pain and terror twisting out into the night. Boppity added his voice to mine, shaking with grief as he cried out Mila's name.

Bippity pressed herself atop us and lay perfectly still, watching with wide eyes and trembling ears as Sheriff Pete took Mila away.

Chapter Twenty-Nine
The Darkest Night

Mila.

Mila's sluggish mind barely had time to wonder whether the sound of the cell slamming would be anything like in the movies before Pete was unlocking the door to the building.

None of it turned out to be anything like the movies at all.

There was a long walk down a hallway past the Public Works department, the Tax Assessor's office, and Business Administration, whatever that meant. Her cuffs didn't jingle behind her back because they turned out to be zip ties. The only sound was the squeak of her sneakers on the mirror-bright finish of the linoleum hallway.

Pete unlocked the door to the sheriff's department and nudged her inside, flipping on a fluorescent light that revealed a small, generic-looking office, complete with a massive photocopy machine that looked older than Mila and a sickly-looking snake plant in the corner. Next to the plant was a flimsy plywood door with a knob that looked like a scuffed silver ball. When Pete opened it, the concrete and cinderblock room inside was somehow more depressing than Mila had expected, and yet more ordinary.

Everything was painted with the shiny, high-gloss beige that landlords in cheap apartments used for bathroom walls. The room was divided into two small holding cells, with an uncaged pathway on the left that led to a desk in the corner. Instead of bars, the cells were made of chain-link that extended all the way up to the concrete ceiling, framed with the same thick galvanized piping people used to fence in their yards.

It made the same rattling *chink* sound, too, as Pete unlocked the keyed padlock and guided her inside. He took her purse and patted her pockets and ankles. Finding nothing, he waved her toward a rickety folding cot like a cheap hotel would have available for guests upon request. Beside it were a porcelain toilet and sink that looked like they belonged in a divey gas station bathroom. Grabbing a pair of scissors from the desk, Pete snipped off her zip ties, then stepped out of the cage and locked her in.

On the other side of the fencing, he finally turned to look at her. "You heard your rights already. Do you want to make a phone call?"

She stared at him, numb and immobile, trying to get her mind to work.

"Fine," he sighed. "Have it your way. Chantelle will check in on you later."

Mila didn't remember moving, but somehow she ended up on the lumpy cot with its scratchy navy-blue blanket and its pancake-thin pillow. She stared up at the shiny beige ceiling flickering in the fluorescent light.

How had she ended up here? Becca was probably fighting for her life. If she was still alive at all. Brandon was dead. At least she knew she could trust Ms. Fi to take care of the kittens.

But she would never see them again.

For some reason, this was the thought that broke her. As the strip of light beneath the door to the sheriff's office flickered off and the front office door closed with a faraway *thunk*, Mila began to shake.

Her shoulders heaved and a terrible wail broke from her throat, echoing against the hateful sheen of the holding cell. All she wanted was to hear their tiny kitten yowls and their curious little chirps. Boop tucking themself under her chin, drooling all over her and purring like a happy thundercloud. Bippity sitting on her shoulder and snuffling into her ear. Boppity jumping and pouncing and then finally settling on her chest like her own personal bodyguard.

She knew Ms. Fi would give them a good life, but she wanted to be the one to open their wet food and hear their little galloping paws. She wanted to watch them grow up, and leash train them, and figure out ways to include them in her magic act. She wanted to travel the world with them. See magnificent places, and stay in huge soft hotel beds, and order tuna tartare from room service menus.

"I want my kitties," she moaned. She wrapped her arms around herself and rocked, repeating it again and again, like a mantra. "I want my kitties. I want my kitties. I want my kitties . . ."

In the windowless room, with no clock, Mila lost all sense of time. She knew she wasn't going to be able to sleep, and suddenly it felt like each second, each breath, dragged on for years. She didn't know how she would cope with being locked up for the rest of her life.

What even happened next for someone like her?

Pete probably had to file some kind of paperwork. She assumed she would be transferred to an actual holding cell in an actual jail somewhere on the mainland where they had a courthouse and a judge and all of that business.

There would be a lawyer, right? And a trial? But no chance of success. Just her fingerprints on her trick knives, the one that killed Brandon and the one that stabbed Becca, would surely be enough to convict her. Unless Becca somehow survived and could identify her attacker.

She shook her head. That was too much to hope for.

Everything had been going wrong for her since Brandon's death. There was no reason to think her luck would change now. She would be convicted and sentenced.

And then she would be remanded to prison. Maybe that would be more like the movies. She assumed it would be grim. For murder, it would certainly be decades. She would sit in a cell, living with the knowledge that she was paying for someone else's crimes. Someone who had killed Brandon and burned down Scarborough Farms and smashed up her apartment and attacked Mugsy and stabbed Becca. Someone who was trying to set her up.

Not just trying. Succeeding.

Her parents had always told her that without their money and connections, she was worthless. The night she finally left, they had warned her that if she walked out the door, she'd be dead to them. As her fingers had closed around the perfectly polished brass door handle, they'd made a final, dire prediction. Since that night, she'd been driven by determination to prove them wrong. But they'd been right all along.

The life of joy and love and adventure she had always dreamed of, the one she'd left Chicago forever to go in search of, had finally come to an ignominious end, just as they'd told her it would.

Chapter Thirty
The Siblings

Bippity.

When Ms. Fi got our kangaroo pouch home, she set us down on her sofa. We were all frozen in shock, as quiet as three statues. Boop wasn't even purring. I knew I should feel something, but all I felt was empty. Numb.

Hylia periodically stalked past, peeking in at us. I couldn't have guessed how much time passed. But eventually, Ms. Fi unzipped the pouch. She had Boppity's little pink Mousie in her hand. When she shook it and the bell in its belly jingled, his pupils constricted and then dilated. His chin jerked toward the sound.

Almost as if he were being driven by raw instinct, he jumped out of the kangaroo pouch.

"That's it, kittens, this way," Ms. Fi sang in her sweet contralto voice. "Hylia and I have prepared a nice little surprise for you."

I couldn't let Boppity go without me. We'd already lost Mila. We had to stick together.

I shoved Boop with my forehead, propelling them out of the kangaroo pouch and toward Ms. Fi, and then followed, making sure Boop kept moving.

Ms. Fi continued to sing her coaxing song. I looked around for Hylia, but the big cat had vanished. Ms. Fi's slippered feet padded softly as she headed down a corridor. When she disappeared through a doorway, Boppity abandoned his careful stalking and raced after her. I poked Boop until they caught up.

Inside was a bed about half the size of Mila's. It had all of the sleeping-fluff from Mila's original apartment atop it, artfully swirled and rumpled and smelling of comfort. An open window let the soft night breeze drift across the bed and into the room. On the far side of the window was a little backyard version of the front porch, except this one wasn't screened in.

Against a wall, a strangely nubbly mat lay beneath our food dishes. Ms. Fi had set out our familiar meat-feasts, along with our water and crunchies. Even our sandbox was there, set in the middle of a second nubbly mat.

In the center of it all sat Hylia, her expression inscrutable. "We couldn't very well have you messing with my things, after all," she tutted. "So we had to find a way to make you feel at home." I almost thought I saw some sort of meaningful look pass between her and Boop. They raced up to her, a purr rumbling to life in their chest. Boppity charged the meat-feast, growling out his fierce contentment around huge, smacking gulps.

Seeing my siblings return to their typical, ridiculous selves released the fear, unnamed until now, that had been building in my chest. The fear that we would be frozen in forlorn misery forever. I drew in a deep breath and let it go.

We would be okay. Even without Mila. It should have been a huge relief, but instead, the thought of Mila brought with it a lance of pain.

Still, Hylia and her human had made a place for us in their home. We were not alone. I looked deep into the majestic Queen's unwavering gaze.

"Thank you," I said. "You saved us."

"Nonsense." Her whiskers twitched fondly. Then her gaze sharpened. "But something is weighing on you."

"We're Mila's protectors." I told her. "But we failed to protect her. She's in the human pound, gone forever." The stab of misery deepened as I said the thought aloud.

"You've only failed if you give up," Hylia told me.

What could that possibly mean?

Boppity finished his meat-feast and trotted over. Hylia called him to her side with a twitch of her ear and began to tidy his food-spattered face.

"I don't understand," I said. "How could we possibly protect Mila now?"

"The answer is the answer!" chirped Boop, popping up from Hylia's floof and trotting over to their own feast-plate. I shot a disgusted look after them. Nonsense, as always.

"Under what circumstances would Mila be released from the human pound?" Hylia asked. I thought hard.

"If they caught the real killer?" It was all I could come up with.

Hylia nodded, and I felt a little surge of hope.

"Mr. Cavendish," Boppity said, poking his face out from between Hylia's paws. "They should catch *him*."

"Maybe not Mr. Cavendish," I told him. "He and Ms. Scarborough stayed home all night when Mila's apartment was smashed up. And they were almost killed in that house fire. The bad guy must be someone else."

He started to argue, but Hylia interrupted him. "It seems clear what your next step should be."

"What?" I asked her. Nothing seemed clear to me.

"We're going to investigate!" Boppity announced.

I stiffened with shock. "Without Mila? How?"

Hylia didn't answer, but she was gazing at my brother with pride.

I gritted my teeth. I was the one in charge. Not him.

The queen turned her gaze to me for a moment, then looked back down at Boppity. "I appreciate your mind for tactics," she told him. "It's a good quality in a general."

He stood, arching his back, and shot me a smug look. "We shall question the humans tomorrow," he said, ridiculously prim all of a sudden.

"We can't question humans," I shot back. "They can't understand us. Besides, if they see us running around town alone, we'll get sent to the pound for sure. They'll think we're strays. We'd have to use Physics to keep from being seen, but we can't. Because of the Law of Cats." I let out a sharp huff, putting him in his place.

"Gently now, little Queenlet," Hylia told me. "Cultivating the strengths of others is an important quality in any leader."

Boppity pinned his ears at her words.

"Ha," I said. "She called me leader and Queenlet."

"Well, she called *me* General," he snapped.

I was about to tell him that a queen or a leader ranked above a general, but then I remembered what Hylia had just told me. I had to bite down on my tongue to keep myself from responding, but I managed to give him a regal nod. A nod fit for a Queenlet cultivating her very own General. "She's right about that," I told him. "You are the fiercest and the strongest of us by far. You're an excellent general."

When he stalked over, I thought maybe he was going to tackle me. But instead, he sat beside me and leaned his side into mine, purring.

I'd never felt him purr before. I squeezed my eyes shut as affection filled my chest. His insight had actually been pretty good. He wasn't so good at seeing the whole picture, but his tactical thinking was fairly impressive. Maybe I could take advantage of that.

"What do you think, General," I asked him. "I've identified some barriers. Do you have a strategy to overcome them?"

He tucked his chin and lengthened his back. "I believe I do," he said after a moment. Turning to Hylia, he gave her a dignified bow, lying down and extending his broad paws in Sphinx position.

"Noble Queen," he began. He was actually rather magnificent. "Might we have an exception to the rule about Physics around humans? We promise to make sure they don't discover us or our abilities."

My eyes widened. What could he mean?

"Certainly, young General," she said. "So long as you do not risk discovery, no laws are broken."

He turned to me. "You can make us invisible. I can move things that are in the way when there are no humans looking. Between the two of us, we can go anywhere. We can even go to the vet's office, where Brutus is, and find out who attacked him. That will tell us for sure who the killer is. Then all we'll need is proof."

He was right! Maybe he wasn't quite as smart as me, but he was very clever at problem-solving. I butted his cheek with my forehead. "I'm proud of you, Boppity," I told him. "That's pretty brilliant. Hylia's right. Your strategic mind is impressive."

"And my purrs are impressive," Boop said, puttering up to Hylia and rolling over to show her their full belly. "You probably want to tidy up the rumbles, right?"

Boppity and I exchanged a fond look as we watched our sweet, silly sibling.

"Listen, Boppity," I said. "I'm not all that hungry. You want to share my meat-feast with me? We can eat it together."

He raced to my dish, and I trotted along behind him, tossing Hylia a grateful look.

The next morning, I awoke to the warm sun on my fur and a drift of breeze that smelled of ocean and lilacs.

Hylia had obviously been in during the night to check on us, because there was a tidy dent in the center of our crunchies. Boppity was already up, and I didn't see him in our room. Maybe he was talking to her.

The window screen was also popped out at the bottom left corner. The gap was narrow enough that Ms. Fi probably wouldn't notice it, but more than wide enough for me to poke my nose through. It widened as I pressed it with my face. Just as I was about to step out, I heard a yowl of terror.

"I'm outside! *Alone!* I'll never get back inside ever, *ever* again!" Boppity yelled. Looking down, I spotted him on the little back porch below the window. He must have investigated the screen and fallen out.

I stepped through carefully and walked along the porch railing until I was above him. "No need to shout," I said.

He looked around wildly until he spotted me. Then he gathered himself and bushed out his coat, trying to look bold and fierce.

"I wasn't shouting," he said. "I just decided to warm up my voice."

"You shouldn't lie," I told him with a fond twitch of my ear. "Your whiskers give you away every time."

I made a little twirl and walked along the broad wooden railing until I came back to the window. Hooking open the corner, I slipped inside.

I kept my ears pointed toward the window until I heard him scale a baluster, then I moved to the center of the floor and sat neatly. He was probably embarrassed. Normally, I'd have enjoyed poking at that vulnerability. But Hylia had shown me a queenlier way.

He pushed through the screen and landed on the bed with a funny little *ploop*. His ears were awkward with chagrin.

Time to lean into the way of the Queenlet. "Bet you can't pounce on me from there!" I smirked, but I also let my fondness show through. Boppity was always at his most confident when he was attacking.

He put on his fiercest war face and flung himself into the air, forearms stretched like wings. When he crashed into me, the momentum knocked the air from both of us, but he wrapped his strong arms around my ribcage and grabbed my scruff, bunny-kicking me with a fierceness that was also just the teeniest bit fond.

I squirmed and twisted, nearly getting the upper paw, until he rolled us forward, tightening his grip and growling playfully.

Just then, Ms. Fi stepped into the room, humming along to the musical sound of a meat-feast lid being peeled. Releasing me without a backward glance, Boppity raced to his dish.

Pride filled my chest as I watched him descend on his breakfast with uncomplicated glee. Boop trotted up beside him, waving their little tail joyfully. I couldn't decide which was nicer: the complex flavor of my lovely turkey-feast, or the warm feeling that I was finally becoming a good leader.

Boppity wanted to leave immediately, but I told him we needed to get directions from Hylia first.

"We can figure it out," he tried to insist as we approached the Queen.

"We can't," I told him. "The world is bigger than the biggest thoughts of the cleverest kitten." Mother had always said that, but I didn't want to mention her and have him fall to pieces again. We didn't have time. Just to make sure he didn't get too full of himself, I told him, "That's me, by the way."

He stiffened, about to argue, but Hylia was already answering.

"The world is indeed immense, but Corvin's Crossing is a very small island about ten miles wide, which means a determined cat can travel it from end to end in a single day at a good, brisk trot. We are only connected to the rest of the world by ferry boats and by the great blue sea."

"The sea is pretty when you're in the sky," Boop told her.

I shook my head.

"Is that why we smell ocean everywhere we go?" asked Boppity.

"Yes." Hylia's whiskers twitched. "I dislike the water intensely. Though I do enjoy fresh seafood. Regardless, my point is that Corvin's Crossing is only a small piece of the world. If you go southeast, past the town green, and keep going, you'll get to the vet's office, where Brutus is."

"Southeast, toward the sunrise and the ocean smashing against the cliffs?" I confirmed.

"Right, little Queenlet. Stick to the tall grass where the town meets the wilderness as much as possible, stay away from the woods, and avoid cars at all costs."

She tilted her head, her eyes growing wider. "Some final advice. It's better to be spotted and thought to be a stray than to be caught doing Physics, but it's best not to be seen at all. Stay away from the rats. Don't go near them. But in case of emergency, follow their example."

"What rats?" I asked.

She smirked. "Exactly."

I shook my head, trying to dislodge a sudden ominous feeling. I considered pointing out to Boppity how wise I'd been to ask for directions, but he was already darting back toward our room and the loose screen. I had to hurry to catch up.

Chapter Thirty-One
Humans and Cats

Boppity.

I wondered why Mother had kept such valuable knowledge about Corvin's Crossing from us. Maybe it had something to do with the dangers in the wilderness. My chest tightened at the thought of Mother, but I shoved it away. I was a General now. No time for yowling. Bippity had pushed past me toward the window screen. I didn't want to be left behind.

In fact, as General, *I* should be first.

Instead, we both fell to the porch together, each pushing to get out front. Boop plooped out behind us, purring and babbling on about the smell of the wind, and Bippity stared up at the sky, tail twitching.

Poor Bippity. She didn't know which way the sun would go. If her body language was any clue, she was beating herself up for not being a good enough leader.

"No bullying," I told her.

"What do you mean by that?" she asked. But before I could answer, she looked back up at the sky. "I don't know which way . . ."

"I know," I told her. "But I do. That's part of my job, so you don't have to be good at it to be a good Queenlet."

The way her whole face softened, and she rubbed her forehead against my cheek and down my side, I guess it must have been the right thing to say.

"Okay, General Boppity," she said. "Take charge. Boop in the middle. I'll bring up the rear and keep watch."

I raised my tail like a flag and dashed into the long grass of Ms. Fi's backyard. "This way!" I called.

I dodged and wove and darted and froze, and occasionally I pounced.

Once, I even caught a tiny frog just the size of my paw, but I let her go so I could sniff her, and she leaped up and punched my nose with her head, then vanished into the grass.

Rude.

When we reached the air that smelled like many animals, I told my siblings to wait while I investigated the vet's office. I returned as soon as I'd found a way in.

"There's a window above a dumpster that I can open with this vomity napkin I found."

"Ooh, that smells interesting!" Boop crept forward.

"I know, right?" I agreed. "I can entangle it with the window and bat it open, and we can slip inside. You and Boop can keep watch, to be sure no humans see, and I'll let you know when it's done."

They followed me into the empty gravel-flattened area behind the building and pointed themselves in opposite directions.

Concentrating, I found a qubit in the window that wanted to bond with a qubit in the napkin, so I introduced them to one another and gave them an entanglement bond. Then the entire window mapped itself across the napkin in my mind, revealing dozens of additional pairs of qubits eager to be entangled across the two objects. Darting my gaze back and forth between them, I obliged, until they were connected by a sturdy, invisible matrix of golden pair-bonds.

"Ready," I called out.

"That was fast!" Boop cooed in admiration.

"I know," I said modestly.

I tried to leap up to the top of the dumpster, but I didn't even make it halfway.

"How about that old box?" Boop suggested. "It looks like our first home, with Mother."

When I turned and saw it, so similar to the nest Mother had made for us, all of my grief, which I'd been fighting back so nobly for so long, and all of my misery at losing Mila, which felt so similar, filled up my chest and throat and burst out all at once. "Motherrrrrrr," I cried mournfully.

"Now look what you've done," Bippity growled.

"What?" Boop asked. "What have I done?"

She pinned her ears, glaring at them. "He's all up in his feelings now. We'll never get anything done with him like this."

I hid my face. I knew a General shouldn't behave this way, but I couldn't seem to catch all the feelings and shove them away again.

"You have to let things out or you can't heal from them," Boop said calmly. They bumbled over to me, purring.

"It's hard, isn't it," they crooned.

"I miss her!" I wailed. I wasn't even sure whether I was talking about Mila or Mother. Maybe both.

Bippity, her feelings still neatly stuffed, rolled her eyes. I hated being such a disappointment to her.

But Boop just kept purring. "I know," they agreed. "Those feelings hurt. I'm sorry it's so hard."

"She was so warm and soft and kind," I cried.

"She was," Boop agreed. They began to lick my face in broad, fur-disheveling swatches, just like Mother had done so many times.

"And now Mother's gone and Mila's gone, and I'm never going to feel that special kind of warm ever again!" I curled in on myself as Boop continued licking.

"Yeah," Boop agreed sadly. "They're gone."

"This is a waste of—" Bippity started. But Boop raised their head and shot her such a fierce glare that she was startled into silence. I'd never seen them look like that before. They gave me a gentle forehead-butt of solidarity.

I looked at them with sad eyes. "I'm glad *you're* not gone," I said.

"I'm right here," Boop agreed.

"And Bippity," I turned, looking at her impatient form. Boop looked at her, too, their ears pert and expectant.

The impatience dropped from her posture, replaced by something softer. "I'm here, too," she said. She even gave me a little lick on my ear, starting to purr. Instead of being swallowed up by my misery or having to shove it down, I was surprised to find myself starting to purr, too. As we sat in silence, rumbling in harmony, I almost thought I could feel our three hearts beating in perfect synchrony.

And then something surprising happened. That special golden warmth grew in my chest. The one I had thought was gone forever. It had been here, inside of my siblings, all along.

I sat up. "Okay," I said. "Let's do this."

I cracked open the window, then disentangled it from the napkin. Next, I entangled the napkin and the box. Lifting my paw, I gave the napkin a swat, and the box tumbled end over end, crashing up against the dumpster with a little *thud.*

It was tall enough to get us about halfway to the lid. The jump was hard, but we all made it. In the vet's office, we found ourselves in a dimly lit back room lined with cages.

"Is this the pound?" I gasped. Was Doc secretly evil? Was *she* the murderer?

A metallic *thud, thud, thud* reverberated inside one of the cages.

"Hello, kittens!" came a snuffly *muuffph* of greeting from the cage. Brutus was lying on his side. A stretchy purple bandage decorated with golden bones went from his forehead to the top of his neck and wrapped around under his chin. His ears poked out through narrow gaps in the sides, swiveling and flicking with joy as he told us how happy he was to have us visiting him.

Bippity stepped forward. I shouldered past her. I should definitely lead the interrogation. It was a generalish sort of thing to do.

"Hiiiiiiiii hero!" Boop trilled. "How is your human doing?"

What a useless first question. We already knew Mugsy was fine.

But Brutus's tail went *thud, thud, thud.* "He's good. He visits me a lot. He says they're keeping me here for observation, and Ms. Fi is keeping him for observation, too. We can go home tomorrow."

"I bet he tells you how brave you are every time he visits! You saved him!"

"He does! I did! Want to hear about it?"

"I do! I do!" Boop trotted in place, their little tail shivering with enthusiasm.

"Mugsy—" *thud, thud, thud,* "—was reading those paper file things," Brutus said, "and grunting about Brandon and fraud and conspiracy and greed and such. I was keeping his feet warm and getting a good snore going, when suddenly there was a *thwack*. Mugsy grunted and fell over."

"Someone snuck past you?" I asked sharply.

Brutus's ears fell and his tail went limp. Before he could answer, Boop trotted in front of me. "Because you're not supposed to be in guard mode when the door is unlocked, right?"

He picked up his ears. "Yes. That's true. Mugsy always scolds me if I guard when the front door is unlocked." His tail gave a tentative wag.

Boop shot me a look kind of like the one they'd sent Bippity when I was sad and she was grouchy. My hindquarters plunked to the floor before I even had a chance to think about it.

"So you were being a good dog, and Mugsy got thwacked, right?" Boop was standing on their toes, leaning forward, eyes wide with anticipation. "What next?"

"Well, I heard the thump and Mugsy made a grunt and started choking, so I attacked. I got a mouthful of blood and muscle, and I was just about to crush bone when I got several ouches, and then everything went dark."

"Do you remember anything else? Any idea who the attacker was?" Boop asked gently.

"I remember foot thuds moving away through the dark fog. The human smelled like desperation."

"Was it Mr. Cavendish?" I asked.

Brutus tilted his head, considering. "I mostly smelled that panicky violence smell, and then the terror smell after I attacked. But Mr. Cavendish smells a little like leather polish and a lot like that stinky wax he uses to make his hair and nose-swirls shiny. I didn't smell the wax, just the leather polish. So it can't have been him."

"Are you sure?" Bippity asked.

"Of course you are," Boop purred. "Poor dog. Brave. Good Brutus."

The dog rested his head on his paws. He looked exhausted. "That's what Mugsy—" *thump, thump, thump,* "—said to me when he woke up. He was crying. *Brave dog,* he was saying. *Good Brutus. There's my brave boy. Just hang on.* I think he thought I was going to die. I'm way too tough, though. No way I'd leave him behind like that." His tail thumped again, weakly.

"Good dog," Boop purred as Brutus drifted off to sleep. "Good Brutus."

I rolled my eyes at my ridiculous sibling, but deep down, I had to admit I'd underestimated Brutus. I'd always thought of him as a goof, but he'd been fierce in battle and brave when wounded. He was a true warrior.

* * *

Back home, Bippity and I were a roiling mass of confusion.

"If Mr. Cavendish isn't our killer, who is?" Bippity asked.

"I don't know," I said, shaking my head.

"Becca!" she exclaimed.

"Uh, no," I told her. "Becca got *stabbed* by the killer. That makes her innocent for *sure.*"

"No, silly!" she batted at my nose, but it was a gentle swat, not a battle-challenge. "I mean Becca knows who the killer is! You can't stab someone in the chest and not get spotted."

That was a good point. I started to get excited, until something occurred to me. "But that means the killer is going to finish her off as soon as he gets a chance."

Bippity's eyes got wider than I'd ever seen them. "To save Mila, we have to save Becca."

"And to save Becca," I continued, "we have to find out who the killer is so we can stop them before they attack her."

"But all we know is it wasn't Mr. Cavendish," Bippity said. "That leaves a lot of other people it could be."

"Maybe Brutus was wrong," I suggested. It didn't seem likely, though. Mr. Cavendish did smell like the acrid, bitter tang of nose-tail-wax.

"I don't think so," she said. "Remember, Ms. Scarborough said he was in his trailer when Mila's apartment got broken into. Plus, he almost died in that house fire. I don't think he would've started it, then gone back inside and gotten all crispy waiting for someone to rescue him, no matter how brave or determined or desperate he was."

"Who else smells like leather polish?" I asked. "The sheriff, when he's in his uniform with the shiny shoes. Becca, when she's been at the barn. The mayor. Mr. Cavendish would, if he left his head at home."

"Don't be ridiculous," Bippity said. But the tension in her whiskers lightened a bit.

"Ask the Queen?" Boop suggested.

Bippity tilted her head. "Actually, that's not a bad idea."

Hylia's tail curled around her as she sat in queen pose at the foot of Ms. Fi's bed. She peered down at us. "Why do you wish to keep investigating, kittens?" she asked.

The question startled me.

"We're supposed to take care of Mila," Bippity said. "We can't fail. She's our responsibility."

"I don't care so much about responsibility," Boop said. They were creeping toward the outskirts of Hylia's fluffy tail, eyes wide with hopeful affection.

I turned to them. "Why not? What do you care about?"

They paused midstalk. "Love," they said. "Joy. Fun."

"A wise response, little one." Hylia casually flicked her tail, allowing it to settle in front of Boop. They scurried forward and lay atop it, eyes closing in bliss.

She turned her piercing gaze to me. "And you? What do you care about?"

"I . . ." I blinked. "I don't know. I've been . . ."

"You've been focused on surviving," she said. "Your whole lives, you and your sister have been reacting to what happens around you. That's a way to go through life, certainly. But is it really a way to live?"

My bones sagged. She was right.

"So what would *you* do in our place?" Bippity's ears were pinned in anger. "Or do you get your fun by picking on my brother and me?"

I felt a great welling of warmth in my chest for my bold little sister.

Hylia tried to twitch her tail in irritation, but Boop was still lying on it, burying their face in its soft fur, so only the tip wiggled. She sighed. "If you want to live a good life, one that truly belongs to you . . ."

She half-stood, sliding her tail out from under Boop and bending to lick their back comfortingly. "You're going to have to figure out what you want to live for. That's the single biggest factor in what human you choose to bond with."

"You mentioned this before," Bippity's ears popped back up curiously. "But I didn't know what you meant."

"There's a unique, ineffable thing that happens between humans and cats." She settled herself again into an elegant queen pose, her gaze distant. "For all of their quirks and faults, humans change the world around them in ways we cats could never imagine. And we change the world in ways they can't understand. When a human and a cat find a special connection, a harmony of purpose, their bond is the closest thing in this world to magic."

Hylia's eyes squeezed shut affectionately for a moment, then opened again, searching my face. "Find your human. Find your purpose. Once you do, everything else will make sense."

She stood to leave.

"One question," Bippity interjected.

Hylia turned, flicking an ear toward her inquisitively.

"What if we do love Mila? She's in the human pound. We'll probably never see her again. Is that really someone we should love?"

"Maybe," Hylia twitched her whiskers thoughtfully. "Only you can know that. But I'm not sure you should be so ready to accept the premise underlying your question."

With that, she flowed out of the room.

I sighed.

"Do you know what she's talking about?" I asked my sister.

"I do," said Boop.

My ears flattened. "No, you don't."

"Yes, I do," Boop insisted.

I looked at Bippity. She looked at me. "Fine," she sighed, turning to Boop. "What does she mean?"

"It's all okay," Boop said. They began to purr. "We don't have to be afraid. Mila is a good human. The best. We all know it."

I blinked.

They were right.

My mind filled with memories of Mila.

Her dismay, holding Becca in her arms.

Her radiance as she and Reverend Bak spoke with their Divinities.

Her pride when we unraveled each of Brandon's dark secrets together.

Her discomfiture at Q's generosity and the kindness of the delicious-smelling chef.

Her determination as she interviewed Mr. Cavendish and the mayor and everyone else.

Her courage as she charged toward the fire to save her sheriff-friend who was trying to put her in jail.

Her pain every time he accused her of killing Brandon.

Her anguish when Brandon's body fell from the sky.

Her joy when we performed magic together.

Her hair slipping into our cardboard box and her careful hands lifting us away from certain death and carrying us home.

Her warmth.

Her kindness.

Her meat-feast.

I turned to Bippity and watched the same light dawning in her eyes. Boop was right. Mila was our human. Like it or not, we already *were* bonded to her. I closed my eyes, shaking.

We *loved* her.

"Love." Boop looked between me and Bippity. "Now you understand too. Love. Joy. Fun." Their purrs filled the room. "Mila."

Boop was right. Mila was our person. Our purpose.

But if we didn't find the killer, we would lose her forever. I straightened my tail. "Come on, siblings," I said. "Let's save our human."

Chapter Thirty-Two
The Culprit

Boop.

After a snack, we had a strategy session with Hylia.

"Maybe we should just guard Becca until she wakes up." Boppity suggested.

"How are you, three little kittens, going to guard a human in a hospital bed night and day until she recovers, without ever getting spotted and taken to the pound?" Hylia asked.

She had a point.

"I guess we have to figure out who the murderer is," Bippity said.

She also had a point.

"Which means we need to be detectives some more," Boppity said.

He had a point, too.

"It's definitely a human," I said. Now I had a point, just like everyone else. I purred at myself.

"To find your suspect," the Queen advised, "Ask yourself who stood to gain from the bad things that have happened. You've been focused on one human. See the bigger picture."

"How do we find out who would gain from Brandon dying and Luxe going broke?" Bippity asked.

"Humans are fascinated with the details of each other's private lives." Hylia said. "When they are together, they say all sorts of things about each other. *Gossip*, they call it. Ridiculous creatures. No finesse."

Boppity and Bippity exchanged a look. Their eyes glowed with enthusiasm and their ears perked up with joy.

"We'll find some humans," Boppity said, "and we'll sneak! Listen! Spy!" He darted back and forth across the room, leaping and crouching and tumbling.

"Let's go to the place with the baker who makes Mila feel safe," I suggested. "That seems like a good place to detectivate."

"Actually," Bippity said, turning her clever gaze on me, "that's not a terrible suggestion. There are always lots of people there. But we can't get spotted, so . . ."

Bippity squinted and we all vanished.

It was sleek and mysterious having all of that light stream past without touching me. And when I looked at my siblings, all I could see was the tiny black slits of their pupils floating along beside me. It took a bit of practice to walk on paws I couldn't see, so I stumbled and flooped out the window before I got the hang of it.

As we approached Q Tea Pie, I spotted a strange white ladder painted on the ground. There was a very tall, very thin tower on the corner, near the ladder, with three eyes stacked one atop the other. The top eye was red. The other two were blank.

Below it was a little white symbol. But as we approached, it dimmed. Another symbol, orange this time, flashed a few times and then solidified.

We stepped onto the ladder.

Suddenly, a car was zooming right at Bippity's little pupil-slits.

"No!" I yelled. But I forgot to use a meow, and Bippity couldn't see my body, so she didn't notice my shout.

I stood frozen on the curb as sour-sharp terror spiked the air all around me. Boppity's pupil-slits crashed into the invisible Bippity, and both pairs of eyes squeezed shut in shock, disappearing them completely.

The car rushed directly over the spot where they'd vanished.

I howled in anguish as my nose reappeared between my eyes. A glance downward confirmed that my whole body was now visible.

Bippity's Physics-bending had ceased.

I knew I should look over at the white ladder painted on the ground. I owed my siblings the honor of witnessing their passage to the Next Place. But I couldn't make myself. I squeezed my eyes shut and began to cry. I was alone. No Mother. No Mila. No siblings.

Just me, alone in the world, with nobody to love and snuggle and purr on.

Then a forehead bumped into mine. My eyes flew open and the first thing I saw was that my nose was gone again. I spotted four slitted pupils hovering in the air in front of me. I staggered toward them. Their bodies pressed into my sides as they leaned into me. My purrs rumbled through their ribs and love flowed between us, warm and comforting.

I heaved a sigh of relief. They were okay. We should definitely go home and take the day to snuggle and think about what had happened.

But before I could say so, my siblings set off, their focus on their goal unshaken.

"Hey, wait up," I tried to tell them. But they still couldn't see my body. I meowed my dismay and they stopped, looking at me.

There was an awkward moment. Everyone was trying and failing to say stuff all at once. Our eyes darted back and forth. "Listen," Boppity said with a meow.

"Problem," Bippity's chirp carried notes of frustration.

She adjusted the photons so eddies of light flickered against the edges of our ears and whiskers, the curves of our chins and tails. We were illusory, like mother's stories of mirages in the desert, but we could make out one another's contours enough to communicate.

"Finally," Boppity said. "I was wondering why you'd been ignoring me all morning."

"Well," Bippity snickered, "at least now I know I can silence you if you get annoying."

"Just try it," Boppity growled.

I laughed. They were so silly, always bickering over nothing. My joy that they were alive, that we all were, bubbled from my chest and filled the air with fizzy glee.

We had made it across the treacherous ground-ladder, and were now approaching the glass front of Q Tea Pie Bakery.

Bippity had been right. Or had it been Boppity? Whoever had suggested we should come here. It was full of chatting humans eating little human treats.

A cool gust of air swept past us. "Smells like rain," Boppity said. He reached out for a nearby pebble, darting his gaze between it and the door.

"Stop that!" Bippity ordered.

"What? Why?" Boppity's tail twitched. "It's about to—"

There was a cracking sound in the sky, and rain began to pour down on us.

"If you open the door with Physics, the humans will see," Bippity insisted. "I promised Hylia I'd make sure we didn't break the Law of Cats."

Boppity huffed miserably, his ears sticking straight out to the sides. I opened my mouth to yowl, but Bippity shot me a glare. "Hush," she told me with her whiskers. Her ear flicked forward. "Humans are coming."

There was a tinkling sound as they pulled open the glass door. Dodging their feet, we rushed inside and shook our fur.

"Do you think they'll see us?" Boppity asked.

"I doubt it," Bippity assured him. "We're all but invisible to their eyes, and humans aren't very observant anyway. Now spread out and let's see what we can learn."

My sister padded over to a table, seating herself beneath it. I wandered through the room, looking around. There were clusters of humans chatting, sipping, and nibbling, and more bustling around the warm, cozy space.

Q sat in their customary throne at the center of the room, heavy burgundy combat boots propped up on a short stool, sipping from a delicate cup as they turned the pages of a book that said *Kolm* on it.

As a very short human approached the counter, Q stood, golden light illuminating the swirly chaos of their hair like an artfully wrought crown.

"Hello, little one!" Their voice was rich and buoyant. My nose bumped into something cold, and I realized I'd been walking slowly toward them, drawn forward as if by their gravitational pull. My face was pressing into the glass of their display island.

"Hiya, Q!" A little voice issued from the little mouth of the little human. It must be a human kitten. How cute! "Mama said I get a treat for being good during homeschool!"

"You were good at homeschool?" Q asked, tilting their head and raising their eyebrow skeptically. "Really?"

"I sure was, Q! Honest!"

"Well, then, my friend, you can have anything you want. On the house. Your mom isn't the only one who's proud of you!"

"You are too?"

Q nodded, smiling. "So, what can I get you?"

"I like that rainbow one!"

"Pride cake! Nice choice! What kind of tea do you want with it?"

"Caramel, please. Can I have the elephant pot? I was learning about the savanna in Africa today. It has some of the most amazing animals on Earth, including the largest elephants!"

"Whoa! I sure am lucky to know such a smart kiddo!" Q winked at the kitten-human. "I'll bring it all to your table. You want to pick out a surprise for your mom? They probably deserve a reward, too, for being a good teacher."

"Oh!" The kitten-human's voice dropped to a whisper. "Yeah. Mom's really good and hardly ever gets rewards. But she loves your one pie . . . um . . . the one with hazel-something."

"Maple bourbon hazelnut and pecan pie?" Q whispered back.

"Yeah. Warm, with whipped coconut cream on top." The kitten-human grinned and trotted back to a sofa that held a tired-looking adult bearing a giant, affectionate smile.

I strolled back to Bippity's table to share the fascinating conversation I'd overheard.

"I have clues!" I announced. "About elephant teapots and rainbow cake and something exhausting called homeschool!"

Bippity shushed me. She was concentrating on freckled Jenny from the vet's office, who was chatting with the tidy lady from the desk in front of the mayor's office.

"Conflict of interests?" Jenny was asking. "Why do you say that, Larissa?"

The tidy lady shook her head, the russet tips of her beautiful black corkscrew curls bobbing gently. "Because the Land Trust was being managed by Brandon. But it had to have a successor trustee, so Mayor Adams is next in line."

"How do you know this?" Jenny's eyes were wide.

"It's public record." Larissa looked into Jenny's gaze, smiling. I liked the look of that smile. It was fond and hopeful. "I had to photocopy it all yesterday morning for a FOIA request."

"FOIA?"

"Freedom of information." Larissa shrugged. "Anyone can request public documents."

Jenny made a humming sound in her throat. "So that means . . ."

"With Brandon gone, Mayor Adams is in charge of what happens to Luxe when it goes bankrupt." Larissa shook her head again, but her smile stayed hopeful and her eyes stayed on Jenny. "That's what I mean about a conflict of interest. Because Mayor Adams tried to buy the land where Luxe is going up, but Mr. Cavendish outbid him. So now he can get it after all."

Jenny grinned. "Wow. You sure are smart. I wish *you* were Mayor."

Larissa laughed. "I wouldn't know where to start."

Jenny held out her fork, offering Larissa a bite of the creamy pink and orange confection on her plate. Watching them, I couldn't help purring.

Bippity was shushing me when Boppity charged up. "I learned that Ms. Scarborough's cookies make people sleep well," he announced.

"Useless," she scoffed.

"Well," Boppity spluttered. "I also learned about the schedule for guarding Becca in the hospital."

"That might be useful, but I learned that Mayor Adams could be the killer!" She lifted her chin proudly, but something seemed wrong with her eyes, and her ears looked a little droopy.

"What? No!" Boppity stiffened, his tail thrashing. "Deputy Chantelle said that Mayor Adams offered to take a shift guarding Mila, since he has a military and security background. Sheriff Pete is guarding her until 10 PM. Then Mayor Adams is taking the night shift from 10 PM to 6 AM, and Chantelle takes over at 6 AM."

"What?" Bippity bushed out into a cactusy poof of anxious ferocity. "Mayor Adams will be guarding her tonight? We have to get the humans to . . . whoa . . ." She wavered. "I think shooing photons is taking more out of me than I thought."

Before my eyes, she and Boppity flickered into semiopacity for a moment.

Boppity pushed her toward the door, bumping her sharply with his head, then walking so close beside her that his ribs pressed into hers. "Lean on me if you need to."

I followed his lead, pressing against her other side and purring low and deep.

The human-kitten and her adult were heading toward the door. We darted past them and outside as soon as they pulled it open. Bippity tripped, landing on her side with an audible *umph*. Icy rain soaked all three of us instantly.

Bippity's third eyelids slid out partway. Something was horribly wrong.

The human-kitten pointed. "Look, Mama! Ghost-kittens!"

The big human popped open a colorful umbrella. "I love your creative mind, hun-bun."

"But one of them is sick, Mama! We should help!" The human-kitten rushed over and scooped Bippity up, setting her back on her feet and running a tiny hand down her spine, which arched in response.

The mama murmured how proud she was to have such a kind and imaginative child.

Boppity and I barely kept our sister upright as we shoved her toward a parked car. As soon as she collapsed into its shadow, she lost hold of the photons altogether.

I started to yowl, but Boppity shushed me.

"Hang on." His eyes squeezed shut. "Hang on. I've got this." His voice was frantic, his whiskers rigid.

"I believe in you," I purred. His ear-tips softened and his whiskers relaxed.

"Wait! I've got it!" he shouted.

He opened his eyes and darted away, returning with a slightly crushed plastic cup. A straw clung to its sticky, vanilla-scented interior. The hull read *Q Tea to Go!*

Boppity drew out the straw and set it slightly to the side. His eyes darted back and forth between the two objects. Then he seized the straw in his mouth and made a little scooping motion, and the cup slid under Bippity and tilted, dropping her down inside.

She scrambled weakly until her nose peeked out of the cup, which was hovering above the ground at a slight angle.

"Look," Bippity said, staring under a nearby car. Her pupils were huge, doomy discs of black. I followed her gaze.

Something darted from shadow to shadow, making for a gutter in the curb ahead.

It had a short, humped body covered in a steel-colored pelt. Its face was pointed and its ears were round and paper-thin. There was something strange about its long and sinuous tail. It was pink and scaly-looking, like a sunburned snake.

An evil one. A shiver of pure dread juddered through my bones.

"Rat," Bippity hissed weakly.

In case of emergency, Boppity muttered to himself, *follow their example.*

I watched him swallow, wrapping his courage around himself like armor. "Time to move," he told me. "Stick close, Boop! Fast as you can!"

He raced into the street, darting from shadow to shadow in a zig-zag pattern. His broad, nimble paws slapped the pavement and he held the straw cocked upward, so the cup zoomed along behind him. I dashed madly, trying to keep up and avoid as many raindrops as I could.

I barely kept myself from howling again when Bippity's mouth yawned open, splattering the ground with steaming glop. Then her eyes fell shut, and she slid down into the cup.

"Bippity is dead!" I screamed. "She opened her mouth and her insides came out and she died!"

Boppity's huge paws moved even faster, like a blur.

We splashed from bush to tree to parked car until we reached our backyard and Boppity leaped up onto the porch. His neck twisted sharply to keep the cup level as he scrambled up the baluster onto the railing.

"Aah! Don't dump our dead sister!" I hollered helpfully.

He pushed through the screen, but the cup crashed into it. I pushed the screen open as wide as I could.

He twisted his head, ducking and weaving, to finesse the cup into the small gap. Unsuccessfully.

He blinked, concentrating, and tried again.

"No . . . almost . . . a little more to the left and . . . wait, twist it . . ." I muttered.

"It's not as easy as it *looks*," he snapped. "Keep your commentary to yourself. Unless you think you can do better."

"Sure, okay!" I dropped through the screen and onto the bed, carefully taking the straw in my teeth.

"Wait, no, I wasn't . . ."

"Thanks," I purred. "Would you get the screen, please?"

He pushed the screen open. "So what you want to do is . . ." he started.

I twisted my head down and to the side while keeping the tip of the straw high, then sidestepped twice and rolled my neck, snaking the cup through the narrow opening and popping it into the room, then gently dumping Bippity onto the bed. He stared at me, shocked.

"Yay!" I purred. "I helped!"

"Unghhhh . . ." Bippity moaned.

"You're not dead!" we both shouted at once. She blinked up at Boppity, who was going vague just like she had. "You okay?"

Before he could answer, his third eyelids slid half shut, and he wobbled and fell beside her.

I groomed them both, wringing as much ice-cold water as I could from their fur and licking it up into crests with my tongue-combs to let warm indoor air past their topcoats.

They slept harder than I'd ever seen them sleep before. When they woke up, it had been dark for a long time. They went from groggy to frantic in an instant.

"Becca!" Bippity jumped up. "She's Mila's only hope, and Mayor Adams is going to kill her!"

"We have to save her!" Boppity hollered.

And they were out the window before I could point out that they were in no condition. All I could do was follow.

Chapter Thirty-Three
The Decision

Mila.

"Listen," Deputy Chantelle told Mila, pulling the door to the holding area shut behind her. "Don't say *anything* about your case. Nothing about Becca, nothing about Brandon. Nothing. You're getting transferred to the mainland tonight. Ms. Fi arranged an attorney to meet with you tomorrow morning. Until then, keep doing what you've been doing."

"What, nothing?" Mila pressed her lips together, forcing back the words that wanted to come spilling out.

She'd been struggling all night and all day to accept her fate, but her mind kept traveling back to the way she'd felt sitting in her loft with Ms. Fi and Mugsy and Becca and Brutus and the kittens, surrounded by ridiculous pink and purple fluff, lit by the glow of a lava lamp, laughing and chatting and nibbling on Q's pastries.

She'd felt cared for. Loved. Supported. She'd felt safe. She wondered if she would ever feel that way again.

Their faces filled her mind.

Big gruff Mugsy with his loyal goofball dog and his bushy brows and his rumpled vest and his wry, crooked grin. He was always there for her, even when he'd just been knocked out and nearly killed for trying to help her. In her mind, he whispered, *I'd do anything for you, kid. Anything.*

Ms. Fi, who had started out as a neighbor and landlady, and slowly become so much more. Who scolded and laughed with equal love, always filling her plate with food and her soul with comfort. Her sweet contralto voice murmured, *You don't even have to ask, dearest. Make yourself at home.*

Becca, her first best friend, so ashamed of loving Brandon she'd buried her own pain at his death so she could put Mila first. She'd shown up again and again for Mila, baring her soul with eyes full of remorse and hope. *You're a star. You've always been a star.*

And the kittens. Sitting on her shoulder and snuffling her ear and scolding her, pouncing and leaping and tumbling, purring and chirping and slobbering. Riding in their kangaroo pouch and sleeping on her chest and causing adorable chaos everywhere they went, and somehow making her feel like she was worthy of love just exactly as she was.

She'd finally found the family she'd been searching for all her life, and before she'd had a chance to appreciate them, they were gone.

Taken from her by the murderer.

The realization built up in her chest, stronger with each breath she took. She wanted them back. Even if it meant she had to fight. To throw an unseemly tantrum, the kind her mother would have been ashamed of. To scream at the sky until someone finally believed that she hadn't done anything wrong.

Now Chantelle was telling her to stay quiet. To be good. To do nothing.

She knew it was wise advice. She knew she should listen.

She drew in a deep breath and blew it out slowly. "I need to know how Becca is."

Chantelle's round alabaster face softened. She tucked a strand of blonde hair behind her ear. "She's out of surgery and resting comfortably. They said she might not wake up for a few days, but her prognosis is good." She bit her lip. "Don't tell Pete I told you. He's freaking out. The mayor has been furious about the escalating violence and Pete's lack of action to keep the people of Corvin's Crossing safe. He's been putting us under a microscope for how we've been handling the whole thing, so Pete says we have to do everything strictly by the book."

Mila sighed. "That's why you told me not to say anything."

"Yeah." Chantelle nodded. "We'll be forced to use anything you say as evidence. We don't want any more nails in your coffin. So to speak."

Mila swallowed.

"Can I do anything for you before I head home for the night?" Chantelle asked. "Pete will be off his watch shift at ten, so he should be here in about . . ." she looked down at her watch. "Fifteen minutes or so. He'll be accompanying you to the mainland for your transfer to pretrial holding."

"I'm okay," Mila started. "I—wait. You're heading home and Pete is going on the ferry with me? Who's guarding Becca?"

"Mayor Adams volunteered to take the night shift. Given his service record, we . . ." Chantelle's eyes narrowed. "Why do you ask?"

Mila's restraint cracked. "That's my best friend in the whole world, Chantelle!" She hooked her fingers through the chain link, giving it a furious shake. "And contrary to the beliefs of the bumbling local constabulary or the angry mayor or whoever is calling the shots around here, I didn't have anything to do with her getting stabbed."

Chantelle's face went tight with anger, but Mila couldn't seem to stop herself. "Even if I were the selfish, heartless monster you all seem to think I am, she's my only hope of clearing my good name, since nobody here will believe me." Mila's shoulders slumped. "I just need to know she's safe. I don't think some aging politician is—"

"Mayor Adams is retired Navy. He earned a silver star for valor in combat," Chantelle snapped. "I'm sure he can handle guarding a hospital room. Not that it's any of your business."

Then her face softened. "Look. This is all really hard. On everyone. The pressure they've been putting on Pete and me, it's . . ." She shook her head. "Never mind. My point is, I don't know who did what, but we're all just doing our best to find a way through this thing. I really do hope Becca clears you." She gave Mila a crooked grin. "If so, you're going to be getting so many apology casseroles, you'll never have to cook again."

Mila couldn't force herself to smile. She wouldn't. She held Chantelle's gaze until the deputy gave her a last awkward half-smile and departed.

Her feet carried her back and forth across her cage. In fifteen minutes, Pete would be zip-tying her wrists again and driving her out to the marina, where a ferry would be waiting to take her to the mainland. She just had to wait patiently for Becca to wake up.

Wait. Becca!

Mila shook out her wrist, but the crumpled ball of paper she'd slipped into the secret pocket up her sleeve didn't move. Reaching inside, she pulled it free. It was sticky with dried blood.

She worked carefully at the crusty, half-dried ball, coaxing it open without ripping it. It wasn't even an entire sheet of paper. Less than half. But when she realized what she was holding, she gasped.

Beneath the brighter red that had soaked into the paper, there were dots of dark crimson. The page was mostly blank, but toward the top it held a single line with a messy signature. Below the line, it read *Quincy Adams, Member 2 (Secretary).*

Mayor Adams! Of course! The mayor hadn't just been taking bribes, he'd been in on Brandon's whole scheme. But the payouts Brandon had been making to the mayor were relatively small, especially considering how big his risk was.

Maybe the mayor had wanted a bigger cut. That would explain the meeting at Rousseau's. Brandon had mentioned whatever dirty little secret was in his file, to keep the mayor in his place and force him to put through the paperwork for the Land Trust.

But now, as the only surviving member of Commodore Holdings, Mayor Adams could take over Brandon's entire scheme. He would have sole control of what happened to Luxe once Mr. Cavendish's bankruptcy filing went through.

Only one thing still didn't make sense. How did Becca get her hands on this crucial bit of evidence? Surely, she—wait. Becca!

Mila's heart jumped into her throat.

Mayor Adams would be going on shift as her guard in ten minutes or so. As soon as the hospital staff left her room for the night, he'd be free to finish her. He'd probably make it look like an accident. Mila would go to prison for his crimes, and he'd be off somewhere living like a king.

The fury that had been building in Mila's chest ever since Pete had locked her in this cage erupted like a volcano. She couldn't let her best friend be murdered, and she wouldn't stand for that slimy mayor stealing her life from her. Focusing her rage like a laser, she rolled her neck.

"I'm coming, Becca," she whispered.

Grabbing the lid of the toilet tank with both hands, she flung the heavy hunk of porcelain to the floor, where it exploded with a massive crash. She took apart the assembly, pulled out the flapper hook, and straightened it, using a jagged shard of porcelain to bend its tip at a right angle.

Now she had a lockpick.

"Can't cage a magician," she smirked.

She grabbed the long, thin flush lever and poked it out through one of the chain links, feeding it between the arms of the lock shank. When she twisted it toward her, the bottom of the lock was forced upward so she could reach the keyhole from inside her cell. In a matter of seconds, she had it open.

She let herself into the office to retrieve her purse. Moments later, she was darting through the shadows of the alley behind the station, heading for the green.

Her heart hammered in her ears. She was officially on the run from the police. For the first time in her life, she'd broken the law. She knew she should feel ashamed or afraid. But all she felt was elated and furious.

"Hang on, Becca," she said as her car's engine sputtered to life. "I'm coming."

Chapter Thirty-Four
The Fall

Bippity.

"Where are we going?" Boop asked.

"To rescue Becca!" Boppity growled. "Weren't you listening?"

"Boop is actually right," I said. "We don't know where we're going. We just know the hospital is in Wilby's Woods somewhere. But Hylia said to stay away from there."

"But we have to save Becca, or we'll never see Mila again!" Boppity set his feet. He was ready to fight.

"Easy, General," I told him. "You're right, but I need another strategic recommendation from you. How can we get protection and help finding our way through the forest?"

Boop waved their tail wildly from side to side.

Boppity snorted. "You don't even look like a cat. You look like a—that's it! A dog! Brutus! Maybe he'll know where the hospital is and how to be safe in the woods!"

My chest swelled with pride at my impressive brother. "Excellent, General Boppity. Lead the way."

Boppity raised his chin and led us back to the vet's office, and it was easy getting back in through the window.

Inside, a human lay snoring on a cot in the room full of cages. Boppity darted from shadow to shadow, practicing his rat tactics, and we followed along.

Brutus was in his cage, sound asleep.

I lifted a paw to poke him.

"Wait!" Boppity jumped between me and the cage. "If you startle him, he might bark and wake the human. Boop?"

I turned to my sibling, who sidled up to the cage. A low, even purr rumbled in their chest, wrapping us in a sound-blanket of soothing safety. They trilled gently.

Brutus's ear twitched and his eyes opened. "Kittens?" He wagged a friendly greeting. "What are you doing here?"

"Hello, friend." I offered him a little bow. "We came because we know you understand the importance of protecting our humans from harm."

"And you have the courage to do what it takes to keep them safe," Boppity added.

"Yes." I nodded. "Our human is in trouble."

"Mila?" Brutus leaped to his feet. "Oh no! What's wrong?"

"Becca got stabbed, and Mila was arrested. Now Becca is the only one who can identify the real killer. We have to save her or Mila will be trapped in the human pound forever."

"No!" Brutus's tail drooped and his eyebrow whiskers rose up like worried peaks in front of his purple bandage. "That's terrible!"

"Can you tell us how to find the hospital?" Boop widened their eyes, their pupils dilating. Suddenly, they looked irresistible. "Please?"

"I know where it is." Brutus tilted his head. "But I can't let you go alone. You'll never make it through the woods."

"We have to try!" Boppity insisted.

"Can you open my cage?" he asked. "I can protect you."

Boppity and I were examining the cage door when Boop shouldered in. They pushed their paw into an indentation in the handle, pressing it in and lifting. With a tinny click, the latch released.

"Hey!" Boppity turned to them. "How did you do that?"

"With my paw, silly," Boop purred.

We hurried to the front of the office, where Boppity entangled a coffee cup on the front desk with the front door lock. After a few tries, he got it unlocked and pulled open a few inches. Brutus shoved his muzzle through the gap. While Boppity untangled the mug from the door latch, Brutus shouldered into the gap and leaned against the door, pushing it wide. We darted out into the night.

"Let me check my scent map." Brutus lifted his nose into the cool breeze. Its tip twitched a few times, and then his posture went rigid and his ears perked up. "Got it! Let's go!"

We followed his huge, dark form, running as fast as we could.

As we ran, a new fragrance began to build on the briny air. It smelled secret. Clever. Dark. Old.

Brutus turned to check on us. "The forest is up ahead. Stay close."

Soon, trees rose up on either side of the road. Brutus darted sharply, heading into the thick of the woods.

"Why are we going in here?" I asked. I was the leader. I shouldn't be afraid.

"It's safer than the road," Brutus shouted over the thud of his galloping paws. "No cars. And it'll get you to the hospital faster. But when we get there, I need to go back. I can't be caught out of my cage like this."

I swallowed my fear. I couldn't imagine how we could protect Becca from Mayor Adams all by ourselves. But if anyone could find a way, it was Boppity.

Something huge leaped from the top of a tree and soared toward us. It was impossibly fast, with huge yellow eyes.

And it was heading straight at me.

I froze, panic rampaging through me. My fur stood on end. My mouth opened and a scream built in my throat.

Before it could get out, though, there was a rustle and a thump. Abruptly, Brutus was standing over me, fearless and powerful and gloriously fiery.

"Fight!" he barked out. His voice was bold and sharp. It echoed through the dark.

The huge beast veered in midair and swerved off through the woods.

"Chase! Chase!" he called, leaping after it. His tail whipped through the air behind him as his paws shushed against the leafy forest floor.

"Chase!" Boppity agreed, matching his land-devouring strides with shocking speed. Before I knew what was happening, their paw-falls had faded into silence as they vanished into the night.

"Wait!" I yowled. "Stop!"

But I was too late. I stared at the maze of trees and bushes and thorny brambles that no longer showed any sign of their passage. I strained my ears, but all I could hear were the songs of small creatures wooing the moon and each other.

Cold, prickly fear grew inside me, freezing my paws to the ground. Boop was still and silent beside me, their eyes as wide as two dark moons.

One coyote or fox or lynx was all it would take to vanish Boppity from the world forever. What if he couldn't keep up with Brutus? What if something snatched him in its jaws, faster than—

My thought was cut off by a crashing noise racing toward us. Before we could react, Brutus burst through a bush, Boppity close on his heels.

"It got away!" He shook his whole body, flinging motes of dirt and leaf into the breeze like a sideways tornado. "It won't come back." He wagged proudly, then turned. "Now come! This way!"

I swallowed my chaotic panic, listening to the bouncing cadence of Boop's deep purrs, louder each time their paws hit the ground and softer as they flew through the air between gallops. The wind whistled in my ear-fur. This whole thing was terrifying, but maybe it was a tiny bit magical, too.

After the right number of trees and bushes and thorns, Brutus stopped in front of a big square building made of very old logs. The ocean smell was all around us.

Brutus wagged with joy when Boop told him how brave and noble he was. He zagged off into the darkness before I could even say thank-you.

I examined the boxy wooden building. "There's an open window," I said. "But it's got a screen, like ours at home."

"Don't worry," Boppity assured me. "I'll handle it."

He leaped directly at the building, hooking his claws into it and scaling it until he reached the window. Nestling his hindquarters into the corner of the window-frame, he swiped at the screen, his huge, gleaming claws unfurled.

"Take that!" he shouted. "Ha! And that!" Soon, there was a generous hole. He pushed himself through easily.

"Ooooooo!" Boop said when their claws hooked into the wood. They clambered up and down, this way and that, hopping and catching themself, snickering under their breath about gravity and how it had no power here.

"Boop! Focus!" I scolded. They pushed through the opening and vanished.

The climb to the window was indeed fun, but I was far too dignified to play. On the other side of the screen was a long drop. I froze, fear stiffening my muscles.

It was so dark, I couldn't even see the floor. It was too far. The long, terrifying fall from Mila's shoulder replayed in my mind, over and over. My belly felt like it was dropping out of my body. I remembered dead Brandon, who had looked hollow, like the life had been punched out of his body by the ground and nothing was left.

I couldn't do it. I couldn't jump into the darkness.

I tried to order the photons in the room to show me the floor, but there were too few of them. The effort made my head pound.

Jump, I commanded my body. *This is for Mila. We have to save her. Jump!*

But my paws wouldn't move.

A rumbling purr rose up from somewhere below, washing over me. "Trust," came Boop's chirping voice, high over the deep, soothing vibrations. I couldn't see their body language, so I only had their voice-sounds to go on. "Safe. Catch."

I started to shake. Boop's purrs deepened until I couldn't hear them anymore, but they vibrated through my bones, like warmth and comfort. Like snuggling under Mother's floof, or being groomed by Hylia. Like Mila's laughing voice and her low chuckle when I whispered in her ear.

"Safe," Boop trilled again. "Trust."

I wanted to be the kind of leader they could be proud of. The kind who put her family first. The kind Mother had always said I could be. I wanted to make her proud. More than that, I wanted my family to be safe. My siblings needed me. And Mila needed us.

Boop's words at Ms. Fi's house filled my mind. *Facing scary things is the bravest,* they'd said, their round face full of sweet, uncomplicated love. *I believe in you.*

I could be worthy of them.

I could, and I would.

Blowing out a deep breath, I threw myself into the darkness. My eyes squeezed shut as gravity clutched me in its hateful fist, whipping me down toward the hard floor with vicious, murderous glee.

Foomp!

I landed in something fluffy and felt myself sinking slowly to the ground.

I wasn't dead!

I could barely believe I'd done it. I had jumped for my family. Finally, I'd shown that I had the courage of a true leader. Boop padded up to me, eyes wide disks of black rimmed in deep sky-blue.

"I knew you could do it," they purred. "You're the bravest. We're so lucky to have you as our Queenlet."

Boppity held something long and thin and wooden in his mouth. "Your majesty," he said, offering me his most courtly bow. He tilted his head and a door swung open, spilling blessed light in from a hallway, and revealing our room. It was clean and empty, with two white beds. One was missing its pillow.

Looking down, I saw that it sat beneath me. Boppity's gaze leaped between a pencil in his teeth and the lever-style knob of the door he'd just opened.

My chest swelled with gratitude for my siblings. How could I ever hope to express such a momentous feeling?

Pencil in mouth, Boppity flew out of the room. He zigged and zagged, darting nimbly into a shadow before I could say *wait.*

Or *thank you.*

Boop squeezed their eyes half shut, rumbling their purr through me like a hug for one deep breath, then raced after Boppity, making their best effort to mimic his sharp, tactical darting.

They looked like a fluffy black tumbleweed.

I zipped out behind them, bringing up the rear and scanning the area for danger.

In front of us was a hexagonal open space with an island-shaped desk at its center like Q's cases of baked goods, but this one had computers and files. Above it, a sign read *Inpatient East Wing.* Instead of canisters of tea, the back wall was lined with drawers of tools and supplies. The whole place smelled sharp and unpleasant.

There were no humans in sight.

Around the sides of the open area were three other doors and two long hallways. Above one corridor was a sign that read, *Intake, Triage, & Emergency Medicine.* The other said, *Diagnostics & Inpatient West Wing.*

In the shadows ahead, Boppity lifted his nose and flared his nostrils delicately, sniffing. I almost told him not to be ridiculous. He wasn't a dog. But I didn't want to scold him when he'd just saved me, so I kept quiet. He'd figure it out soon enough.

"I smell Becca," he said. "She smells like barn. Leather polish and hay and horse sweat and sunshine."

I took an exploratory sniff, but I couldn't smell anything.

"I smell the mayor, too," he continued. "Cologne and wool and sea air."

Sea air? Wool? Cologne? But Brutus had said the attacker smelled like . . . "Wait!" I shouted. "It's not him!"

But he was already running again, his gaze leaping between the pencil in his mouth and the lever-handle of the door he was approaching. I barely had time to shoo away his light as he tilted his head and the handle dropped.

Clenching my jaw against the shocks of pain arcing through my head as I pushed my command of physics to its limit, I shooed away Boop's light and mine, too.

The door flew open. Inside the large hospital room, a bed near the back wall held an unconscious Becca. An empty chair sat near the bed, and in front of it sprawled Mayor Adams, also unconscious.

And standing between the wall and the bed, bending over Becca and holding a syringe, was Ms. Scarborough.

Chapter Thirty-Five
The Hero

Boppity.

The murderer was unconscious, a partially eaten cookie beside him on the floor. The nice cookie lady was looking down at Becca, holding a syringe and a little bottle. I was invisible, pencil and all. It had happened before I could blink.

I disentangled my pencil and darted into the room, tucking myself into the shadows beneath the chair. My siblings arrived beside me, leaning into me for comfort.

Bippity was swaying like she had at Q's. She was going to lose her grip on the photons any second. Boop was shaking with fear for some reason.

"What the . . . ?" the cookie lady, Ms. Scarborough, looked at the open door with wild eyes. "Who opened the door? Hello? Who's there?"

She craned her neck, throwing her gaze over our hiding place and out into the empty east wing.

"Huh," she grunted. "Missy's on break for at least ten more minutes. Must have been a draft or something."

She turned her attention back to Becca. "As I was saying, dear, I hope you can hear me. I need you to know how hard this is. So much harder than that crooked lawyer. Especially after he figured out what had happened to my husband. Vern was easiest of all." Her lips twisted in a humorless smile.

Why was Boop shaking so hard? Everything seemed to be okay. Ms. Scarborough had already defeated the mayor. It seemed like she was protecting Becca, too. Clearly, she'd defeated some other villains in her time. But the trembling beside me increased, and now there was a scratchy, anxious feeling building in my chest.

Bippity gave a nearly inaudible meow, crawling into the deeper shadows under the bed. "Trying. Can't. Soon."

Poor Boop's pupils grew as wide as full moons beside her nearly closed ones.

My brave sister was pushing herself to her limit, trying to keep me safe. I wanted to join my siblings under the bed, but I had to stay here. I had to see what was happening. The jagged feeling in my chest was growing, and Boop was shaking harder and harder.

I had to protect Becca.

Footsteps thundered toward us.

I turned to see the most beautiful human in the world racing toward the doorway, lit from behind by a nimbus of flickering fluorescent lights.

Mila!

My joy at seeing her again was so powerful, I nearly raced out of the shadows to greet her before I remembered that Becca was in danger.

"Ms. Scarborough!" Mila exclaimed. "Of course! Becca found that ripped paper from the murder scene hidden at the farm. And you've been drugging your cookies so Mr. Cavendish wouldn't hear you coming and going. That's why I was so wobbly the night your house caught on fire. I only had a little nibble, but . . ." Mila's eyes drifted from the unconscious mayor on the floor to the mostly-eaten cookie beside his still form.

"Mila!" Ms. Scarborough exclaimed. "How . . . ?" She shook her head, her eyes taking on a piercing, intent focus, like a hunter locking onto prey. She grabbed the tubing beside Becca's bed and lifted her syringe. "I just need to . . ."

"Stop!" Mila lurched forward, but she was all the way across the room.

I knew there was danger. But all Ms. Scarborough had was a vaccination. They only hurt for a minute. I couldn't see the threat, so I didn't know how to stop her.

"I can't . . ." Bippity shuddered, her legs buckling. Reappearing abruptly, I shoved myself into the darkest shadow under the chair.

Boop stared at me from beneath the bed, eyes so wide with fear their irises were practically swallowed in black. "Murderer!" their eyes screamed from the pitch-dark. "Stop her!"

The itchy feeling in my chest expanded until it swallowed me whole. My teeth sank into the shaft of the pencil as time slowed to a virtual standstill.

Abruptly, my body buzzed with unfamiliar sensations.

I realized with a jolt that I was feeling three sets of lungs and twelve shaky paws. I'd only felt this way once before, at the vet's office, when we liberated the water and avoided the broken glass on the floor.

But this time, the connection was absolute. It overtook me entirely. I struggled to hold onto myself in the chaos of being in three places at once. Bippity's exhaustion pulled at me like a black hole, drawing me toward the quiet calm of unconsciousness.

Rage filled my chest. *Nothing* was going to stop us from protecting Mila. I felt three sets of lips curl back against three sets of sharp, furious fangs.

There before me was my own body, bold and tiny and clutching a pencil longer than his long, stiff tail.

My tail.

I was looking at myself through two sets of eyes. One view was bright and chaotic, overrun with vivid colors and shards of light like nothing I'd ever seen before. The other was blurry and nearly closed, pushing back at the darkness with a will as strong as steel.

I squeezed my eyes shut, confused. What did it mean? What was I supposed to do? I was ready to fight for my family. Ready to die for them, if that was what it would take to save them.

But I didn't understand how.

Through the darkness, the image of a syringe filled my mind. It was surrounded by a terrible black haze, and razor-fierce lines of venomous green shot out of the fluid it held.

That's the weapon. Bippity's voice rang clear and certain in my mind, drained but determined. *Poison.*

I opened my eyes to see Ms. Scarborough poking the tip of her weapon into Becca's tubing.

Poison.

The itchy feeling in my chest burst, severing the connection. I was back to being just one tiny kitten with two eyes and four paws.

A kitten who had to stop a murderer.

Fast as a flash, I entangled my pencil with the syringe, still forging the qubit bonds as I whipped my head upward, *fyooing* it into the air.

My skull was suddenly pounding like rocks being smashed together. The bonds I was pulling together snapped like rubber bands breaking. My jaw went slack and the pencil fell from my numb mouth. The syringe flew over the bed and landed in the chair above me.

I wavered, but managed to stay on my paws.

"What?" Ms. Scarborough looked at her empty hand, confused.

Then her gaze snapped to Mila. "Trickery." Her voice was cold. She pulled something oily and black from her pocket and aimed it at Mila with a metallic click.

A gun.

"Actually," Ms. Scarborough said, "this might be a blessing in disguise. Get in here and shut the door."

I trembled as Mila walked in and pulled the door closed. Now I had to protect her *and* Becca. And I was barely on my paws. I tried to draw in a deep breath, but all I managed was a shuddering gasp.

"It was you arguing with Brandon in the back alley," Mila said, spreading her hands in the air. "You must have figured out that Brandon and the mayor were conspiring to bankrupt Luxe."

Ms. Scarborough waved the gun in the air, guiding Mila toward the chair. "I knew all along. But Brandon told me he was doing it to save Corvin's Crossing. To keep it from becoming just another tawdry Vegas knockoff overrun by tourists. Now pick up that syringe. Bring it here."

No, Mila, I wanted to shout. But I couldn't seem to move. *Poison. Death.* My paws were too heavy. I swayed, fighting to cling to consciousness.

Mila lowered her hands. "You were trying to save your home." She nodded. "But Brandon had something on you. Mr. Scarborough's illness, plus the real estate listing for . . . wait. Did you poison him?"

"He was going to sell my farm to a developer. He didn't care what it would do to Corvin's Crossing. He just wanted to be rich. I tried to talk sense into him, but back then, the way mortgages worked, I couldn't stop him."

Awareness dawned on Mila's face. "You threatened to reveal Brandon's corruption, and he pulled you inside of Mugsy's. You held up your proof, but he snatched it. Probably said something condescending. I can picture the sneer on his face."

"Yes. He said he'd show the sheriff his evidence, and they'd exhume Vern and test his hair. Then they'd know I'd killed him." Her eyes narrowed. "Men always underestimate what I'm capable of. What I'll do to protect my home." Ms. Scarborough shook herself and jabbed the gun toward Mila. "The syringe. Grab it! Now!"

"Okay! Easy!" Mila reached over to the chair and lifted the syringe. "Here it is. I'm bringing it over. I'm—whoa!" Mila stumbled on the mayor's foot. "What exactly did you put in that cookie? Is he dead?"

Ms. Scarborough's eyes darted to the prone form of the mayor. "No. At least not yet. It's my usual recipe, just double-strength. Ketamine from the farm. It's used to sedate horses."

"Is that what you're going to give Becca?" Mila twisted her wrist, gesturing toward the bed. "Ketamine?"

Ms. Scarborough nodded. "Yes. It's painless. She won't feel a thing. Now hurry up. Get over here!" She shook her gun again.

Mila drew in a deep, shaky breath. "I can't. I can't do this."

"You don't have a choice." Ms. Scarborough's voice was hard as ice.

Beneath the bed, Boop's irises widened until their pupils were tiny black points. I felt their purr rumble through me, as low and deep and comforting as pure, endless love.

Mila's breathing steadied. I thought I heard her whisper, *I'm a star. I've always been a star.*

"What?" Ms. Scarborough growled.

"Nothing. I'm here." Mila stepped up beside Ms. Scarborough, holding out her hands.

They were empty! Mila had vanished the syringe like Mr. Cavendish's watch. My chest bloomed with pride.

"Where's the syringe?" Ms. Scarborough shouted. "Give it to me!"

Mila held up her hands. "I don't have it, ma'am. I—"

Ms. Scarborough jammed the gun against Mila's chest, her face twisting with fury. Mila drew in a gasp of terror. I tried to launch myself from the shadows, but I was too weak. My paws wouldn't budge.

But Boop's purrs rumbled on. Love as deep and steady as the bones of the world flowed from their core in waves and vibrated through me.

"Okay! Don't shoot!" Mila panted, eyes wide. "Here!" She twisted her wrist and rolled her hand over to reveal the syringe.

Ms. Scarborough snatched it, pocketing her gun and reaching for Becca's IV tube.

Mila stumbled again, catching herself on the bed. She barely grazed Ms. Scarborough's arm, but the woman screamed in pain. Brutus must have done some real damage to it.

"Clumsy girl!" Ms. Scarborough hissed through clenched teeth. "Watch it." She shoved Mila away.

"I'm sorry." Mila shook her head. "I know you're only doing this to protect Corvin's Crossing. I even understand why you framed me. Why you broke into my apartment and stole my other knife. But why did you burn down your own farm? Surely not just to make me look guiltier?"

Ms. Scarborough squeezed her eyes shut. "No. It was partly that, of course. But I didn't plan on killing Brandon. I just wanted to stop him. Once he was dead, there was nothing to keep Mayor Adams from taking over his scheme. I needed time to figure out what to do next."

Mila nodded. "I see. Mr. Cavendish's death would have frozen Luxe's finances until they cleared probate. No bankruptcy filing. No corrupt sale to the holding company in the Caymans."

Mila offered a sympathetic smile. "I get it, Ms. Scarborough. Corvin's Crossing is special. It needs to be preserved. And if you're not here to look after it, nobody will."

Ms. Scarborough's chin trembled. "That's right." She looked down at Becca. "You're a good girl. You never deserved the hand life dealt you. And you don't deserve this. But I have to do it. Corvin's Crossing is more important than any one life."

Lifting the syringe, she grabbed the IV tube.

She fumbled for a moment, confused. Then her face contorted in rage. "Where's the tip?" She wheeled to face Mila.

Clever Mila! How had she done that? She'd broken the needle off of the syringe. Becca was safe!

"You!" Ms. Scarborough screeched, whipping the gun from her pocket and pointing it at Mila's face.

Mila froze.

My heart hammered in my chest. I watched as Ms. Scarborough's expression slowly melted from fury into a calm that was a hundred times more terrifying.

"This is better, actually," Ms. Scarborough murmured. "I can say you attacked me and I was forced to defend myself. I'll get two new syringes and give Becca and the mayor fatal doses of ketamine. I'll put your prints on the syringes and the bottle and put them in your pocket. When I call 911, they'll put it all together. A final tragedy, but at least your rampage will be at an end. We'll all be safe." She was nodding to herself. "So all I have to do . . . is shoot you."

"No, Ms. Scarborough," Mila's eyes were huge. A tear streamed down her cheek.

Mila was going to die.

Forcing my paws to move felt like ripping myself apart, but Mila was worth it. I bolted out from the shadows beneath the chair and flew under the bed, racing toward her.

Mila shook her head. "Please," she begged. "No."

But Ms. Scarborough was nodding slowly. "Yes. I'm sorry Mila. But this is it. Goodbye."

I hadn't even made it out from beneath the bed. I wasn't going to get to her in time.

I was too weak. Too slow. *Mila!*

Click.

My paws skidded against the icy linoleum and my eyes squeezed shut.

I couldn't make myself look.

"Really?" Mila asked. "You were really going to shoot me in the face?"

Mila?

How was that possible?

I opened my eyes. Her face looked as perfect as ever.

Click. Click.

"I don't understand." Ms. Scarborough sputtered, shaking the gun and squeezing it again and again. "I—"

Click. Click. Click.

The door to the hospital room flew open. Sheriff Pete burst through, gun drawn, with Deputy Chantelle behind him. "Hold it right there, Mila! Don't move a . . ." Sheriff Pete's voice went from ferocious to confused as he took in the scene.

Understanding dawned on his face and the tip of his pistol swung from Mila to Ms. Scarborough. "Drop your gun and put your hands up," he said. "You're under arrest for murder, arson, breaking and entering, vandalism, and attempted murder."

She deflated as the sheriff pulled her arms behind her back and zip-tied her wrists together.

Mila lifted her empty palms into the air. "Sorry, Ms. Scarborough, but I had to stall you until Pete got here."

"But . . ." Ms. Scarborough spluttered. "But where did my bullets go?"

Mila's lips quirked up into a crooked smile. "Becca, if you can hear me, thanks for believing in me even when I didn't. This is for you."

She held her palms out toward Ms. Scarborough, wriggling her fingers.

"Bippity . . ."

Drawing herself up tall, she arced her hands through the air like she was tracing the contours of a big ball of light.

"Boppity . . ."

As her hands curved down into a bowl shape, she suddenly clapped them together with a resounding *smack.*

"Boop!"

Bullets fell to the floor like rain.

I couldn't believe my eyes. It was magic! Real magic! Maybe Mila was a kitten in human form. That was the only explanation.

When they heard their name, Boop raced out from under the bed and flung themself onto Mila's leg, scaling her in a flash and shoving themself up beneath her chin. I nudged my stirring sister, propping her up as we staggered out behind them.

"Kittens!" A shocked laugh escaped her. She knelt to scoop us up. Salty rain raced down her cheeks, mingling with the warm, beautiful sound of her laughter.

The purr that rumbled to life in the chest of my exhausted sister was almost as loud as Boop's. As I grabbed Mila's face with my paws, licking her tears joyfully, I realized that I was purring too.

"But wait!" She pulled back to look at us. "Where did you come from?"

Boop tilted their head to the side, their eyes going wide. "You can never know!" they chirped, waving their tail in the air like a stubby little flag of victory.

Chapter Thirty-Six

The Beginning

Boop.

Mila parked her car in the alley behind Mugsy's theater. Bippity and Boppity leaned into me, vivid with excitement, and I purred at the comforting weight of them crushing into my ribs. Behind the dumpster, a gust of wind crisp with an early hint of autumn lifted our old box, now weathered and warped almost beyond recognition, and sent it tumbling. The big steel door to the club banged open.

"Hurry up, kid," Mugsy rumbled. But he was surrounded by his typical cloud of fondness, way too fluffy for his gruff tone. Tonight, there was something new in his energy, something I hadn't noticed during the shows we'd been doing five nights a week all summer.

Mugsy hefted Mila's shiny new case, which bore a cartoon image of a human magician in a purple cape. Three large black kitten faces peered in on the image from the edges. Emblazoned across the case in glittery purple was the name of their new act: *Mila's Magic Kittens.*

Brutus raced up, wagging, as Mila followed Mugsy into the backstage area, lugging the rest of her gear.

"Good dog," I told him. He wagged. I purred.

I closed my eyes, allowing the sudden awareness of the many, many humans on the far side of the big red curtain-wall to wash over me. The sound that shushed off of them and into the air was like a friendly, excited mix of purring and humming.

All of the humans we knew were out there. I could feel them. Gentle Doc who had taken such good care of us when we were weak and sick, and who had saved brave Brutus. The delicious, mysterious Chef Rousseau. Becca, with her hay and sunshine smell and her quiet, complicated hope. Q, wrapped in a cloud of cinnamon and comfort.

The staff at the hospital where Becca had stayed.

Jut-chested Mr. Cavendish with his shiny nose-tails, and the many mourners from the church, and Reverend Bak with his golden glow, and spotted Jenny who had been so generous with her water and who had helped Mila name us. All of the firefighters and rescue workers from the farm fire. Sweet, stern Ms. Fi with a smile as bright as a sunrise. Even remorse-soft, hopeful Sheriff Pete and his deputy, Chantelle.

Over and around my awareness of these familiar humans, though, between and beneath them, were the smells and moods and emotions of strangers. More every time, crammed into the crannies around tables where there was only room to stand. Too many to count. None of them knew us now, but by the time we were done, I was certain that we'd have filled them all with wonder.

As Mugsy helped Mila set up her props and check the lighting panel, I once again felt that new something hovering around him. It flitted like a songbird, bright and fleet. There was a secret in the air. The good kind. Mila set the three of us on our little table in the center of the stage.

"Secret," I said to my siblings.

"What?" Bippity asked.

"Boop is just saying random stuff again," Boppity told her. "Focus." My siblings were reviewing the act for the evening to make sure there was no way for the humans to detect their tiny bursts of physics. Mila and Mugsy were convinced that well-trained kittens and perfectly timed lighting changes were the keys to her success as a magician, and my siblings were careful to maintain the illusion.

The first Law of Cats was honored.

I trusted them to keep it that way. They were getting really good at it.

I thought about telling them again that there was a grand secret zipping around in the air, waiting to be named. But I figured they'd find out soon enough.

I watched them fondly, my purr deepening in my chest.

Once everything was set up, Mugsy clapped Mila on the back as usual. But this time he said, "I've got something to tell you, kid."

"What is it?" she asked, her eyes fixed on the red curtain.

Mugsy made a hairball noise in his throat. "I got a call last night from the Royal Theatre in London. They want to book you for a six-week run with an option to renew." He grinned. "You're on your way, kid."

"What?" she squeaked.

"Yup," he nodded. "That big-time life is calling you. Champagne and caviar. Sky's the limit. Don't forget us little folk when you get there."

She launched herself at him, flinging her arms around his neck. "I can't believe it!" she squealed. But I could tell by the burst of brilliant elation in her chest that she believed every word.

She buried her face in his shoulder, and I felt the happiness flooding from her in waves. "Thank you, Mugsy," she whispered into his shirt. "I could never forget you. You're my family. You and Becca and Ms. Fi."

"And us!" I trilled.

"And of course you kittens," she agreed. I purred my delight at her wisdom. We knew who our family was. And we knew something else, too. Something important. A cardboard box, a car, a duplex, a loft, a theater . . . as long as we were together, anywhere we went was home.

He patted her back awkwardly. "Okay," he grunted. "Okay, kid. Alright." Extracting himself from her embrace, he stepped back. A *rumph* sound escaped from his throat. As he shuffled over to Brutus, I heard him mutter, "Proud of you, Mila."

Mila whooped as she leaped up and down. Hope and glee bloomed gloriously from every inch of her.

"See?" I said to my siblings.

Bippity's eyes grew wide. "You know what this means?"

"What?" I tilted my head and purred.

Bippity tried to give me a disgusted look, but only for a moment. Then she turned to Boppity, the excitement in her eyes electric.

I knew she wanted to tell us. She was bursting to. I looked at her expectantly, my face carefully blank, even though I did know what it meant.

I knew exactly what it meant.

Love. Joy. Fun.

Adventure.

Names and Places

Becca Varma—bartender at Mugsy's Club, housekeeper and barn-worker at Scarborough Farms

Bippity—female kitten of the litter, generally considers herself to be the leader

Biscuit—one of Ms. Scarborough's goats (along with Cookie)

Boop—kitten who eschews the human concept of gender, source of all the best purring

Boppity—male kitten of the litter, master tactician, world's fiercest warrior

Brandon Jameson—Mila's boyfriend and manager, and Corvin's Crossing's all-purpose lawyer

Brutus—Mugsy's brindle pit bull

Chantelle—Sheriff's Deputy and second-in-command of law enforcement in Corvin's Crossing

Chef Michon Rousseau, owner and chef of Rousseau's, a fine French restaurant and possibly the closest thing to Heaven on Earth

Names and Places

Cookie—one of Ms. Scarborough's goats (along with Biscuit)
Corvin's Crossing—the small island on which our tale takes place
Doc—short for Dr. Ladonna, veterinarian of Corvin's Crossing
Fi—aka Ms. Fi, Mila's neighbor and landlady
Hylia—the cat living next door to Mila and Brandon, owner of Ms. Fi
Jenny—veterinary technician/office assistant at Doc's veterinarian office
Larissa—Mayor Adams's administrative assistant (shhhh . . . she has a crush on Jenny)
Luxe Hotel & Resort—high-end resort hotel under development on the southern coast
Mary Scarborough—owner of Scarborough Farms B&B and maker of delicious bedtime cookies
Mayor Quincy Adams—mayor of Corvin's Crossing
Mayor's Office—the front portion of the front building in the municipal complex, where Mayor Adams and Larissa work
Mila MacAllister—stage magician and Bippity, Boppity, and Boop's human
Mitchum Cavendish—Mainlander and corporate bigwig; owner of Luxe Hotel & Resort
Mugsy—owner of Mugsy's Club, human of Brutus, and cranky old bear
Mugsy's Club—a pub and performance venue; our kittens are discovered in the alley behind it
Municipal Complex—a two-building red-brick complex hosting Corvin's Crossing municipal offices and services, including the mayor's office and the sheriff's station
Municipal Parking Lot—a free parking lot at the end of the alley shared by Mugsy's pub and the Municipal complex
Pete Goff—sheriff of Corvin's Crossing

Q—Owner of Q Tea Pie

Q Tea Pie—Corvin's Crossing's local tea shoppe and bakery, a favorite place for gossiping

Reverend Bak—Leader of the Corvin's Crossing United Church of Christ

Rosemary—one of Ms. Scarborough's horses (along with Sage & Thyme)

Rousseau's—fine French cuisine (see Chef Michon Rousseau)

Sage—one of Ms. Scarborough's horses (along with Rosemary & Thyme), living lie-detector

Scarborough Farms Bed & Breakfast—local B&B and barn/farm run by widow Ms. Scarborough

Thyme—one of Ms. Scarborough's horses (along with Sage & Rosemary)

Wilby's Woods—spooky but lovely mixed evergreen and deciduous forest in the northwestern quadrant of the island

Content Warnings (including spoilers)

As a trauma survivor, I appreciate when authors give me the option to prepare myself for potentially triggering content. Below is a partial list of such themes and subjects. Spoilers are included, so please decide what's best for you.

No animals are killed in this story, unless you count food.

Corpse (human), on-page
Death (human), off-page
Falling (human, dead body), on-page
Falling (cat, non-fatal), on-page
Fire, house and barn, on-page
Food, described and eaten (human, feline, and canine), on-page
Grief, loss of mother (feline), on-page
Infidelity (human), off-page

Content Warnings (including spoilers)

Injury (canine), off-page
Medical care and first-aid (human), on-page
Murder (human), off-page
Needle vaccination (feline), on-page
Needle, IV (human), on-page
Negative self-talk (human and feline), on-page
Orphans (feline), on-page
Sedation, narcotic, involuntary/nonconsensual (human), on-page
Sexism, historical (human), off-page
Stabbing (human, nonfatal and fatal), off-page
Strangulation (human, nonfatal), off-page
Verbal abuse (mild), on-page
Veterinary care and first-aid (feline and canine), on-page

Acknowledgments

First, I want to offer my most heartfelt thanks to you, reader. Every good book is an act of co-creation between the author and the reader who interprets and imagines the story it holds, filling in details and letting it unfold in your mind. Whoever you are, wherever you are, my deepest thanks go out to you for being my partner in bringing Mila and her kittens to life. I couldn't have done it without you.

There are more people to thank for helping this book make the long journey from my mind to your hands than there are furs in the longest, floofiest tail of the queenliest queen who ever was. Here are some of the shiny ones:

April and Kaya, there isn't a big enough word for *gratitude* in any language I've studied. I know you're in my dedication, but it bears repeating. Your love, support, enthusiasm . . . heck, just the sheer number of times you read new drafts of the dang thing . . . I'm boggled at how I got lucky enough to have you both in my life. You're miraculous, and I adore you.

Acknowledgments

Every writer needs a community of others whose writing inspires us and whose feedback shines a new light on our work. Along with April, I want to thank Alice, whom I met in the querying trenches, Lily, whom I met in a flash fiction competition, and Em, whom I met a million years ago because of soup fairies. You are the cornerstones of the great library in my brain, and without you, it would soon crumble to dust.

Marisa Corvisiero, my agent, for being wise and honest and kind, and for always having my back.

Denise Zaza, my editor, for falling in love with my kittens and encouraging Mila to be the hero of her own story, for your brilliant editorial vision, and for your unflagging support, clarity, and patience as it came to life on the page.

The entire team at Crooked Lane Books, whose professionalism, positivity, and commitment to excellence are matched only by your delightful personalities and your passion for bringing stories to the people who love them. Thaisheemarie Fantauzzi Pérez, Marcia Santore, Dulce Botello, Mikaela Bender, Megan Matti, Rebecca Nelson, Stephanie Manova, Julia Abbott, Lexi Baker, Bethany Pullen, and Matthew Martz, you make the world a better place every day.

Dave, for your music recommendations, your wit, and your willingness to play video games for me and April and Kaya late into the night. It takes a lot of media to keep my hungry mind fed, and you always have the tastiest morsels. Even that terrible one with the bear.

Nathan & Jenn, whose shared love of cats and puzzles continues to be a source of inspiration, and whose meowvelous kitty pics always remind me of how wily, wonky, and wonderful our feline companions are.

Mom & Dad, for quite simply everything.

Dr. Becker and the whole team at Veterinary Associates of North Branford: you got me through the worst year of my life with courage, wisdom, grace, kindness, and mercy I will never forget.

Iris and Titan, our dogs, who love everyone unconditionally, and who snuggle and groom and obey and gently wrestle the tiny, sharp, floofy, rumbly not-puppies, and who snore when I need white noise and squash me flat when I need comforting and lick my feet when I . . . well, let's be honest. I don't need that. But you do it anyway, including right now as I write this, Iris. Thanks. Gross.

Finally, I'm endlessly grateful for the cat ancestors and spirits, the cats who are with us now, and the cats who are yet to arrive in our lives.

And for all the things they know, but will never tell.